"In beauty of face no maiden ever equaled
her. It was the radiance of an opium-
dream - an airy and spirit-lifting vision
more wildly divine than the fantasies
which hovered about the slumbering souls
of the daughters of Delos."
—- *Edgar Allan Poe*

THE ELEMENTS OF PANDOVERSE
WARRIOR

PROLOGUE

"RISKY ISN'T THE WORD FOR IT, REALLY." Sighed Zeus.

Athena smirked at the God. She wore a black floral summer dress and black pumps. It wasn't the stereotypical God-attire, but the stereotypical behaviour and fashion was left behind in Olympus, many years ago. "You know how far they've come, how much potential they have? Come on! Please!"

Hecate glowered at her, "If you go, I go too."

Zeus gave a hearty laugh, "Now you're being ridiculous. Hecate, sending you to Pandoverse would be most daft."

"Daft?" The Goddess of witchcraft said with mocking shock and disbelief. "I've changed a lot over the years, you know?" Unlike Athena, who was dressed like a happy girl in the summer, Hecate wore black jeans and a loosely grey t-shirt. It was just Zeus, who dressed in the traditional attire.

"Perhaps."

"Oh, hardly." Athena huffed, brushing her loose blond hair from her face, "Just send me down. Genesis wouldn't want to come face to face with a goddess from the underworld now, would she?"

"I live in the same city as you!" Hecate snapped, gesturing to her surroundings. "Seriously, what is wrong with you?"

"Ladies, enough!" Zeus roared. The room shook slightly, causing the Goddesses to silence themselves in an instant. Even though they had adapted to the modern world, Zeus still had alarming authority over everyone. He spent hours in his home, doing stuff that the Goddesses weren't even aware of what, and being practical. "Hecate, Athena has a point." He responded, resting his head in his hand, "You can be …intimidating, especially if Genesis see's you as the bad guy here. Athena you will go, but you mustn't be seen by anyone other than Genesis. It is too risky at this time. Find a way to get her alone."

"Sweet." Athena smirked at the God, who shot her a look of disapproval.

Both women nodded a curt goodbye and walked out of the throne room and into the hall. "I will help you get her alone." Hecate admitted, "I want to help as much as I can."

Athena smiled, "Thank you, Hecate." She squinted her eyes at the sunshine as it shone down on them with intense heat. "We should get planning on what I must say to her?"

Hecate agreed as they descended the steps and onto the streets of Evlogimenos. The Gods moved to the city three centuries ago, when Olympus fell. After Hades became allies with the Titans,

Olympus became a target of a great war and it soon became a shattered remainder of what had once been. Zeus swore revenge on his brother, before creating Evlogimenos, or as the Gods called it, *Evlo*.

"Morning Athena, morning Hecate!" A lady greeted as she passed.

"Morning Artemis!" Athena chirped to the Goddess of the hunt, as she strolled past them on the sidewalk. She wore Roman sandals, ironically, that laced up to her thigh. Her pure white dress hung to her waist elegantly, tied with a simple ebony string. She had auburn hair that trailed past her hips in loose tousled curls, a thick braid around her head like a halo.

"How's everything going?" Artemis asked, pausing briefly to interact.

"Well," Hecate grinned, "Athena's been granted the opportunity, by your father, to visit Genesis on Earth, or perhaps Pandoverse. It all depends on wherever is safest"

"That's incredible, finally things are looking up?"

Athena gave a long sigh, "I hope so. For centuries we've waited for the right one to come along and rescue us all in Evlogimenos, she must survive, before the next great war."

"Well she's doing well so far I hear, she's strong." Artemis smiled, "And I'm highly impressed you managed to speak with my father without him causing the sunshine to falter, that's a real talent.

"We just knew what buttons *not* to push." Hecate laughed, "It'll all be okay in the end, just watch, just wait and see when we run those dirty Titans into the ground."

"They're our ancestors," Athena reminded her, "Despite everything. But I do agree, and our Genesis will help with such battle!" She added proudly.

Artemis gave a smile, "I must run, I have to meet with Aphrodite. Speak soon!" She walked off, leaving Hecate and Athena to themselves once more.

Hecate turned to her fellow Goddess with a grin, "So, let's get planning, shall we?"

ONE

IT HAD BEEN TWO YEARS. SINCE IT HAPPENED.

It, being Genesis Bella Valencia's arrival in Pandoverse. Pandoverse was the world outside Earth, that inhabited supernatural creatures and intensely-trained warriors blessed with the four elements, Earth, Air, Water and Fire. Genesis had found out about her element abilities only the summer before last, when Theo Benedict, a young warrior, brought her to Pandoverse for her first time. She had been in danger almost her entire stay. She had made new friends, fallen in love and learned that her own brother, was not to be trusted. This knowledge came after a series of events that almost brought her to her death, with no thanks to him. She had also found out that after almost three years of believing her parents were dead, they were very much alive, and living with a group of Elements whom were waiting for the Great War to begin.

Immediately, when she found out such news, she began to prepare for her journey to the place they were staying, on the outer boundaries of Pandoverse. She was stopped instantly and told to wait. Apparently time would be a necessity as she would have a lot to prepare for. The battles. The journey. And the whole concept of getting out of the centre of Pandoverse, without getting caught and possibly murdered, by the governing leaders, the Elders. The Elders were those who led Pandoverse, those who wanted those like Genesis, the Quadrupedia, dead. Theo's father was now the leading Elder and her brother was working alongside them also.

This meant that Genesis and her friends had to continue their original plan of moving back to Earth. They took the atrium, the portal between worlds, to Earth and moved into Margaret Pelagius' old farmhouse. After Margaret was killed by her ex-husband, Elder Markos, she had left the farmhouse to Genesis, along with her Chevrolet truck, shares in her family supermarket, and a closet full of Pandoversian warrior gear and weaponry. Genesis had killed Elder Markos to avenge her friend's death. That was the first person she had killed, and it haunted her always, despite knowing it was the right thing to do.

Now, a couple years on, from all the havoc and pain, it was a chilly Sunday September afternoon in Central Park and Genesis had taken a stroll through the park with Theo. It was then, that Theo asked her to marry him. At first she was sure he was joking, but he was entirely serious.

"I don't mean now," He said quickly after acknowledging her expression, "I mean soon– well, kind of. One day– One day, soon. I want to know, that if I die in this war, I die with you loving me unconditionally, tied to me forever." Theo explained, as he walked alongside her, his hands in his pockets and her arm through his.

"But then I'd have to go through so much paperwork after your death so I can remarry after?" Genesis teased, her laugh receded when she saw the look on his face. "I love you unconditionally anyway! Why would you think otherwise?" She added, her eyebrows knitted in anxiety.

"I'm sorry I asked. I just thought that with everything going on, you would want it too." He sighed, looking down.

Genesis stopped and turned him to face her. "Theo, I do want to marry you. I want to spend the rest of my life with you. I just don't want you to ask me, because you're worried that you're going to be killed."

"I'm not worried."

"Then we can have our nuptials after the war." She said with a smile, leaning forward to kiss him gently.

Theo pulled back, "If we survive." He said sternly.

"We will survive Theo. When it's over, I will become your wife. Although I doubt the Elder's will marry us now." She laughed. The Elders were the governing leaders of Pandoverse, there were always four. One for each element. Of course, they had killed two back in Pandoverse. Theo's father had replaced one, and the other had been replaced by a middle-aged man from Fotia, the town for firements.

"We will do it here, on Earth." Theo began. "A mortal wedding. The big white dress, the flowers, the celebrations. All as you have dreamed of since you were a little girl."

"We can? Isn't that against the law for us or–"

"I don't quite think the law is a problem at the moment, do you?" He laughed.

They reached a large rock and he began to climb, reaching down to help her up. When seated, she cuddled into his side with a sigh. "When are the others coming?"

Theo looked down at his wrist-watch. "Any time now."

And he was right. The first person to appear, was Felicity. She was eleven years old and Genesis had saved her life back in Pandoverse, when a guardian was sent by the Elders, to destroy all those with quadrupedia. She skipped forward, her long hair, alike to Genesis', bouncing behind her in loose curls.

Following Felicity, were the twins, Eliza and Elijah Kaimana, they both had dark hair, olive skin and bright blue waterment-eyes and lean bodies. Built for battle. Xavier and Tom followed behind, alongside Noah and his younger sister Paisley. All of Genesis and Theo's friends, all alive and well, on Earth.

"Ready to go home?" Tom asked breathlessly, staring up at the pair on the boulder, his thick scarf huddled around the lower half of his face.

"I miss the sun." Xavier sighed. He wore light-blue skinny jeans, with a black sweatshirt, cream scarf, brown Chelsea boots and a black flat cap. He looked like a true British gentlemen.

"Of course." Genesis replied. Theo slipped down and held his arms out to catch his girlfriend as she followed.

The group all huddled together behind the trees, out of the public eye. Tom, being the son of Hermes, was able to transport them from place to place, using his mind. The group split, each half holding onto each of his arms, as he took them back to Los Angeles, California.

Eliza sat on a stool in the attic of the farmhouse, her elbows on the large table, looking up at Tom. They had begun dating when they first came back to Earth. Although he had family there, he lived in the house with everyone else.

"So that's where we're headed?" Eliza asked, pointing at the red pin on the map of Pandoverse. Over the past year, the boys in the house had spent endless hours creating a 3D map of their word. They constructed miniature versions of all the significant buildings and landmarks in Pandoverse out of clay, and drew on pathways, the beach and the borders. Now they had to decide the best route to take, to get through Pandoverse and out of Fotia safely. Of course, if Tom had more knowledge of Pandoverse, it would be easier. But with his basic knowledge and lack of memories of the world, he could only transport them to one place that he remembered clearly. The Benedict house.

"Yes, that's roughly where the Artillery are based." Tom explained.

The Artillery, were an organization of elements whom were against the Elders, and wanting to fight for their own. No one knew of the whereabouts of the Artillery, until Genesis had found the message from her father in the back of the Compendium, explaining how he and her mother, were part of the group, alive and well, and living in the borders of Pandoverse.

"No one's ever been there." Eliza said, almost in a whisper. "I mean, loads of people have travelled south, toward the Valle Mortis, but not north, east nor west."

"Well these guys have, hence why we're going." He explained, standing up and walking around the table. He wrapped his arms around the front of Eliza, and rest his chin on the top of her head. "We're going to the governing parts, and we will use a vision dome to keep us unseen as we travel to the volcanoes in Fotia."

Before Eliza could explain, Genesis and Theo burst in, Genesis grinning like a Cheshire cat. "I have an idea." She said. "So I'm the daughter of Hecate, Goddess of witchcraft and whatnot, correct?"

Eliza and Tom nodded.

"So what if I can find a way of transferring my memories to you?" She said, directing herself at Tom. "So you can get us to the Fotia, as close to the borders as possible."

"Gen, I don't think getting through Pandoverse is the problem here, is getting out of Fotia, that is." Eliza said with a sigh.

"Why is that the problem? Only a few hundred vampires around them volcanoes, I think we'll be okay." Theo said sarcastically, as usual.

"Well I suppose all we can do is try?" Tom suggested, heading toward Genesis.

She took his hands in her own and closed her eyes, willing herself to show him what was in her mind. But nothing happened. "Well, it sounded like a good idea." She mumbled.

"We'll try again after dinner, don't worry." Tom comforted, rubbing the top of Genny's arm.

She smiled at him, although she wasn't too convinced. "Very well." She turned to Eliza, who was sipping contently on a glass of red wine. "Theo and I are engaged."

Eliza choked on her drink, before placing the glass down and walking over to the couple. "Excuse me?"

"I wouldn't so much say engaged, I haven't got her a ring yet." Theo explained. "I'll need your help with that."

Genesis looked at him with a smile, before turning back to her friend. "It wasn't done properly, but we aim to get married after this is over."

Eliza's face dropped. "Gen, that's a while away, I mean–"

"It'll be okay." Genesis interrupted. "I know it will."

"Well then. Congratulations, I look forward to helping you shop for diamonds." Eliza smiled at Theo half-heartedly.

"Thanks." He replied, before taking his girlfriend's hand in his own, and leading her back downstairs.

Tom turned to Eliza, his expression sullen. "I can't help but worry there won't be a wedding."

Eliza shook her head. "Maybe we should persuade them to have it before the battle, just in case."

"Do you not think they're too young?" He asked.

"They're twenty, Theo's nearly twenty-one. In Pandoverse, that's the average age of marriage." Eliza explained.

"They'd get married in Pandoverse? Is that safe?"

"I doubt it. Perhaps, for Genesis' sake, they'll have a mortal wedding, here on Earth. That would be nice." She said dreamily, a smile creeping onto her face.

"That would be, maybe you should suggest it. If something happened in the war, to either of them, the other would regret not doing it sooner." Tom shrugged, his tone dull.

"I will, after dinner." Eliza said, before sauntering downstairs, with Tom close behind, to find the rest of their friends.

"I found something." Xavier said loudly, running in the room with a dirty old leather book in his palms. When they had left Pandoverse, Genesis and Theo had been the ones to insist they brought half the library from the Benedict house with them.

"The book of the enchanted." Elizabeth Aurelia, Theo's mother, explained.

"What?" Genesis asked, turning to her future mother-in-law with bewilderment.

It was Claudia, Theo's aunt, who responded. "The Book of the Enchanted. All about The Children of the Ocean, The Children of the Night and The Children of the Moon."

"What have you found?" Said Elijah, standing up and wandering to his friend's side.

"I think," Xavier began, "That we may be able to bring one more Element into our army."

"One more?" Theo asked.

"One more." Repeated Xavier. "Perhaps, the daughter of Artemis. Goddess of the hunt. I believe she would be useful?"

Elijah's eyes widened. "But the daughter of Artemis is Amethyst?"

"Correct." Xavier pointed at a specific page in the book, titled: Reversing a mermaid spell. "It says, and I quote, the only one who may have the ability to reverse a mer-potion, within the first decade of it happening, is any child of Poseidon."

"Does it say how?" Eliza asked. Her brother was the son of Poseidon and she knew what this meant to him.

"It does. Elijah, you must go into the sea of Nero and you must collect three items. A pearl, a leaf of kelp and the pine of an urchin."

"Well that's easy isn't it?" Genesis said cheerfully. "I mean as for the urchin you should wear gloves but–"

"It's not." Theo interrupted. "Mermaids are nasty work, they guard their underwater kingdom like you couldn't imagine."

"So if they're nasty, why are you saving one?" She asked Elijah carefully.

"They only become bitter in time. I doubt that Amethyst has reached such stage in her immortality just yet." Elijah replied smoothly.

"You're going to take away her immortality?"

"If she wants me too." He replied.

"What makes you think she would?" Genny asked, cocking her head to one side in interest.

Theo turned to her, his eyes glistening in the flame from the candelabra. "Because some people will do anything, for the one they love."

16

Eliza sat opposite Genesis atop a bale of straw, in the almost burned-down barn. "I think you should do it now."

"Do what now?" Genny asked, fiddling with a piece of straw between her finger and thumb.

"Get married, to Theo."

"Eliza, it's too soon. I would rather wait until after all of this is over and done with." She replied, shaking her head in slight dismay, "I love him, but I'm not ready."

"But what if–"

"What if one of us or both of us dies?"

Eliza nodded.

"I– I don't know, I guess I just hope we won't." Genesis said nervously, realisation looming over her.

"Either of you could die not being bound to the other, doesn't that make you sad?"

"I would like to wait. I would like to marry him the traditional-Pandoversian way."

"I doubt that will ever be the case, even if we all win and survive. The Elders would no longer stand, who would hold the ceremony?" Eliza asked.

Genesis shook her head. "I don't know, I haven't thought about it that much really."

"I think," Eliza said, "You should wait until we find the artillery and when we return here to prepare for the final stages of battle, you should marry him. With your parents there, your father can walk you down the aisle and everything.

It may not be traditionally Pandoversian, but it will be traditionally mortal, and that's what you believe you were for so long. Did you grow up dreaming of silver and gold gowns? Or white? Think about it Genesis. Think about it."

Genesis pondered for a moment, before smiling. "I suppose," She began, "I could. We could. When we return."

"You should go tell Theo your plans."

"I will right now." She headed out of the barn, turning to face her before she left, "Eliza, I'm getting married."

"Yeah, you are."

TWO

"TODAY IS THE DAY, GEN!" FELICITY CHIMED, jumping onto Genesis and Theo's bed.

Genesis groaned and sat up to face the young girl. "Huh?"

It was Theo, who replied. "We're going to find your parents, remember?"

Genesis jumped up and out of the bed in excitement, almost knocking Felicity off the mattress in the progress. She ran downstairs, only dressed in Theo's shirt, and into the kitchen to the others.

"I doubt your parents want to see you wearing that." Elijah commented, looking her up and down.

Theo appeared behind his fiancé, passing her some jeans and giving her a quick chaste kiss on the temple. She headed out of the room to change, leaving everyone to wait for her return.

"Are you excited to be going back?" Elizabeth asked her son. She took a sip of her tea and stared up at him.

She and Claudia were going to stay behind and wait for the group's return. Despite her worry for their little adventure, she had high hopes for them all.

When Genesis returned, she looked flustered and excited for their journey. "Let's go!" She chirped.

Genesis, Theo, Elijah, Eliza, Tom, Xavier and Felicity stood in a huddle. Tom held his arms out in front of him, and the others held on, preparing.

"See you." Elizabeth and Claudia chorused from the table.

"See you!" They replied in unison, before disappearing into another world.

They were at the edge of the governing parts, on the borders of Nero. It was what Tom could remember.

"It's been so long." Eliza said quietly, absorbing her surroundings. "Feels like a lifetime."

Genesis nodded. "Where to first?"

"Amethyst." Elijah said, wrapping a vision dome around the group and gesturing them toward the beach. It was relatively quiet, being so early in the morning. A small handful of Elements were having a laugh and a paddle at the water's edge, but it seemed not a lot was happening elsewhere. The sand was a soft, crisp white, with very little stones or shells mixed upon it. The beach was along a vast stretch and Genesis thought it was far beautiful than many beaches she had ever journeyed to before.

When they arrived, he headed straight for the water.

"Not alone." Theo said abruptly, "I'm coming too."

"So am I." Eliza said.

"Well then I am too." Genesis added sternly.

"Hell no." Theo said, putting his arm to stop her before turning to face her. "Over my dead body will you be going in there."

"Well then," Genny said smartly, "You better get digging yourself a grave. If you're going, I'm going."

"What about the others?"

She moved her hands, taking the vision dome off of her, Theo and the twins, leaving it over the others. "Let's go."

Theo shook his head, there was no point in arguing. Regardless to what he said, she would be going. "Here." He huffed, handing Genesis a lamina. "It's the only weapon that can be used underwater."

Genesis nodded in understanding, taking the blade and sheathing it in her belt. "Has anyone got towels?"

Theo laughed.

"You don't need a towel. You're airment, you can dry yourself off instantly– and us too." Elijah explained, standing in the water knee deep.

"Not to mention," Eliza said, "That being waterment means you can breathe, speak, see and stay dry underwater. It's somewhat magical."

"Right, okay." Genny said. "Let's do this." She took Theo's hand, as the four of them waded into Nero's ocean.

The ocean was dark. Not that Genesis really knew what to expect, but it was barely dawn and under the surface of the water was dark and gloomy.

It was Elijah, who produced a light that guided their way. He held an orb-like object in his hand, swimming in between Genesis, Theo and Eliza. Eliza created a bubble around the group, giving them the ability to speak to one another under the tide.

"How do you know where to get these items?" Genesis asked, swimming beside her friends.

"I don't. But I know someone who does." Elijah responded, swimming forward haste and eagerness.

They resurfaced quite far from the shore, climbing up onto a small island.

"This is pretty incredible." Theo admitted, staring at his surroundings.

Elijah sat on the sand, his feet in the water, staring out.

"What now?" Genny asked.

Before anyone could reply, there was a screeching sound from beneath the waves. A sudden figure appeared, flying out of the water and diving back in again. The figure approached, jumping up from the ocean and snapping it's fangs at Elijah. He stepped back and held his hands up defensively. "Woah, Amethyst, it's me!"

The figure, which Genesis could now tell was a mermaid, calmed down, circling the low tide and swimming to Elijah's feet. "Eli?"

He nodded, gently reaching forward and brushing a strand of wet blond hair from her face. She flinched, but eventually eased up to a human's touch. "I missed you."

She pressed her cheek into his palm. "I missed you too." She scanned her eyes across the others. "Who's this?"

"You remember Eliza and Theo?" He asked.

She nodded.

"Well this is Genesis." He continued.

"My fiancé." Theo added.

Amethyst's eyes widened. "Theo Benedict, you fell in love with someone other than yourself?"

He shot her a look. Genesis just laughed.

"Amethyst." Eliza spoke up. "If you could be an element again, rather than a mermaid, would you?"

"And give up my immortality?" Amethyst replied. Elijah's expression became sullen.

"Of course I would!" She exclaimed, making Elijah perk up again. "I'd do anything, anything at all. Is there a way? Please tell me you guys know a way?"

"We may do." Genesis said sweetly. "But we're going to need your help." She continued before explained what they needed, and how they needed to do it.

Amethyst sat on the sand by the waves, her tail dipped in the water. "The kelp is easy enough to get. I can safely get you the pine of the urchin…"

"But the pearl?" Genesis said in a mumble.

"The pearl is protected."

"By what?" Theo asked.

Amethyst shook her head. "Not what, whom."

The group stared at her inquisitively. It was Eliza who chose to speak up. "Whom being?"

"The Draco Mare."

Genesis shuddered. "What is that?"

"The sea dragon." Theo translated. "It's a large reptile-like creature that lurks around the bottom of the Pandoversian Ocean. It's around thirty-foot in length, from teeth to tail. It feeds on human flesh and bone."

"That sounds nasty." She responded. "Why would it protect a pearl though, I don't understand?"

Theo gave a sigh. "It's not just one pearl. Zeus' brother Poseidon, has a lot of, you could say– properties– down there. One room in particular, is made solely of pearls. The Draco Mare sleeps in there. Protects the pearls with her life."

"Well, if the room is made of pearls, surely we could take one from the outside?"

"No can do." Amethyst said simply. "If you take a pearl, you disturb the beast."

"I think we could do it." Genesis said with confidence.

Theo laughed. "This is why I love you. Always overestimate us all. I don't think we could."

"Doesn't Zeus' prophecy almost state that we are all meant to do something extraordinary."

He shook his head with furrowed eyebrows. "Doesn't it also state that most of those before us drastically failed?"

"Most of them didn't come this far! We can't just drop this. Amethyst needs us, and we need her too."

"Gen–"

"No. I'm doing this, whether you are joining me or not."

He took her hand in his own. "Well if you're doing it, I guess I am too, huh?"

The pearl room was more beautiful than Genesis could have imagined. Despite the sleeping giant sea-dragon in the centre.

"So we just pick a pearl and go?" She whispered to Amethyst, "That doesn't seem hard. She's sleeping."

"Go ahead." Theo smirked. "Try it."

She leant forward to pluck a large shiny pearl from the door, when Elijah shot his hand forward. "Don't, it'll wake him."

"Do you have any better ideas Elijah Kaimana?" Theo asked with a light laugh.

Elijah shook his head.

"Thought as much." Genesis said proudly. She place a thumb and forefinger on the pearl, watching over her shoulder as the dragon lay sleeping, before pulling it from the door.

Everyone tensed, preparing to fight. But the dragon didn't move. "Oh, maybe ol' son of Poseidon here just saved our lives!" Eliza chimed, patting her brother's back.

They began moving out of the room, checking over their shoulder's frequently, to see if the dragon moved.

"Why didn't it wake him?" Genny asked Theo, as they made their way back.

"I'm not too sure." He replied, looking over his shoulder once again. "Um, guys–"

Everyone turned to look behind them. In the distance, they could see the pearl room.

And it was empty.

A sound came from behind Genesis, she carefully turned to face the thirty-foot long reptile. "Theo." She squeaked.

A flash of light passed her eyes as Theo's blade swung by her face and toward the dragon. "Stay back."

The dragon roared, which made the water vibrate around them, and advanced on the group, its jaw snapping toward them, bearing its meter long pointed shark-tooth-like teeth.

She staggered backward, reaching for her weapon and slashing it towards the beast, Elijah and Elijah doing the same. "Where's Amethyst?"

Elijah looked around, his expression worried.

When suddenly she appeared. "Elijah!" She screamed, revealing a large metal trident. "This is your call."

He looked confused, "What?"

She didn't have time to answer when the dragon passed her and advanced on Genesis. She threw the trident to the boy and smiled. "You know what you've got to do."

He nodded, lunging forward toward the reptile, the trident glowing in the darkness of the ocean. The dragon swayed, avoiding the sharp points and knocking into Theo.

Theo dropped his lamina and watched as the faintly glowing blade sunk down toward the sea bed. "Well shit." He mumbled as the Draco Mare headed his way.

A whistle cut through the brief silence. "Over here!" Genesis bellowed, waving her hands to catch the dragon's attention.

"Gen don't–"

The dragon began her way, its large scaled tail swishing in the water.

"Come and get me!" Genesis continued, swimming away as fast as she could.

She reached a cave and swam inside, allowing the dragon to follow and get stuck in the small entrance to the rocks. It thrashed its large body in the crevice, becoming stressed. Genesis could only pray that the others caught onto her plan and helped her, or she could be stuck for a really long time.

A flash blinded her momentarily as the trident sunk into the dragon's skin. Light crept through every orifice on its body, creating new cracks in its scaly skin, before it exploded before her eyes. She shrank back, covering her face until the ordeal was over.

"Genesis?" Elijah called into the cave. He picked up a fallen tooth of the Draco Mare and swam toward her, "Let's get back to the surface, I hate being underwater for too long."

She nodded, taking his spare hand and swimming out of the cave and up to the air once again.

Athena sat crossed legged on the floor, her brother, Ares, beside her.

"So they did it?" He asked, watching tentatively into a glass sphere. It had been brought to them by Hecate many years ago, as a way of watching what went on it Pandoverse.

"They did." The Goddess of wisdom said sweetly, "And so effortlessly too. I can't believe how easy they make this. They're going to succeed, they will, I'm so sure of it."

Ares grinned, "I get the excitement, I mean– they're doing great. But please don't get your hopes up, there is still room to fail."

"My Genesis doesn't fail." Athena stated abruptly. "Ever."

"*Your* Genesis has only been in this world for a small amount of time, if she had been born and raised in Pandoverse, she probably would have made plenty of mistakes and failures by now."

"But not one that would cost her life?" Said Athena, in somewhat shock.

"Well I should hope not, or she wouldn't be here now to fight for the prophecy." Ares responded in a sarcastic manner.

Athena rolled her eyes before glaring at the God of War, "She won't fail. Theodore might, but never Genesis."

"Theo is a highly and sufficiently trained Elemental fighter. He is of soldier status and has every ounce of potential. He is the least likely of that social group to fail. Theo can't fail. He also can't do wrong by Genesis."

"Okay," Replied Athena, "So what if he has to choose between his father and Genesis. Then what?"

"He wouldn't go on his father's side, obviously, how stupid do you think he is?" He laughed.

"With you as a mentor, it's hard to put into words."

"Enough bitterness, Athena."

Athena went to respond, when a knock came from the door, "Come in!" She called, in her usual sweet tone.

Artemis strolled in, her twin brother, Apollo, at her heels. "Did you see?" She squeaked, "They rescued Amethyst! I'm so happy!"

Apollo took a seat beside Ares and scowled, "So they have added a sea creature to their squad, big deal."

"It's a huge deal, thank you." Artemis countered, sending vicious stares her brother's way.

"Genesis and Felicity could have fought this war single-handedly, and won, you know that, right?"

"How?!" Both Artemis and Ares replied in shock horror.

Athena grinned, "He's right. I mean, Felicity is a pretty strong girl, she has a lot of potential. And Genesis may be new to all of Pandoverse, but she sure is adapting well, I'm extremely impressed."

"Oh, sure. The kid and the newbie are so great." Artemis responded, her voice dripping with sarcasm. "Young and inexperienced is certainly the recipe for success."

Ares smirked, "Considering Genesis was so smart– she forgot to bring clothes to Amethyst."

"They all did, don't blame Genny." Athena scoffed.

Another visitor caused the quartet to break away from their bickering.

Hecate.

"Are you done fighting?" She snapped, drawing their attention to her, "In any given moment, our Element's will head off into the wilderness to find the Artillery, we need to keep watch."

"We are." The group replied in unison.

"Athena, we need to consider setting our plans in motion, when you're done arguing, come see me."

And with that, she exited, leaving the Gods in silence.

THREE

WHEN THE GROUP MADE IT BACK TO THE SURFACE, they all collapsed in relief.

"Oh my Zeus." Elijah gasped, "That was–"

"Petrifying?" Eliza said.

"Haunting?" Added Theo.

"Exhilarating!" Genesis grinned.

They all turned to her, including Amethyst, who was half in the water, leaning on her elbows.

"What is honestly wrong with you?" Theo said in disbelief. "You're crazy."

Amethyst smiled. "I like her."

"Thank you." Genny replied. "I'm not crazy, I'm just living my life the way I should."

"The ingredients!" Eliza said in shock.

They all jumped up, running to the water's edge.

"One spine of an urchin. One leaf of kelp. And," Amethyst turned to Genesis, who pulled out the pearl from her pocket. "One pearl."

"Now what?" Genny asked, placing the pearl with the other items.

"Mix it together, add a mermaids tear and drink." Elijah explained.

"Oh well you make her cry whilst I find a tumbler won't you?" Theo smirked.

Elijah grinned, holding up the tooth. "They're hollow." He poured some water it the thicker end, and watched as it trickled out of the pointed end.

"That's kind of disgusting." Amethyst pointed out.

"Well do you want to stay all fishy or what?" Theo asked, seemingly annoyed.

Genesis shot him a look, before turning back to the mermaid and tilting her head to the side. "How can we get a tear?"

Amethyst shrugged. "Punch me?"

Theo gave a hearty laugh, earning another look from Genesis.

"Or," The mermaid said softly, "A sad story."

Everyone looked at one another in confusion, hoping someone had an idea of some sort.

"I got it." It was Eliza who spoke, "Elijah, tell us the story, the complete story, of how you met and fell in love with Amethyst. Tell us how you lost her too, tell us everything."

Elijah paled slightly. "I, um–"

"That would make her cry, it will probably even make me cry. I love a good romantic story." Genesis said dreamily.

Theo shook his head. "She has a point though, tell us it all."

Elijah let out a heavy sigh, passing the ingredients to his sister so she could begin the mash up the ingredients and prepare them. "Okay." He said.

"Where do I begin?"

"I was sixteen, she was fifteen. Of course, Eliza and I had no parents, we are orphans. We lived together and helped each other whenever we could. I was going to the school to collect a group of students for their swimming lessons, Eliza usually helped me, but she had caught the flu and couldn't attend. I was informed that another waterment would take her place. At this point, unaware, I was annoyed. I didn't want to work with anyone else but my sister, we did everything together. But I had no choice than to agree.

I began to start the short walk to the governing parts, strolling along the beach until I reached the road. I heard a girl's voice calling from behind me. She kept saying, 'excuse me!' I stopped to turn to face her. Standing there, was the most beautiful girl I had ever seen. She had long red hair, that was still damp from either a shower or her morning swim, and it fell down to her hips. She had huge eyes, shocking blue, like the rest of us. 'I'm Amethyst' she said, 'I'm working with you today.' I realised then that today was going to be a lot easier than I thought. I told her it was nice to meet her, and held my arm out for her to hold, so she could walk beside me. She took it, and smiled. And it was then, I felt my heart contract, I realised that I was going to fall crazy in love with this girl.

When we had reached the governing parts, I had learnt a lot about her, as she had me. I knew that her parents lived in one of the larger houses in Nero, and that she was an only child.

She was a year younger than me, and had a duplex called Shox, with an 'X'. I laughed at this, and she said 'don't judge me, I was only young'. I didn't judge her, I just thought it was adorable, and creative. I had also learnt that she was the daughter of Artemis. Although she seemed more impressed with me, being the Son of Poseidon.

After the lessons were over and we had escorted the young elements back to the school, I asked her if she'd like to come for dinner. I said that I had a twin sister who wasn't feeling too good, so I would understand if she didn't want to accept the invite. But she said yes and that she had to quickly pop home to let her parents know and that she'd meet me at mine in thirty minutes time.

She turned up dead on time. That night we had smoked salmon with salad.

From that day, our relationship bloomed, and I had fallen well and truly in love with her. When she turned eighteen, I asked her to marry me. She said yes. She, myself and even Eliza were delighted. Her parents on the other hand, were not.

They forbade her to marry me. 'You're far too young!' they said. Even when we said we didn't plan to marry anytime soon, they still seemed to be against it. I didn't quite no how much they forbade it until they told her we weren't to see each other ever again.

We were both heartbroken. We didn't want to be apart, so we snuck around to be together. I would climb through her window at night just to lay beside her and hold her. I did this almost every night without fail, and her parents never knew, or so we thought.

One night, I didn't visit, not for any particular reason other than I was extraordinarily tired. I awoke around two in the morning, from a piercing scream. My first thought? Amethyst. I jumped out of bed and ran to her home, climbing through her window as I would any other night. I found her crouched in the corner, shivering. I ran to her side, taking her hand and asking her to face me despite her pleas to leave.

Eventually she gave in and turned to me.

I saw it.

Her eyes were purple, her teeth were pointed, and scales were forming along her waist and thighs. She was a mermaid. They had turned her into a mermaid. They wanted her to marry into Government, it was obvious. Not some orphaned swim teacher. I thought they would see past it, for her happiness. I didn't realise this was the length they would go to, to keep me from their daughter.

From that night forward, I barely saw her, only occasionally when I was out in the ocean, but that rarely happened. I had lost her forever. Until now."

Genesis turned to Amethyst, who had tears streaming down her cheeks. "Eliza, go!"

Eliza placed the tooth under Amethyst's eye, collecting drop of tears and pulling away proudly. She quickly mixed the ingredients in and passed them to Amethyst to drink.

She gulped the concoction down, wiping her mouth with the back of her hand afterward.

Nothing happened.

"You have to be kidding me!" Eliza shouted, "It has to work, it's got to work!"

Amethyst stared blankly at the group, "I don't think–"

Before she could say another word, she doubled over with a scream.

"Amethyst?" Elijah cried. He reached for her but was held back by his sister.

"Don't, she's changing, you mustn't touch her." Eliza said, calmer than before.

"She's in pain!" He said breathlessly.

"I understand that, but it'll be over soon."

And surely enough it was. After around a minute or so, Amethyst lay crumbled and groaning on the floor. Her hair was a shade or so darker, her skin looked more tanned, her eyes were once again blue and her face looked more mature than before. Her teeth were no longer pointed and her tail had disappeared, leaving her with two long human legs.

"Amethyst!" Elijah said, rushing to her side.

Genesis turned to Theo with a look of pride as he came to her side to hold her. "That's thanks to you that is." He said sweetly

"How so?" Genesis asked. "Elijah killed the Draco Mare, not me."

"You trapped her, you thought of the idea, you played a massive part in this."

Genesis smiled, resting her head on his shoulder. "Theo…"

"Yes?"

"Amethyst has no clothes on."

They both look over to the young girl, surely enough, she was naked, huddling around herself to protect her dignity.

"Do something!" Genny whispered, "You can make money can't you make clothes?"

Theo gave a light laugh. "Unless she wants to be wearing twigs then no."

Genesis glared at Theo, before pulling off his sweatshirt. "She can wear this."

"Apparently so." He replied, just following her lead without question.

They wandered over to the young girl, who was huddled into Elijah's side.

"How're you feeling?" Genny asked, crouching down at her side and passing her Theo's sweatshirt. It was long like a dress so it covered her modesty, although they didn't have much other choice anyway.

"I feel a bit dizzy, but I feel okay." Amethyst replied.

Eliza came over, "We should head back to the others. Perhaps Paisley or Noah could help you feel a bit better?"

They all agreed, making their way to the water. "You going to be okay?" Theo asked Amethyst, gesturing to the water.

"I was a mermaid for four years, I think I can swim." She said sarcastically, before diving in after the others.

Theo turned to face Genesis, "Next stop, your parents."

She smiled. "They're going to love you."

"How do you know?"

"Because," She said, "I love you."

FOUR

BACK ON THE SURFACE OF NERO'S BEACH WAS chilly. Genesis felt sorry for Amethyst, who was wearing just a large sweatshirt. They wandered up to the others, reapplying a vision dome for their safety.

"You did it!" Tom said in awe.

"That's impressive." Xavier responded.

Felicity grinned at them. "You beat the Draco Mare didn't you, who did it?"

Genesis pointed to Elijah, who she noticed was pointing at her. "It was a joint effort," she said, "I trapped him, Elijah killed him."

"That's incredible, no one's ever managed to even come close to killing him before." Paisley smiled, before turning her attention to Amethyst. "Thankfully I thought ahead here."

She reached into her backpack and pulled out so clean clothes. "I figured if everything went to plan, you may need these."

Amethyst's face lit up in appreciation. "Thank you so much!"

"I'll take you somewhere to get changed." Eliza said quickly, leading the girl away whilst the others prepared to move on.

"So where to next?" Tom said blissfully, "Fotia?"

"Can you remember it there?" Genesis asked.

"Roughly, I can try, I guess. There's no harm in trying?" He said.

Theo shook his head, "In this situation, there could be a lot of harm in trying. More harm than good, actually."

"That's true, but I don't see what choice we have." Elijah commented.

Genesis looked up at Tom, "Let me try something quickly."

"If you're going to try the memory thing again, there's no point, it didn't work before." Theo snorted.

"Just let me try." She snapped.

She placed her hand on Tom's cheek and closed her eyes, channeling her thoughts and memories of Fotia to his mind.

Tom jumped back in shock. Blinking to refocus himself into reality. "It worked."

Theo stared blankly at Genesis. "You just–"

"Wow." She replied.

"That was incredible," Said Tom, "I can see it, remember it, as if it was my own memory. It's like I was there?"

Theo grinned. "Well if any of them piss you off, at least you can give them some memories of us." He teased.

Tom gagged, "Please don't!" The group echoed with a disgusted groan

Even Felicity, who was only young, contorted her face is disgrace. "Stop that."

Genny and Theo laughed as they watched Eliza and Amethyst arrive back.

"Ready?" Tom asked confidently.

"Where we going to go to?" Eliza questioned her boyfriend. "How close can we get?"

"How about the volcanoes of Fotia?" He said with a mischievous grin.

"But you've never been th–" She looked over at Genesis. "Oh, it worked?"

They all nodded.

"Amazing. You're truly amazing." She turned back to Tom, "Well then, let's go shall we?"

They all held tightly onto Tom, including Amethyst, who turned to Genesis last minute and said: "Is this safe?"

It was Theo who replied instead. "Nothing we do is ever safe, but we sure as hell do it anyway."

And with that, they disappeared.

Fotia's volcanoes were how everyone remembered. Dull, eerie, and extremely hot to stand around.

"I say we get through these then set up camp on the borders?" Eliza suggested.

Everyone agreed in unison, beginning their trek across the terrain.

"Genesis." Theo said in a shouted whisper.

Genesis turned to him with a questioning look as he beckoned her over with his hand. "What's up?"

"I just wanted to talk to you." He said, taking her hand walking close to her.

"That sounds concerning." She said awkwardly, "Need I be worried?"

"No, of course not!" Theo laughed. "I just wanted to know how you feel. In the next day or so, we will be with your parents, with the Artillery."

Genesis nodded her head slowly, "Yeah I know. I'm kind of scared. I feel like I should be mad at them. They led me to believe they were dead. In fact, they lead me to believe that I was not who I really am. That my brother was in London! Everything they've said and done is a lie. I should be so mad. But I'm desperate to see them again." She looked down at the floor.

"I understand." Said Theo, his gaze still fixed forward. "You should be mad, but you should understand their point of view also. Imagine if you had a child, or a younger sibling."

Genesis looked over at Felicity, whom was like a younger sister to her. Ever since she rescued Felicity from the wrath of a Guardian, she had been extra protective of her at all costs, even more so because she too, was pure quadrupedia.

"Exactly, look at Felicity, she's pure like you, and you protect her with your life." Theo said, as if he had read her mind. "You protect her more than you would if she was just waterment or airment. Because they're not at risk. They just wanted what was best for you, even if that meant keeping you in the shadows."

"So why," Genesis began, "Did they choose now to bring me to Pandoverse?"

"They didn't, my mother did."

"I get that. But they knew that I would come eventually otherwise they wouldn't have left that note for me in the back of the compendium. It wasn't just a standard letter, left for me to find or be given. It was hidden. We had to solve riddles to find its whereabouts. They knew I would come here, so why did they choose now?" She said, disappointment etched into her voice.

"Maybe they wanted you to be old enough."

"But if they thought about it properly, they could have allowed me to be here my entire life, to train like all the others from a young age. My duplex would have been stronger, I would have been stronger. Bringing me here now isn't in anyone's favour." She said evidently.

"Maybe you could ask them all this when we see them? Once you've managed to catch up." Theo suggested, looking down at Genesis with a worried expression.

"Perhaps I could." She replied. "I don't really know what to expect to be honest."

"I don't think anyone knows what to expect." Said Theo, "We're all just young and dumb with oblivious expectations and high hopes."

Elizabeth walked out of the supermarket with Claudia. Both carrying several carrier bags of shopping in their hands.

"I wonder," Claudia said, "If they had any luck with Amethyst?"

"I hope so. She could be a really big help to them in all of this. She could be a help to all of us." Liz replied with a small smile.

"Does any of them, including Elijah, know about her? About how she was demi quadrupedia beforehand?"

Liz shook her head. "Not that I'm aware of. That story always upsets me. What kind of being puts their young child through that, taking about one of their abilities?"

"I know, it does me too." Claudia replied despondently, "It would be even more convenient if they could reverse it, so she could be airment as well again."

Elizabeth shot a look at her. "What if she has reversed it now? If she's element again, maybe she could've changed back with both abilities?"

"We need to contact them!" Claudia almost screamed, "They need to know!"

"But she needs an elder to brand her?"

"No, she was branded for both abilities as a baby, she should be okay, if what we believe is true."

Elizabeth smiled proudly. "I hope it's correct, I really do."

Her smile soon faltered, catching Claudia's attention. "What's wrong Liz?

"They're here."

"Who?"

"Jaspar and the other Elders. They're on Earth."

Genesis sat down on a boulder, rubbing at her knees. They were tired, worn out, and there was a sky full of stars already.

"How much further?" She asked Elijah and Eliza, as they stood beside her.

"Not too much, about another twenty minutes or so and we'll be on the other side." Elijah comforted.

"Great," Theo said, "We should get going then, get there sooner rather than later."

"I agree." Xavier added, "This place gives me the creeps."

A mumbled chorus of 'yeah's' were enough to persuade Genesis off of the rock and back onto her feet. "Let's go." She said with a half-hearted smile.

They all began in the direction Elijah said when a sound brought them to a stop.

"Uh, guys." Felicity squeaked. "Are all element-born vampires good with people? Or only some."

"Some." Amethyst said. "Some are still deadly, and then those who are born vampires, are the worst of them all."

"Born vampires?" Genesis questioned, she'd never heard of such a thing.

"Those." Theo replied, pointing at the few dozen vampires that were slowly closing in on them.

"Why are they here?" Claudia growled.

"I don't know, we need to hide." Liz said softly, "We don't have weapons."

"I don't even have abilities!" Claudia panicked.

"Where can we go?" Liz cried. "They've spotted us, we need to go, now!"

Before they could run in any direction, a large car pulled in front of them. The window came down and a middle aged woman leaned out. "Quick! Get in, now!"

Liz and Claudia shrugged at one another, before sliding open the back door and climbing in.

In the back of the car was a large leather case, and a young girl sat beside it. Liz looked questionably at the girl, "What's this?"

The girl smiled, before clicking the lock and opening the case. "Weapon of choice?" She asked.

Inside the case lay rows of laminas, una's and reditum's.

"I have a gladio and an arcus also, your choice." The girl said innocently.

Liz looked over at the woman driving the car. "You're Margaret's daughter and granddaughter, right?"

"That's right. The name's Sophia, that's Maggie." The woman, Sophia, responded.

"Maggie, you know all this?" Claudia asked, curious.

"I do yes. After Grandma died, I met Theo and Genesis and told my family how I wanted to be like them. They've allowed me to learn and train, I just need my sculpes of course." Maggie explained.

"We decided she best know some little bits and pieces of the elemental world, just in case." Sophia added, "She's incredible with a militum."

Maggie grinned. "I'm a ninja!"

"A what?" Liz asked, seeming mortified.

"It's a mortal thing, kind of. Don't worry." Sophia chuckled.

"Oh shit." Claudia mumbled, staring out of the back window.

Behind them, walking at incredible speed, was the Elders. Followed by two guardians.

"How are they following us?" Liz asked, becoming angry.

She grabbed a lamina and gladio with two scabbards to sheath them in. Claudia followed, taking the arcus also.

"Maggie, you ready?" Sophia asked her young daughter. Maggie nodded, her hand hovering over the hilt of the militum.

"Let's go!" Sophia shouted. She pulled the car up and they tumbled out, weapons at the ready, Liz in the lead.

"Elizabeth!" Jaspar shouted, raising his hands in defence, "Lower the weapon, we're not here to hurt you. Do not make a scene in the mortal world would you, please?"

Liz glared for a moment, before slowly lowering the gladio. "Why are you here Jaspar?"

He clasped his hands in front of him and looked at her with a dangerous look in his eye. "Elizabeth, it's lovely to see you. And you, sister dear." He directed to Claudia. "Who are your friends?"

Maggie hid behind Sophia, avoiding eye contact.

"Are you Pelagius' children?" He asked.

Sophia nodded. "You and your friends are surely aware of who she is, seeing as one of your own killed her."

Jaspar looked over his shoulder at the others. "Wasn't any of us, we can't take any blame for Markos' behaviour. Anyhow, he is no longer with us." He turned his attention back to Liz. "Elizabeth, were is Theodore and the girl?"

"The girl has a name." Liz spat. "They aren't with us, we can't help you."

"We need to find them." Jaspar growled. "And that Tom Rogers boy, where is he?"

"Again, we cannot help you." Claudia added.

"Well I know that they got that young mermaid, changed her back. They killed the Draco Mare." He explained.

"They did?" Liz asked in shock.

"They did." He replied. "Now, I will ask you one more time, where is Theodore and Genesis?"

Liz frowned, "I won't tell you. I cannot help you. I am sorry."

"Very well." Jaspar turned away to his colleagues. "Gregor."

Claudia shot a look at the others in confusion, before Gregor slammed his foot down on the floor. Vines sprouted from the ground, winding their way around the group's torso and limbs.

"Jaspar stop this!" Liz cried, trying to struggle free. "You don't need to do this!"

"I'll stop if you tell me of their whereabouts, and where they are headed." He replied indignantly.

"Never." She spat.

"If you won't bring me to them, I will bring them to you." He said smartly. Within minutes, the girl's bodies were covered in vines, and everything was silent.

Vampires.

They're scary most of the time, Genesis thought. Aeris was quite intimidating, despite how friendly he was. But these, 'born-vampires', were petrifying.

"Food?" One sneered.

Another grinned, showing it's fangs in delight. "Perhaps, I smell quadrupedia."

Genesis backed up a step, whilst Theo walked forward. "Can I speak to your um, leader? Please?" He asked politely.

The vampires exchanged looks, before one stepped forward. "Good evening Mr Benedict."

"Calispar? You're the leader?" Theo said in confusion. "You're not a born vampire?"

Calispar had been a fere-quadrupedia when Theo was young, but soon changed into a vampire. He was an elderly man then, but immortality made him look younger.

"No, but I'm stronger than them all. Why do you pass here Theodore?" Calispar questioned.

Theo stared indifferently at the lead vampire. "You dislike the government, don't you?"

A chorus of hisses came from the vampires around them all, some saying nasty things, others groaning at the words Theo spoke.

"Yes," Calispar said, "Why do you ask?"

"We're trying to reach the Artillery."

"You know there is no such thing, right? Just a silly old myth?"

Genesis stepped forward. "No, it's real. My parents are there."

"And what if they're not?" Calispar asked.

"They left a letter." She said.

"Maybe they left it when they planned to go, but never went because it wasn't real?"

"It's real, and we're going to find it." Theo said calmly. "If you could let us pass, we should be grateful."

Calispar hesitated for a moment, "Very well, just this once. Do not ask to pass again, one time is the only time we give for free."

"We won't, we promise." Genesis smiled, looking at Tom.

"Go quick." Calispar hurried them. "Wait, Theodore!"

Theo turned back. "Yes?"

"What if the Elders come looking for you, what should I say?"

Theo smiled in realisation that Calispar was on their side. "You're intelligent Calispar, I am entirely sure you can think of something."

"Very well." The vampire replied. "Good luck to you all, you will need it."

FIVE

IT WAS DARK.

And no one knew where they were.

"I'm so sorry." Elizabeth whispered into the darkness, hoping her friends were still around.

"It's not your fault." A voice replied. It was Sophia. "We didn't have to help you, we chose too."

"But Maggie, she's so young she's–"

"She's an element, she's strong." Sophia replied. Liz could hear her smile in her voice.

"Claudia?"

"I'm here, I'm with Maggie." Claudia responded calmly. "We're okay."

"Good," Said Liz. "We need to get out of here."

"Where is here?" Sophia asked, her voice strained from her struggles.

"I have no idea." Liz replied solemnly. "I hope the others are doing all okay."

"I know they are." Maggie spoke up for the first time. "They're strong. Born-warriors! They're going to be absolutely fine!"

"Didn't Jaspar say they killed the Draco Mare?" Claudia asked.

"What's the Draco Mare?" Sophia questioned.

Liz coughed. "It's a sea monster, guards Poseidon's underwater kingdom some say. No one has ever even maimed it before, only ever been slain by the beast itself."

"Told you that they're strong." Maggie said simply, followed by silence.

*   *   *

"That seemed too easy." Felicity said to Genesis, as they made their final walk out of Pandoverse. "Why would a bunch of born-vampires leave us to walk through, and not try to kill us?"

"Calispar." Theo interrupted.

Both girls looked at him, but Genesis chose to speak. "How do you know him?"

Theo looked at her without an expression. "When I was a baby. My mother knew him for many years, she brought him to meet me because he too, was fere-quadrupedia. He was a close family friend for many years. It was only a few months after my sixth birthday that he disappeared. In time I learned that he was turned, because of his abilities. That was the first time I realised that I was in danger, that my kind, were in danger. That was the first time I realised something had to be done about it."

Genesis gave a heavy sigh. "It's sad. So sad. That people are being all but killed, for something beyond their control?"

"That's why we're doing something about it." Theo replied with a smile.

"We're here." Xavier said, falling behind to walk beside Genesis. "We just need to set up camp."

Genesis studied her surroundings, it was just caves and rocks, dirt and dust. "Okay." She said. "Where do we need to be?"

Tom approached them next, directing them toward a cave. "The twins just checked it out, it's small, but it's clear. We can sleep there, rotating who's on watch each hour."

"I'll start." Elijah volunteered.

"I'll join you." Amethyst smiled.

"We'll go after." Felicity said sweetly, gesturing to herself and Eliza.

"Then us." Tom, Noah and Paisley added.

"I guess we're going last then." Theo said to Genesis, who was starting a fire.

"I'm cool with that." She said briefly, before turning her attention back to the fire.

Everyone settled down by the fire, using the heat and each other to stay warm.

"So what's going to happen after this?" Eliza said, picking at her fingernails and not looking up as she spoke.

"Well I guess, we keeping travelling, like Genesis' parents said too." Tom replied.

Genesis looked up at the mention of her name. "What if it wasn't real?" She said remorsefully. "What if it *was* a lie? Or it's too late?"

"Don't think that way." Theo mumbled, taking her hand in his own. "They're alive."

She turned to him and nodded.

"Right, let's all get to sleep then." Noah said cheerfully. He turned to Elijah and Amethyst "You got this?"

They nodded and headed to the entrance of the cave, leaving the others inside.

Genesis settled down beside Theo, snuggling into his side for warmth and comfort. "I'm scared."

Theo turned around to face her, pulling her close so their noses were almost touching. "Don't be," He soothed, "I'm with you every step of the way."

"I'm serious Theo, what if they're not there?" She whispered.

"What if they are there?" He said. "Wouldn't you rather find out just in-case? Or you'd live forever in regret?"

"And if they're not, we're wasting time. Everyone's doing this for me." Said Genesis.

"That's where you're wrong."

"How so?"

"Gen, we're doing this not for you, not for us, but for Pandoverse. We're doing this for our future children and their children. We're doing this for justice, equality and faith. What we're doing, is an act of selflessness. Genesis, we're not doing this for you, we're doing this for everyone."

Genesis stared wordlessly at her fiancé, "You're right. I just hope it all works out."

"It will. As soon as we find them, we'll go back to Earth and get married." He crooned, brushing a strand of hair from her face.

"I can't wait." She replied, planting a soft kiss on his nose. "Good night."

Amethyst shivered in the icy breeze.

"You cold?" Elijah asked, wandering over to her side and wrapping an arm around her.

"Yeah, it's been a while since I've been…" She gestured around her, "On the surface."

Elijah laughed. "Mm, it gets a bit chilly here at night, who would've thought? With the volcanoes at what not."

Amethyst rested her head upon his shoulder. "It's strange, really."

"What is?"

"Everything. How everything has turned out. I spent the past three and a half years as a sea creature and I thought I would live out the rest of my eternity like that. But then you come along again, with your new friends, and here I am. I'm here with you. I have legs and no gills. I inhale oxygen and exhale carbon dioxide. I'm human again." She laughed to herself. "Well, as human as an element can be."

"I noticed something earlier." Elijah said softly, lifting her off of him and looking directly into her eyes. "Your irises."

"What about them?"

"They're not just blue. They're ever so slightly grey too."

Amethyst shook her head, "That can't be?"

"It's true." Said Elijah. "I didn't notice it before but you're demi-quadrupedia, aren't you?"

"Was." She replied. "Was demi-quadrupedia. I was turned into a waterment as a child, I never spoke of it to you before because I didn't think it mattered. It was irreversible. That's the main reason why my parents hated me. My Grandma was killed for her Quadrupedia. They thought I was cursed. They somewhat learned to accept me, if I married into Government, I'd always be safe. But when they knew I was to marry you, they hated me. They hated us. They believed we could produce a family which were cursed too."

"When you changed, back to an element, you were somewhat reborn." He said, tilting his head in thought. "You changed back to an element with both your original born powers."

"So you're saying that I'm–"

He grabbed her arm, pulling up her sleeve. Surely enough, on her inner-forearm, were two triangular shapes. "You're demi-quadrupedia."

Felicity sat crossed-legged, drawing in the dirt with a stick. Eliza was pacing back and forth ahead of her, like a soldier. She admired her warrior-like behaviour. Her strength and versatility. "Eliza?"

Eliza turned to the young girl, and wandered over. "Hey." She said. "What's up?"

"How do you think this will end?"

"What do you mean?"

"How will it end? Will we all be okay, do you think? Will anyone die?"

Eliza shook her head, "Don't think like that, negativity produces weakness. We need to be strong, be positive."

Felicity cocked her head to one side. "Strength isn't always a good thing. Theo's strong, so strong, but Genesis is his weakness. If something happened to her, he'd be weak, entirely weak. She's the key that would unlock his insanity. He's our best warrior."

"You're right there." Eliza said. "And you're also right in saying he's our best warrior. And because he is, I know that he'll be safe. And as long as he's safe, he'll keep Genesis safe." She paused, looking out at the stars. "Genesis is pretty strong too."

"She is." Felicity said with a smile. "She's learnt so much in so little time. She survived illecebra poison and managed to keep her abilities. That's practically unheard of. Not to mention the Draco Mare, alongside Elijah, they destroyed it."

Eliza grinned down at her. "She's pretty impressive isn't she? Earlier, Amethyst said something that made me think. She said to Theo, 'you fell in love with someone other than yourself'. And it's funny because no one ever thought Theo would love someone, ever. He's always been so cold toward people. She has really changed him. She put up with him until he realised how special she was. That's strength, real strength. Perseverance is strength."

"When this is over, everyone will remember her as the heroine of Pandoverse."

"They'll remember us as her faithful army too, don't you worry."

"Eliza, we're going to make a legacy." Felicity thought out loud.

"We are the legacy."

Jaspar paced the length of the great hall, his hands clasped behind his back. "Gentlemen."

The guardians all stood to face him, alongside the other Elders, and Seth.

"I still have no location on Theodore and his friends, has anyone found anything yet?" Jaspar asked.

Seth walked up to his side. "Elder Jaspar, if I may–"

"You may not."

"But you'll be intrigued to know–"

"Seth Valencia."

Seth looked up at the Elder.

"Sit back down will you, please?"

Seth smiled and nodded, making his way back to his seat as Jaspar continued.

"I want you to split up. I want some of you to go to Nero, some to Aeras, some to Gi, some to Fotia and the rest of you." He pondered for a moment. "I want you to go to London and California, we must find them and fast."

The guardians scattered obediently, and Elder Gregor chose to speak. "Jaspar, I believe you'll like to hear what young Seth here has to say."

Jaspar waved a dismissive hand at his fellow governor. "We're following my plans right now, if I need any added advice I will approach you all and ask."

"But you just asked us if we had found–"

"Enough!" Jaspar bellowed, causing Seth and Gregor to shrink back in fear. "Seth, go check on the prisoners, see if they're ready to give us any information yet." Seth nodded and headed out of the door quickly. "Gregor, tell the other Elders that we will meet here tomorrow at dusk."

The Elder abided, before scurrying off, leaving Jaspar to his own devices.

"Theodore, my son," He said, mostly to himself, "I will find you and your friends, and when I do," he smiled, an evil twisted smile, "It won't be much of the father-son reunion you'd hope for."

"Gen, wake up."

Genesis groaned and rolled over to face Theo, "What?"

"You remember how we were meant to take turns guarding?" Theo asked.

"Is it our turn?" She questioned with a croaky voice.

"No, it's time to go."

"Really? Why didn't we get to guard?"

Theo laughed lightly, "I tried to wake you but you moaned and said you were too sleepy, I let you sleep."

Genesis sat up straight quickly, almost knocking into Theo in the process. "You guarded alone?"

"It's not a problem, you didn't want to." He replied sweetly, planting a kiss on her temple.

She gave a slight gasp. "You should've woken me! That's so irresponsible Theodore!"

Theo laughed, much harder this time. "The full name? Really? And I did wake you, as I said, you didn't want to do it."

"I don't remember."

"Doesn't matter, get up, we're leaving."

She did as she was told, standing up and gathering her stuff off the floor. "How far is the travel today?"

"We worked out, it's at least four hours." Paisley said, passing an empty water bottle to Genesis, "Can you top up?"

Genny nodded, placing her hand on the plastic and allowing the bottle to fill with liquid. "That's not too bad then I suppose, can't we fly there, wouldn't that be quicker?"

"We'd tire them out." Noah said, gesturing to the quartet of dragons.

"Not much more than they'll tire out flying beside us." Eliza suggested. "After all, they'll be flying slowly. That's quite tedious."

"She has a good point." Xavier said, taking the bottle from Paisley to have a sip.

"Of course I do." Eliza said smartly.

"How much time would it save us?" Theo asked.

"About two hours, if we fly steadily and take a short break in between. That way we can shorten the time and not tire them out." Elijah answered.

"There you go then, let's fly." Genesis smiled, heading out toward the duplexes.

The others followed closely all in deep discussion about the events that could follow.

"Right," Xavier said out loud. "There are four dragons, nine of us, three snakes, one owl and three wolves."

Everyone, including the duplexes, lined up to face him.

"I suggest that I ride Ardebit, alongside Elijah, Amethyst and Elijah's duplex." He continued. Elijah nodded, taking Amethyst's hand and allowing his snake, Tyson, to slither around his shoulders.

"I'll take Theo, and the four duplexes." Genesis added, taking Theo and suggesting for Luna, Sapiens, Fulgur and Axel with her.

Noah stood beside Draco, "Okay then, I'll take Eliza and Felicity with their duplexes."

Lastly it was Paisley, "Tom come on!"

Tom wandered up to Paisley and Flame, "Gen, do you want us to take some of yours, to lighten the load?"

Genesis pondered for a moment. Tom's duplex, Optimus sat perched on his shoulder. They had the least travellers on one dragon, meaning they had the lightest to carry. "Okay." She said. "Luna, go sit with Tom and Paisley." She soothed to the wolf.

Luna jumped down and trotted over to the others without having to be told twice.

"We ready?" Xavier shouted from the back of Ardebit.

Everyone agreed, and within moments, they were soaring through the sky, and further from Pandoverse than anyone had ever been before.

Six

IT WAS WEIRD TO SEE. PANDOVERSE, LOOKING SO small. It was the same as looking out of the window of an aeroplane. Everything was small and minute. The difference was this wasn't an aeroplane, and in the distance wasn't London or Florida. It was Pandoverse, and Genesis was on the back of a dragon. A few years back, the idea would have seemed most unrealistic, but now it was her life. She thought as to why as a kid her parents always told her, if it seems impossible, chances are, somewhere it was real.

Now it made sense.

Dragons, vampires, werewolves, mermaids. They were all real, and of course her parents knew about it.

"We're not far now." Theo whispered into her ear. His hands were drawn around her waist tightly, holding on. Axel sat in front of her, almost on her lap, tied onto Ignis' harness. Fulgur was tangled around one of the harnesses handles, and Sapiens sat perched on another.

"I'm nervous." Genesis admitted, looking over her shoulder at him. "It's been so long."

"Four years is a long time Gen, you're going to seem so different too them, it's frightening. But it'll be okay. We can get them, get back and get planning for the next step to winning this battle." Theo said comfortingly.

"You forgot the part where we get married." She teased.

Theo laughed, "I will have to get your father's blessing first."

Genny tensed, her father had always been extra-protective of her, and would imagine even-more-so now she was in this world. Her heart broke for a moment, the idea of him refusing his blessing to Theo. "No you mustn't."

"I have to Genesis, I can't just go ahead and marry you – as much as I would love too!"

She shook her head, "If we didn't know they were alive you would have."

"But they are alive so I want to." He looked at her questionably for a moment, "Why, what's wrong? Do you not think that he'll like me?"

"I think he'll love you, it's just when they find out about Seth they might become a tad protective of me." She admitted.

"Let's just see what happens, shall we?"

"Are you having second thoughts?" Genesis asked, worry etched into her voice. "Please tell me the truth?"

"Stop being paranoid! I'm not having second thoughts. I'm just trying to get your parents back to Earth, get you a ring, get your father's blessing and marry you before we have to go kick-ass!" He grinned.

Genny shook her head and laughed. "Very well. Let's go get them shall we?"

"Let's."

"You have to let us go Seth." Maggie growled, "I haven't even earned my sculpes yet, how can you keep me here?"

Seth snickered at the young girl. "You're all in this together, you chose to help them then you face the consequences with that."

"Seth," Liz spoke up, glaring his way, "She's right, she hasn't earned her sculpes, Claudia and Sophia are simply just mortal. I'm the one Jaspar wants, let them go, and keep me."

"No way." Claudia said abruptly, "Like hell will we allow that."

"You have no choice." Liz spat, before turning her attention back to Seth. "Let them go, keep me, please?"

Seth pondered for a moment, "I'll speak to Elder Jaspar and see what he says."

"Thank you." She replied softly, watching as he left the room.

When he'd gone, she turned back to the others, "Listen to me. If Jaspar agrees to let you go, you must promise me to get hold of the others. Find Theodore and tell him what's happened, he'll know what to do. But make sure, despite her arguments that Genesis doesn't try to help him. She mustn't end up here, it's far too dangerous. She's who they're really after." She paused. "Promise me that?"

Claudia stared blankly, "Okay, I promise."

Liz turned to Sophia and Maggie, "Promise me?"

"We promise." They replied solemnly.

The door swung open once again, to reveal Seth and two guardians. "I spoke with Elder Jaspar," He announced, "Elizabeth, you must stay. The rest of you are free to go."

"This must be it." Genesis said knowledgably, "Where else could they be?"

She landed Ignis on the outskirts of a forest, the others soon followed.

Sliding off the dragon's back, she stretched her legs briefly, turning to Theo. "They have to be somewhere in here."

"How do you suppose we find them, when we were flying, it seemed like a big forest." Theo said, looking around him.

Eliza wandered up to the couple, "You can work it out Gen."

"How?" Genny replied, slightly perplexed.

"Daughter of Athena? She's the goddess of wisdom and battle strategy remember. Well how can an army fight without navigational skills?"

Genesis stared at her friend in confusion, "Are you saying that I have the ability of navigation?"

"I'm saying that you should have an ability that will help with navigation." Eliza smirked, "You know the drill, use your mind."

"She has a point." Theo said simply. "Worth a shot."

"Okay." Genesis replied. She stared out at the shrubbery ahead of her. She closed her eyes, thinking solely of a route, a pathway, to take her to her parents.

When she opened them again, nothing was different, except she could see a faint glow in the midst of the forest, glowing yellow. "I see it" She whispered.

Theo looked over her shoulder, his eyes level with her own, "I can't see it. What are you looking at?"

"The glowing?"

He shook his head, "Son of Ares, not as blessed as you apparently."

Genesis laughed, "Just trust me."

"Let's just get going," Said Elijah, "Before it gets dark again."

"Oh yeah, I don't fancy wandering this place at night." Paisley added.

Genesis nodded. "Okay, follow me."

They all exchanged looks and shrugged, following her without another word.

"We're so close." Genesis grinned, the glow was only through a small selection of trees.

"I hope your instincts are right, because it's growing dark, and fast." Theo warned, standing beside her.

"We're not even in Pandoverse any longer, I doubt there's anything to be scared off."

Felicity joined at their sides, "That's the thing Gen, we don't know what could be out here."

Genesis looked down at the girl, "You're right, we should hurry."

"I sense something." Amethyst said quietly, "Something's here."

"Sense?" Genesis repeated, looking at her inquisitively.

"Daughter of Artemis, the Goddess of the hunt." Theo explained.

"Oh." She turned to Amethyst again, "What do you sense?"

Amethyst stayed quiet for a moment, staring ahead of her. "That."

Claudia ran carefully through the streets of Gi, Sophia and Maggie at her heels.

"How do you know he'll help?" Sophia asked, keeping a close eye on her daughter.

"Because I know him. Just trust me." Claudia replied, gesturing them to hide around the corner.

She knocked on a door and waiting patiently. It opened, and a tall man answered, his long dark hair falling over his shoulders. "Jax." She smiled, "Is Adrianna in?"

"No she's not, is everything okay?" He replied, looking curiously at his mother-in-law. "It's time, isn't it?"

Claudia nodded, before turning to the side of the house, "Sophia, Maggie, come, quickly."

The pair came from their hideout, wandering carefully toward Jax.

"Come in." He said, "Before anyone see's you."

They abided, scurrying inside the door and into the hall.

"What's going on?" Sophia asked Claudia, as Jax directed them into the sitting room.

"Jax is quadrupedia." Claudia explained, earning a puzzled look from both Sophia and Maggie. "He was born with just green eyes, but he is actually both earthment and firement."

"But he's married to your daughter?" Sophia questioned.

"You're right, I am married to Adrianna." He began, "She never knew about my abilities, in time, she grew to despise quadrupedia, and I knew if she knew about me, she would despise me too. I had told Claudia about it, and she told me to keep my secret safe. To hide my second sculpes, Elizabeth took me too Earth where I got a tattoo over it. Adrianna thought I was just going there for work, she was furious about the tattoo, but in time she got over it and moved on.

Thankfully my secret stayed safe even then. When everything began to kick off between the quadrupedia and the government, Adrianna decided to behave indifferently toward everyone, including her own mother. I spoke to Claudia about everything, and we realised we weren't on the same team as the girl we loved. Despite everything, if the time came, we would have to leave her, she wouldn't allow us to take her with us, nor would she keep our whereabouts safe. And now I know, the time has come."

"Now we need to get back to Earth and wait for Theodore and the others." Claudia announced.

Jax smiled, "Follow me. Let's go."

"Haven't you got children?" Sophia asked him, following him as he walked.

"I do, but they're too young to know what is going on. I would take them with me, but it's not safe, it will break me to leave them behind but their safety comes first."

"I'm not allowed to see them. She thinks that I have too much going on with quadrupedia, so she doesn't trust me near them." Claudia explained.

"Don't they have it too, if you have it?" Sophia directed at Jax. "Quadrupedia, I mean."

"No, fortunately for her, they don't." He replied bitterly. "Here we go."

He pulled a metal loop in the wall, pulling open a hidden atrium. The darkness filled the gap, inviting them in. "Ready?"

Sophia took Maggie's hand and went first. Claudia took Jax's wrist and smiled, "You sure about this?"

"Are you?" He asked.

She exhaled deeply, "She had her chance."

"She did."

"Let's go." She replied, stepping into the darkness and allowing it to swallow them into another world.

SEVEN

"WHAT IS THAT?" FELICITY SQUEAKED.

Theo pulled a lamina from his boot, holding it out in protection. Amethyst had her arcus at the ready, alongside Elijah with his Gladio.

Genesis looked around at her friends, they were all prepared to fight. All but herself, Tom and Xavier.

"Gen, why aren't you ready?" Theo snapped in a hushed tone.

Genesis giggled too herself, "Don't hurt him."

"Him? How do you know it's male?" Eliza questioned, "It could be a girl."

"How can you be scared of that?" Tom laughed, "So cute."

"It doesn't matter how cute it is." Noah said shakily, "It could be deadly."

"So deadly." Paisley added.

"Guys seriously–" Genesis began.

"What if there's more?" Amethyst whined.

"Seriously–" Genny tried once more.

"Genesis, please step away from the creature!" Theo cried.

At this point, both Xavier and Tom were laughing hysterically, earning peculiar looks from the others.

"Theo, calm down." Genesis comforted. She stepped forward, "It's just a cat."

"A what?" Elijah asked.

"A cat." She repeated.

"What's that?" Eliza asked.

Tom looked at her, "A c–"

"I know it's a cat but what is a cat!" Eliza screeched.

"It's a pet." Genesis explained. "On Earth, people have animals as pets, such as cats, dogs, hamsters–"

"Hamsters?" Felicity interrupted.

"So like a mortal's duplex?" Amethyst asked, trying to make sense of it all.

"Wait, you had a picture of one of these in your photo book at home." Theo said to Genesis, sheathing his weapon and stepping closer. "A grey one."

"Not quite." She replied to Amethyst, "Pets don't have particular humans, nor do they have any abilities!" She turned back to Theo, "I did. That was my cat from when I was a child." She replied, stroking the cat's head, "Her name was Tabitha."

"Oh." He replied, "Does this cat have a name?" He placed a shaking and under the cat's chin, causing it to purr in content. "Oh my Zeus!" He cried, jumping back.

Again, Tom and Xavier laughed, "Oh dear." Xavier smirked, "You're scared of a cat."

"It growled!" Theo exclaimed. "It growled at me!"

"Oh Mr *I'm-a-big-fancy-warrior*, it didn't growl at you– he was purring. They do that when they're happy." Genesis explained, picking up the cat and walking back to her friends.

"Right." He replied nervously.

"Do you know what I'm confused about?" Said Paisley. "Why, if they are people's pets, is there one wandering around aimlessly?"

"Good point." Tom replied, rubbing the cats head. "Where's your owner?"

"And," Noah said, "Why is an Earth animal here?"

"We're closer than I thought." Genesis said quickly. She held the cat close to her chest and began heading through the trees. "Come on."

Jax sat at the end of the long mahogany table, studying carefully at the pages of an old leather book. "It says," He began, turning to Claudia, "That it isn't unheard of. A quadrupedia with only one colour in their irises. It's very rare, mind you."

"Rare as in Zeus'-blessed-warrior rare?" Claudia asked, sitting beside him with a mug of hot chocolate. "Or just rare?"

"I don't understand?" He replied, seeming perplexed.

Claudia set down her beverage and stood back up, heading to the book case. She ran a finger across the spines of the books, until she found the one she was after, and picked it out.

"Here," She said, returning to her seat, "Read through this." She flicked to a particular page and pointed at a paragraph. "It will make more sense to a lot of things."

Jax took the book from her hands and began to read. Moments later he looked up at her in shock, "They're the ones this book talks about, they're the chosen ones?"

"Correct, they've made it further than any other element in the history of Pandoverse, we just have to hope and pray they continue forward." Claudia said half-heartedly. Despite how much faith she had in them all, she couldn't help but worry. She also worried what was written in the book. The final paragraph of the prophecy was coated with a smudge of ink. Whatever was written beneath it, could possibly impact them all.

"They'll do it." He replied. "How do you find out, if you're you know… blessed?"

"You just know." She smiled, before heading back out the door in search for Sophia and Maggie.

Jax stared after her in bewilderment, he wanted to know whether he too, was what they all seemed to call – *blessed*.

It was like a camp site.

Genesis placed the cat onto the floor before taking Theo's hand in her own and wandering into the centre of the huddle of tents and huts. The others stayed on the outside, keeping their distance with weapons at the ready in case they were necessary.

"Hello?" Genesis called out.

There was no answer.

"Perhaps they've moved on, we should keep looking." Theo said sympathetically.

"No, they're here. I know they're here." Genny replied adamantly.

"Not at the moment they're not, we should wait it out, see if they return." He suggested, pulling her close, "We will find them, I know we will."

"I just want to get this battle started," She whispered, "And get back to ordinary life."

"If we win," Theo began.

"We will." Genesis interrupted, "So, when, we win."

He looked down at her for a moment, "*When* we win, would you like to move back here, or stay on Earth?"

Genny stared blankly ahead of her for a moment, comprehending the idea. "Where do you want to go?"

"Anywhere you are." He smiled, kissing the top of her head.

"Enough of that, lovebirds." Xavier shouted from the trees, "What's going on?"

The pair wandered up to their friends. "Nothing." Theo announced, "We're going to wait here though."

Eliza stepped forward, "How about, we all split up? We can look in the other three directions, whilst Genesis and Theo stay here."

"Good thinking," Elijah complimented his sister, "Then if we find anything, we can send up a signal?"

"Okay." Theo said, "We need a different signal each though, to save confusion."

"Right, I'll go with Eliza and Felicity." Tom decided, "We'll signal with the trees."

"But how will we find you?" Genny questioned.

Felicity said softly, "You'll know."

"Elijah and Amethyst?" Theo asked, turning to the pair, "Signal?"

They exchanged looks for a moment, "Rain. We'll signal with rain."

"Okay." Genesis replied, "Follow the rain. Noah and Paisley, I'm guessing your signal is fire."

The siblings grinned at one another, "Of course."

"And I guess we'll be using air." Genesis said to Theo, who looked annoyed. "Well, I'll be using air."

"Right!" Eliza smiled, "Let's go!"

The group split up and wandered to three sides of the camp, disappearing into the trees. Genesis turned back to Theo, "Now what?"

"Now we wait."

Liz sat in the corner of the room, her back against the corner of the concrete walls. She didn't know, until very recently, that this part of the governing hall existed. It was dark, damp and cold. She was worried for her son and his friends, she was worried for Claudia, Sophia and Maggie. Did they get out of Pandoverse?

"Elizabeth." A voice echoed throughout the room. "Stand."

She looked up at the direction of the voice, to see Seth standing in the doorway, two guardians at his side. "Why?"

"Because you're wanted, so stand." He spat, "Or they will make you."

Liz looked from one guardian to the other. They looked evil. Their faces were taut and expressionless, their postures were plain and robotic. She was more than glad that Theo never accepted the offer of being a guardian. They were simply just brainwashed minions.

"Who wants me?" She asked, staying seated.

"Elder Jaspar."

"Why does he want me?"

"He wants to talk with you Elizabeth, please don't make this any harder than it needs to be." Seth said calmly.

"Just to talk, huh?" She replied.

"Just to talk." He repeated.

Liz sighed. "Very well."

She stood and walked toward him, brushing off the guardian's as they attempted to lead her forcefully. "I can go myself."

They walked to the stairs, descending them into another room, where Jaspar stood beside a wooden chair, waiting for her arrival. "Elizabeth."

"Jaspar, what do you want?" She growled.

Jaspar gave a wicked grin. "I want answers. Lack of cooperation has disastrous consequences."

She turned to Seth, who was halfway out of the room, "You said he just wanted to talk?"

Seth bowed his head, as the guardian's took her and sat her down on the chair, strapping her wrists to the wooden arms. "He does just want to talk, but as he said, if you don't cooperate, talking will be set aside."

"What do you mean?" She said between her struggles, she turned to Jaspar, "What are you going to do to me?"

"That," He said, "Is your choice."

Genesis peered inside one of the huts, it was dark, but clearly lived in– and recently.

"Theo," She whispered, "It smells like my parents."

Theo chuckled, leaning over her shoulder, "Gen, I think you're imagining things now."

"I'm not, I know what they smell like! They're my parents." She cried, turning back to him.

She walked over to two small dishes on the floor, one full of water. "Don't tell me someone hasn't been here recently? The cat has been fed and hydrated."

Theo stuck his finger in the bowl to be sure, "Yeah, that's water."

Genesis rolled her eyes at him, "Figured."

"Then where are they? Why aren't they here?" He asked her, raising a singular eyebrow.

"I don't know." She sighed, sounding exasperated. "I really don't know."

Theo stepped back out of the hut to analyse his surroundings, Genesis following close behind. She placed her gloved hands in her jacket pockets, resting her head on his shoulder.

"I say we check out the others." She suggested, pointing at the tents and huts in the area, "See what we can find?"

"Yeah okay." Said Theo, "We'll check them out together."

Genesis smiled, walking toward the first tent with Theo at her side. She pulled open the entrance of the first tent, ducking inside. It was quite spacious, with a total of four sleeping-bags spread around.

"A girl's tent." Genesis acknowledged

"How do you know?" Theo replied, looking at her in confusion.

"Because it's far too tidy." She laughed, stepping back out.

She climbed inside the next tent, peering around. "Two guys." She said briefly, before clambering back outside.

"I really don't understand how your brain works." Theo mumbled, following her again.

She approached the other hut, pulling open the door to glimpse inside. "A family lives in here." She explained.

"How do you know?" He laughed, shaking his head, "Is there name tags I can't see?"

"No," Said Genny, "It's just obvious, by the clothes laying around, the colours, the lay outs, I don't know how to explain it, I just know."

"Oh." Theo said.

Genesis smiled at him, before heading back to the hut she assumed was her parents, "For example," She began, "I know this belongs to my parents. This hut is clearly lived in by two people, most possibly a couple."

She wandered up to the table beside the bed and a gasp left her lips, "And there's a photo of us."

"Photo of who?" Theo asked, appearing at her side, "Oh."

She held the frame in her hand, the photograph of her, Seth and her parents stared back at her.

"They're alive." She whispered, as if to confirm everything from the past year.

"Alive and well." A voice came from the door. Genny and Theo spun around to face the two figures that casted silhouettes in the doorway. "Genesis," One voice said. "Welcome home."

EIGHT

"MUM? DAD?" GENESIS SAID, BARELY AT A whisper.

She stepped forward hesitantly, Theo's hand at her waist. "Go on." He said softly, encouraging her.

She looked up at him quickly before leaving his side and wandering toward her parents. Her dad opened his arms, awaiting her embrace.

She stood just a step away from them both, silently staring.

"Genesis?" Her mother said calmly, "Are you okay?"

"You lied." She croaked, tears forming in the corners of her eyes.

"Gen–"

"You lied to me. You lied to me and I thought you were dead!" She cried. "You led me to believe that you were dead. You allowed me to grieve and to mourn when all the while you were here, alive!"

Theo stepped forward, placing a hand on her elbow, "Gen, don't do this come on."

"No!" She snapped, pushing his hand away, "They lied!"

"Genesis we had to, for your safety, for the sake of Pandoverse." Her father explained, "We never meant to hurt you."

"But you did." She replied bluntly, "You hurt me bad. You left me alone with just Seth for family, Seth of all people!"

"Seth is your brother." He said. "In fact, where is he?"

"In the underworld for all I care!" She spat.

"Genesis!" Both her parents said in shock.

"He's dead to me!"

"Genesis you need to explain everything to them before you start throwing out comments like that." Theo whispered.

"Okay then," She said smartly, "My brother, tried to get me killed. He tried to split Theo and I up so he could get me alone and have me murdered!" She began to head out of the door before turning around one last time, "Oh! And where is he you ask? Why, he's at the governing hall with the Elders, his leaders, the men he now works for!" She stormed out, leaving Theo and her parents in shock.

Theo turned to them and awkwardly smiled, "I'm Th–"

"Theodore Benedict." Her father said proudly, shaking his hand, "Thank you, for taking care of our daughter."

"I love her more than anything on Pandoverse and Earth combined Mr Valencia, I will protect her no matter the cost."

"Call me Alex." Her father smiled, "And welcome to the family."

Genesis sat on a fallen tree, stubbing the toes of her boots into the mud. She had cried, for around twenty minutes straight. No one had come to find her, so she just stayed put. It was growing cold and dark, and she was quite deep into the forest.

She pushed together a handful of sticks and twigs, throwing a small fire-bomb into the pile and causing it to light.

"Much better." She crooned, placing her hands above the flames and embracing the heat.

"You've always been one for getting cold." A voice said from behind her. She turned to face her mother, standing quietly beside a tree. "Never could feel the heat! No matter what."

Genny laughed, "Yeah at least something's still the same."

"May I?" Katherine asked, gesturing to the log.

Genesis nodded, moving over to allow her mother to sit beside her. "Mum I'm—"

"Don't worry." She interrupted, "I understand why you were mad, and Theo has filled us in with the Seth situation, I'm in shock. I'm disgusted."

"I was too." Genny admitted, "I thought he was on our side. Theo seemed to dislike him, for a long time, I couldn't quite get why. But he's an intelligent boy, he knew what Seth was capable off."

"He is," Katherine said, staring ahead into the trees, "Well I don't want to reminisce of the bad things for now, but I've missed you and I've missed being your mother. So tell me about Theo?"

Genny laughed, "What about him? He's an incredible guy."

"Right he is, he saved your life I'm told. Tell me how you ended up together and about your date in Paris! I want to know it all, I want to catch up."

"How did you know about Paris?" Genesis questioned.

"He mentioned it briefly earlier." She replied.

"Oh."

"So? Tell me."

Genesis smiled, "Well he came to me when I was living in Los Angeles, of course I detested him to start, he all-but magically appeared in my kitchen, I was petrified!" She grinned at the memory,

"He was so cold toward me for a long time, then he kissed me one time, and it kind of developed from there. Xavier took me to dinner in Areas once, it was amazing, such an incredible view. Theo got jealous, so when he came to taking me on a date, he wanted to outdo Xavier's efforts. He took me in the atrium and we arrived in Charles De Gaulle airport. He took me for dinner on the Eiffel Tower, and bought me an opal necklace for my birthday." She pulled the necklace from beneath her coat, showing it off. "We got together after that, and then everything was perfect. But I had a vision of him killing Seth and I left, back to Earth, where Seth tried to get me killed."

"Hold up." Katherine said, turning to her daughter in confusion, "Vision?"

"Yes, daughter of Hecate and Athena, you must know?"

"Of course I know, is that your gift then? To see in the future?"

"And past." Genesis stared ahead for a moment, it was entirely dark now, just the light from the fire keeping their surroundings aglow. "I'm sorry, you know. About Seth. I know he's my brother, your son, but I really don't care for him no more."

"I understand, it's hard to love someone when they've done such bad things." Her mother responded, staring down at her hands.

"Mum, I forgive you." Genny said softly, "And Dad. I understand why you did it."

Katherine smiled, "Let's go back, I have some people who want to meet you."

Genesis stood, linking her arm through her mother's and heading toward the camp. "Wait," She said, quickly turning around and raising a hand, the fire extinguished and she turned back to Katherine with a grin, "Safety first."

"That's going to take a while to get used to."

When they arrived back at camp, Genesis was met by her friends. They all stood huddled in a group, all but Felicity. And they all wore a solemn expression.

Genesis' stomach dropped, "Where is she?"

"Gen–" Theo began, before he could say anything more, Felicity wandered over, beside Alex.

"Oh thank-god, I was worried about you for a moment." Genny laughed, Felicity stayed silent, before looking straight at Katherine.

Genesis followed her gaze, seeing her mother's expression looking blank.

"Mum?" She asked, trying to catch her attention. She looked back at Felicity and her father, "What's going on?"

Felicity let a tear fall down her cheek before running to Katherine, who awaited her with open arms.

"You know Felicity?" Genny asked, becoming increasingly confused.

Her father came to her side, "Genesis, you know in that letter, in the Compendium?"

She nodded.

"I mentioned you had another sibling?"

Genesis stared at him wide-eyed, catching on to what was happening.

"Genesis, Felicity is your younger sister."

"Don't touch me." Elizabeth spat, thrashing her head to one side when Jaspar's fingers grazed her cheek. "Get your filthy hands off of me."

"We were married once dear Elizabeth, how could you be so cold toward me now?" Jaspar snarled.

"What do you want from me?" She asked, looking down at her shackled wrists.

"I don't want anything." He replied sharply, "We don't need you in our lives."

Elder Gregor stood forward, lifting his hands to form vines around Elizabeth's feet, causing her movements to decrease.

"Then why am I here?"

Jaspar gave a wicked grin, before joining his Elder friends as they brought down their wrath on Elizabeth Aurelia.

"My…sister?" Genesis said, barely at a whisper.

"Gen, isn't this great?" Felicity squeaked.

Genny gave her a half smile and nodded, "How come I don't recall any of this? The pregnancy, you raising her?"

"Mermaids," Felicity said, before their parents could speak. "They enchanted us. They were worried about raising us together due to our quadrupedia, so they enchanted us."

"Did Seth know?"

Katherine took her elder daughter's hand, "Yes dear, I'm so sorry, it was for your safety."

"Everything was for my safety." Genny said with a sigh.

"And mine." Felicity added, "We're sisters, isn't this awesome?"

Genesis pondered for a moment, it all made sense. When she had first met Felicity, she always noticed their similarities, their hair, their mannerism, their accents, the fact they both had lost their parents, presumably. "It's pretty awesome," She replied, pulling the young girl in for a hug.

She heard her parents exhale heavily in relief, before turning to Theo, "Let's eat?"

He nodded, "I believe we have roast hog?"

"My favourite." Genesis and Felicity said in unison.

Theo laughed, "Come on."

Genesis sat upon a log beside Amethyst, she turned to the girl and smiled, "How are you?"

"I'm good, I feel human again." She chuckled, "What about you? A lot has gone on. You found your parents, you found out that Felicity was your sister–"

"I'm surprisingly great." Genny said with a smile, "It's a bit of a shock, but everything is ok–"

Before she could say anything more, a bunch of images crossed her, mind. She saw Liz, laying lifeless on the floor. Her brother and another Elder standing over her body, "Dispose of her." Seth spat, nodding to the Elder before heading out of the room, and closing the door before him. He looked ahead, "You and your posse are next." He growled.

Genesis gasped for air, blinking back tears. Seth was talking to her, in her own vision. Liz was dead. Everything was going wrong. She brought her focus back to everything around her, finding Theo kneeling at her feet, his hands around her own. "Theo." She breathed.

"What did you see?" He asked, brushing some hair from her face, "Gen, what's wrong?"

She looked away from him and at all of those around her, her friends, her family and the rest of the artillery she didn't yet know. Shaking her head, she stood, "I need to go for a walk."

"Genesis." Theo called after her, grabbing her wrist, "You can't go alone."

Genesis stared at him for a moment, not ready to tell him what she saw. She tapped her thigh, calling Luna to her side. "I'm not alone." She said, before heading into the forest with the wolf at her heels.

NINE

GENESIS LAY AT THE LAKE EDGE, LUNA AT HER side. She stared up at the stars, thinking about everything that had gone on. How would she explain to Theo what she saw? She felt hot tears fall down her cheeks at the thought, her heart broke into a thousand pieces at the memory of the lady who was her guardian for the past year and a half.

"Genesis Bella Valencia." A voice came from the trees.

Genesis sat up, looking over at the shadows in anxiety, "Who's there?"

A figure appeared from the darkness, it seemed to be sort of aglow. A tall blond woman elegantly swayed toward her, wearing jeans and a hiking jacket. "Just me."

Genesis raised an eyebrow, "I really do apologise, but who are you?"

The lady laughed. "You know me better than you think." She sat beside Genesis, reaching out a hand to pet Luna. "You must tell him, you know. It's his mother."

Genny stared ahead, "How do you know about my vision?"

"Because I know the lady whom gave you the ability to see such things."

Genesis snapped her head in the woman's direction, "You know Hecate?"

She nodded.

"Wait, you're–"

"Athena, the goddess of wisdom and battle strategy."

Genesis gaped for a moment, before shaking her head, "But how?"

"You've come farther than any other in history Genesis Bella, Zeus granted me this opportunity to visit you. Hecate wanted to come along, but I refused, she can be awfully intimidating. She gave you the vison so that you would wander off alone, so I could talk with you."

"Does this mean the vision wasn't real?"

Athena bowed her head in dismay, "I'm afraid it is real. Elizabeth Aurelia is deceased, I am very sorry."

Genesis felt her heart contract at the words as they left the Goddesses mouth. "Oh…"

"We need to think ahead Genesis Bella, I am here to help you plan the next step in this war, a plan that'll defeat Hades' nasty minions once and for all. A plan that will restore happiness, light and faith into all of Pandoverse, for good."

Genny shook her head, "I don't know if I can go on. I might just move back to Earth with my family and friends and stop, before anyone else is hurt!"

"That would be down to you, to protect them!" Athena cried, "Genesis Bella, we all have faith in you, you were chosen for a reason."

She felt tears fill her eyes and a lump form in the back of her throat as she looked up at the Goddess. "It's so hard."

Athena pulled her in for a comforting hug, "I know it is. But you've come further than anyone else in history, you mustn't give up now. When this is over, I will ask Zeus to bring you and your friends to visit us, you will be gifted and treated like one of the Gods, as you deserve."

Genesis pulled away from her, wiping her cheeks with the backs of her hands, "Do you live in Olympus, in the clouds?"

Athena let out a snort, "In the clouds? You mustn't believe all the stories dear! And we left Olympus a few centuries ago I'm afraid, we live in a place called Evlogimenos."

Genesis laughed, "The stories, huh? They've all been just stories until not too long ago." She pondered for a moment, "Evlogimenos?" She nodded slowly, taking everything in, "So we need a plan. Any ideas? Because I'm all out."

Athena smirked, "Genesis Bella, I'm the Goddess of battle strategy, of course I have ideas."

"Have you heard from Elizabeth?" Sophia asked, pouring a mug of coffee for herself, Claudia and Jax.

"Not a thing, I'm growing concerned." Claudia replied solemnly.

"How can we contact her?" Jax questioned, taking the mug from Sophia's hands.

Before anyone could respond, Maggie walked into the kitchen, her expression pained.

"Mags, what's wrong?" Sophia asked, running to her daughter's side.

"I just spoke with Genesis."

"What?" Jax said hurriedly, "How? When?"

"In my dream." Maggie replied.

Sophia let out a sigh, "Mags, if you dreamt it–"

"–It may be real." Jax interrupted, "Maggie, what happened, and what did she say?"

"She said she spoke with Athena, and they conjured up a plan. She said something about Morpheus. And Elizabeth."

Claudia stepped forward, "Is Liz okay?"

Maggie looked up at her with tear filled eyes, before carefully shaking her head, "She's not. Genesis had a vision, she can see the present as well as the future and the past. Liz is dead."

What happened next happened slowly. Claudia fell to her knees, as Jax's arms wrapped around her torso to hold her up. Sophia let out a cry of anger and hurt, taking her daughter and cradling her in her arms.

Claudia sobbed into Jax's chest, so loud the room fell silent beside the painful sounds. "Why? Who would do such a barbaric thing?"

Maggie gave her a soft and apologetic look, "Jaspar did it."

"It can't be true." Claudia cried, "What if it was just a dream?"

Jax pulled her back, to look her in the eye. "Claudia, you know who Morpheus is, right? The God of dreams? Genesis told Maggie that because I believe Maggie is blessed by him."

Claudia let out another cry.

"They have a plan?" Sophia asked.

Maggie nodded, "She said that she has found her family and the Artillery, they are all going to travel back here on Friday, and then we will begin preparing for the war."

"Does Theo know?"

"When we spoke, she had not informed Theo, she was with Athena at the time. Athena explained a bit about my ability, but I can't remember the full details, I just remember the name Morpheus."

Sophia nodded, "Okay, we should get the place ready for when they return." She turned to Claudia, "I'm so sorry."

Claudia frowned, wiping her eyes, "Do not apologise for my brother's actions, just know, that I will seek my revenge, no matter the cost."

Genesis wandered back into camp, her head bowed. Her mother was the first person to notice her, taking her aside before anyone else could see she had returned.

"Genesis, where have you been? That poor boy has been worried sick about you!" She soft softly.

Genny stared at her for a moment, before letting the tears fall. "I started this war, and people are being killed because of me."

"Anyone who gets killed dear, they knew the possibility, they came into this fight knowing it could happen. Who are you speaking of anyway?"

"Mum," Genesis whimpered, "She's dead. Elizabeth is dead and it's all my fault."

She began to sob in her mother's arms, before the sound of a heavy breath caught her attention.

She turned, to see Theo standing in the shadows.

"She's what?" He asked quietly, stepping forward. "Where is my mother?"

"Theo," Genesis mewled, reaching a hand out to console him.

He drew away, shaking his head, "No, you don't know this for sure, do you?"

"Theo, Athena came to see me, she told me herself, I'm so sorry."

"No, until we see her, we don't know." He growled, "You could be imagining things, you're pretty creative anyway, aren't you? Is this some kind of sick joke? Or just some bullshit?"

Katherine sighed, "Theodore, I know you're hurting but she wouldn't lie about this."

"Theo please?" Genesis cried, "I was the one who had to see it, it's hurting me too."

Theo gave a half-hearted laugh, "No, you don't get to hurt. You're right, this is your fault. I wish I never came to you and brought you from Earth, then my family would still be almost whole. I wish I never stayed by your side, I wish I never fell in love with you and I certainly wish I never asked you to marry me!" He barged through the two women and into the woods without another word.

Genesis started after him, but didn't make it far when Katherine held her back. "Gen, leave him. He needs to cool down, it's hard news to hear, a death of a loved one." As soon as she spoke the words, she knew what would follow.

"Yeah." Genesis spat, "I would know." She pulled out of her mother's grip, and headed after her fiancé in the woods.

She found him back at the lake she had sat beside earlier in the evening. He had his pants rolled up to his knees and his lower legs dipped into the water below. He sat, leaned back on his palms, staring out into oblivion. "I'm sorry." He whispered.

Genesis went to join him before he spoke again.

"I failed you. I promised you, after Quinton's death, that I would look after the family, I would be the best son you could ask for. Now you're gone, slain by my father's hand. I'm out here, Zeus knows where this is, and I have lost you."

Genesis stayed silently in the shadows, keeping silent as she listened to him speak.

"I shouted at her, I told her wish I never knew her or loved her. I said I wished I never proposed. I don't wish that, I never wish that mom. Genesis is the greatest thing that has ever happened to me. I wish we went ahead and got married before we left, so you could have been there. But then again, her parents wouldn't have been. Either way, if she forgives me, and still wants to marry me, I hope you're going to watch us with a smile, I love you."

"I still want to." Genesis said at a whispered tone.

"Then, one day, she and I will have a beautiful family, and I hope you can look down on them and protect them too. Your grandchildren. We're going to win this you know. I will be orphaned by the end of this war but we will win, for you, for Pandoverse.

Genny and I can move back into the Manor and have a fresh start. It'll be amazing, I just wish you could be there." He paused, sniffling, "Mom, what if she doesn't want me anymore? What if she hates me now? Then I would have lost you, dad, Quinton and Genesis. I couldn't bear to lose you all. She's all I have."

Genesis couldn't allow her heart to break any further at his words. She ran to Theo's side, stumbling at the lake's edge and wrapping her arms around him. He didn't hesitate to take her into his embrace, crying into her shoulder. "I'm sorry." He said, over and over, "I was such an ass, I'm sorry."

"No," She soothed, kissing his forehead, "I understand, I've kind of been there."

He nodded, placing his hands on either side of her face, "I know you have. Not kind of, you have. You lost them, they were dead. What happened here was a fortunate situation, I'm so happy for you."

"Theo—"

"No listen to me. I do want you. I do love you. Meeting you was the greatest thing to ever happen to me, and asking you to marry me was the best thing I have ever done. The minute we leave this camp and get back to Earth, we're going to plan. We are going to get married before we set off for this war. We're going to marry, have a honeymoon and enjoy ourselves for a while. Forget everything! Because I'm so stupidly in love with you Genesis Bella."

He moved back, taking a small box out of his pocket. "I didn't ask you right the first time, so here's to second chances."

Genesis gasped as he lifted the top of the velvet box, to reveal a large white gold diamond ring in its centre. "Theo–"

"Genesis Bella Valencia. Will you do me the honour, of becoming my wife?"

Genny stared helplessly at the ring for a moment, then back to Theo's loving eyes. "Yes," She breathed, "I will happily do you that honour."

He slipped the ring onto her finger, before pulling her close and placing his mouth against hers.

"When did you get this?" She whispered against his lips.

"It was your grandmothers. Your dad gave it to me." He said, lifting his head away.

"He did?"

Theo nodded, "I told him what happened, and how I planned to marry you on our return, if he would give us his blessing. He smiled and gave me a hug, and said he couldn't ask for a better man to marry his daughter, and that I've protected you all this time, and he owes me the world because of it.

 He then told me to wait whilst he went into the hut, and returned with the box, he said 'it was my mother's, but I want Genesis to have it. Originally it would have gone to Seth to propose with, but he doesn't deserve it anymore. If you would like, you can give her this.' So I opened the box, and fell in love with the ring the same way I fell in love with you– instantly."

Genesis felt a tear fall down her cheek at his sweet words, "I love it."

Theo smiled, "I love you."

"Theo, I'm sorry, about Liz." Genny said softly, taking his hands in her own, "And I'm sorry I didn't tell you after the vision."

He gave a smile, the sort of smile you can only achieve when your heart is breaking, "I understand. She really loved you Gen."

"I really loved her too, I feel like I owe her my life."

"Then do so. Give your life to me, her son." He replied, "Let me love you all my life."

"I wouldn't have it any other way."

Back at the camp, the mood was sombre. Everyone sat around the fire, their discussions solemn, and their expressions fairly blank.

Genesis coughed to gain their attention, "I would like to announce something."

They turned to her and Theo in anticipation.

Theo held up their entwined hands with a smile, "I asked her to marry me, properly this time, with a ring and everything." He smiled at Alex, "She said yes."

Everyone stood and cheered, before Genesis hushed them once more.

"I would love to celebrate such a milestone in my life with you all, but now is not the time. Earlier today, Elizabeth Aurelia was taken from us. Taken from Pandoverse, taken from Earth, taken from the universe. She was brave woman, a warrior. She took me in when I had no one else and she helped me learn the ways of an element. She raised two beautiful, incredible, strong children. And even after the loss of Quinton, she still excelled in raising Theo to be the amazing young man he is today.

With such a tragic event happening to someone so close to our hearts, it calls for serious measure. Tomorrow, we will return to Earth, we will begin our battle plan against the Elders. This evening, I was visited with blessing by the lovely Athena, she and I discussed all that had happened and was to happen. We made a strategic battle plan and I will share this with you all in time. We will rise and stand together as one, and we will go against these dark forces. It will be tough. We will have to harm people, people we once believed we loved. But it is for not just ourselves, but for Pandoverse. For the past, the present and the future of Pandoverse." She gave a wicked grin to Theo before turning back to the group ahead of her. "I would like to quote something someone special to me once said because we are the Artillery, and we are the future of Pandoverse."

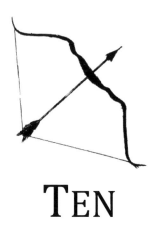

TEN

IT WAS ALMOST MIDNIGHT, AND EVERYONE WAS engaged in celebrations. Despite the death of Liz, Theo approved his and Genesis' celebrations and joined the others in a night of remembering the life of his beloved mother, and foreseeing a peaceful future with his fiancé.

"Do you know, before Alexandrus and I left Earth and Pandoverse, we used to take Genesis on camping trip every summer." Katherine said softly to the group. "She used to bring her guitar and we'd sing songs by the campfire, like your typical cliché in the movies."

Genesis gave a chuckle, "I remember that song we used to sing, *Hold on*?"

"I loved that song!" Alex replied cheerfully.

Another woman, her name was Sally, turned to Genesis with a smile, "I have something for you then." She jumped up and headed to her tent, soon returning with an acoustic guitar in her hands.

Genny shook her head, "Oh no. I haven't played in at least three years! Nor have I sung in front of anyone but my family and Xavier."

Xavier grinned, "We'll sit in front of you, make you feel more at ease."

"Oh stop that," She said, biting back laughter. She turned to Sally with a sigh, "Fine, I will do it."

Everyone applauded, taking their seats back around the fire and facing her with enthusiastic expressions.

Genesis took the guitar, placing it across her lap and arranging herself until she was comfortable and ready to play. "Okay," She said nervously, "I dedicate this to all of you, and Elizabeth," She smiled to Theo, "This is called Hold on."

She began to strum, the melodic sounds filling the air, causing her friends and family to gently sway to the music.

Life gets tough, I know
I've been there before,
And I'll be with you all along,
Don't be worried, when your head,
And heart are at war,
I'll be with you if you just hold on.

Don't be sad, my dear,
Smile for me,
And I'll be with you all along,
Spread your wings, and fly,
Make sure you are free,
I'll be with you if you just hold on.

I know that strength, is hard,

For you to show,
And I'll be with you all along,
But to me, you are,
My hero,
I'll be with you if you just hold on.

She continued the song, her parents singing along peacefully, Xavier whistling in-between verses like old times and the other's joining in with him when they had caught on.

She finished the final chord with tears in her eyes. The small crowd of friends erupted into applause, causing her to cry.

"What's wrong?" Theo asked, taking the guitar from her and placing it aside before wiping her cheeks.

"I'm overwhelmed. So many bad things have happened recently Theo, but then I see you and everyone here, and although so much is missing, I fill like I am still so lucky." She replied, laughing through her tears. "I'm sorry, I know I shouldn't be positive at all given the situation but I felt like something was missing for so long, even before my parents left. Then I met you and I don't feel that way any longer."

Theo smiled, "For the love of Zeus," He said, "I am so God damn in love with you."

Jax stood at the water's edge, looking out at the wide vast ocean.

"It's beautiful, isn't it?" Claudia asked, approaching his side.

"It is." He replied.

"I'm sorry, about everything. I know you must miss her. I miss her, despite all that has happened."

Jax turned to her with a slight smile, "Its fine. Everyone's going to have to adapt now, it's only fair I do too."

Claudia nodded in understanding, "I feel like I've lost so much recently. With my brother, Adrianna, Elizabeth. I just hope and pray that Theo and Genesis make it back safely today."

"They will," He replied, "I have never met two people stronger and wiser than them two. They truly are blessed, literally and theoretically."

"We were all supposed to be blessed. We were all born as Pandoversian Elements for a reason. The gift of the Gods. And we used it, we took advantage of it, and we brought war rather than peace to our lands. Now here we are, I have no abilities, you had to leave your family, and we're stood on Santa Monica beach, on Earth, waiting patiently for our friends to come back home, hoping that they do come back home." Claudia said with a sigh.

It was early, the sun was still rising and on the horizon you could see the yachts of wealthy American's sailing on by. On Pandoverse, money only ever came with authority and respect. On Earth, it was entirely different. Claudia had learned the ways of mortals. How some of them had money from working hard. Some had even won money. She understood that some people just did something outrageous and they found themselves in the spotlight, the money trailing in their shadows.

She would never quite understand why all this happened, but she respected it. It wasn't her world to judge. At least, for now it wasn't.

Jax turned in the sand to head back toward the promenade, Claudia soon followed.

"Maggie said that apparently Theo proposed to Genesis last night." He explained, shuffling through the sand.

Claudia raised an eyebrow in confusion, "I thought he did that before they left?"

"No." Jax replied, "Properly, with a ring."

She stared for a moment, "That's beautiful, Elizabeth would be so pleased."

Jax nodded slowly, "I believe they plan to wed on their return to Earth. Before the battle."

"Life is too short not to, I guess, at least there can be some light within all this darkness."

"When the world becomes dark, you should look for the shining of the stars." He said softly.

"And when rain pours," Claudia responded, "Look out for the beauty in the rainbows."

Genesis stretched out beside Theo, who still lay fast asleep. His hair was all ruffled from sleep, and his arm beneath her neck. She sat up, kneeling on her elbows and looked down at him. "Theo." She whispered, lightly shaking his shoulder, "It's time to get up."

He grumbled, turning over and pressing his face into the pillow.

"Theo." She said again, "We're going to Earth, we're going to get married remember."

At that, he sat up, almost knocking her backward in the process. "Is it today?"

"Yes!" She laughed.

He jumped up from the floor and slipped on some sweatpants, before running outside, leaving Genesis in bed.

"Bye then." She chuckled, throwing the blanket off her body and standing up.

Outside, most of the group were dressed and ready. Felicity was alongside Xavier, who was teaching her to shoot with the arcus, aiming at the circles carved into the trees.

Amethyst was using some stone like object to sharpen a lamina, sat beside Elijah, who was polishing his gladio and scabbard.

His sister sat on the other side, throwing reditum's and catching them as the returned. Tom was watching her with a loving stare whilst another young boy, named Harry, was in deep conversation with him about being the son of Hermes.

Her parents were now talking with Theo and Sally, about the arrangements and plans for the day. Noah and Paisley were attending to one of the group members whose name Genesis couldn't quite remember, he had a fractured ankle, but within the next ten minutes it would be healed and he would be able to walk freely again.

Felicity skipped over to Genesis, Xavier following close behind, and wrapped her arms around her. "Xavier is teaching me to shoot, so I can use an arcus just like you."

Genesis laughed, "How lucky, I was never trained with mine. Just remembered a few things from our school's archery class back in London."

Xavier smirked, "You have definitely improved since then."

Genesis pushed at his shoulder, "Enough of that."

They laughed together as they approached the mass of the group.

"Listen up everyone." Katherine called, gathering everyone's attention and causing them to wander to her parallel. "We leave in the next ten minutes and the plan is as follows."

She went on to explain how we would need to create a particular formation to give Tom the ability to send us all back to the farm house in Los Angeles. It would take two trips, he would take some home, then return for the rest. If any person was to break the chain, themselves and possibly some others, could be left behind. It was risky. If Tom forgot even the slightest detail of the camp, he could lose sight of the location he would have to return too. Due to this, Genesis would have to travel with him both times, in case his memory became significantly blurred, she would have the ability to restore his memories of the came with her own. Two consecutive trips from one world to another was already risky, they would have to portal three times during those two trips, they had to be careful, or it could become fatal.

"Are you nervous?" Theo asked, appearing at Genny's side.

"Not particularly, why would I be?" She replied with a shrug.

He grinned, "Of course you're not Genius– you wouldn't be would you."

Katherine wandered up toward the pair, "Genesis, are you ready?"

She nodded in response, "Who's going first?"

They gathered up their first group. It consisted of Eliza, Felicity, Alexandrus, Sally, Noah, Paisley, Icarus, Xavier, Harry, Sabrina, Yale, Adorjan and Tiberius. Secondly would be Theo, Katherine, Amethyst, Elijah, Konner, Milo, Jessabelle, Fabia, Lacey, Lael, May, Crystal and Paignton.

Genesis approached Tom with a smile, "You ready Tommy boy?"

He nodded, taking her hand and preparing their journey into another world.

ELEVEN

IT WAS WARM BACK IN THE FARMHOUSE.

Claudia had started up a fire in the fireplace and the entirety of the dining room had become warm.

The group were sat dotted around the room, many of the adults were sat at the table, alongside Genesis, Theo, Tom, Eliza and Maggie.

"Firstly," Theo spoke up, "Before we begin to prepare for the battle, Genesis and I have some things we need to say."

Genesis turned to him in confusion, before he continued.

"So it was hard to choose just one of you, but I had to pick." He turned to the boys whom were sat at the far end of the room, "Noah, would you be my best man?"

Noah's eyes widened in surprise, "Of course!" He grinned, walking up to Theo to give him an appreciative hug, "Thank you so much."

Genesis smiled at him, "Right, so, Eliza, Felicity, Amethyst, Maggie and Paisley. Would you like to be my bridesmaids?"

The girls all squealed with excitement and agreement and Genesis hushed them. "Eliza, would you please be my maid of honour?"

Eliza let a single tear fall with happiness, "I would love to."

"Great, that was far quicker and simpler than predicted. Anyhow, now that's settled, I believe we have a war to prepare for." Theo smirked. Everyone cheered, gathering around to discuss the battle strategy that Athena had created.

Eliza stood impatiently at the front of the store, her arms folded over her chest and her foot tapping rhythmically on the floor.

"I just can't choose." Genesis sighed, brushing her fingers through her hair as she wandered out.

"How hard is it to pick two rings? They're best to match, you want platinum, with diamonds? I still like the ones from the other store." Eliza huffed.

Genesis shot her a look, "Fine, we'll go with those."

Theo placed his hand at the small of his fiancé's back, "Come on then, we'll get those."

"Then you have to go with Noah to get those suits whilst Genesis and I have to find a dress." Eliza smiled, walking beside the pair to join Noah who was on the phone to Xavier.

Within ten minutes, they had returned to buy the rings and had gone their separate ways.

"So what kind of dress are you after?" Eliza asked as Genesis pushed open the store door.

"Something fitted, but flared toward the bottom," Genesis said softly, admiring the dresses around her, "Lace."

A woman approached the pair with a slight smile, "Ladies, how may I help you?"

"She needs a wedding dress! Pronto." Eliza grinned.

The woman glanced at Genesis, looking her up and down with slight disgust. "Aren't you pretty young?"

Genny gave a snort, "I'm twenty. Not that it should matter, I'm happy in love."

"Then what's the rush? Who leaves dress shopping until last minute?" The woman responded smartly.

"Well–"

"They are moving back to England. They want to get married over here though, it's their dream location, in her Aunt's old farm house. Therefore it's all rushed!" Eliza said cheerfully, covering for Genesis.

"Very well, seems sweet. What are you after?"

Genesis explained her wish, and followed the lady into the back room where she got the opportunity to select and try a vast amount of dresses. There were ball gowns, mermaids, sleek, lace, silk and more. It was beyond words, every girls dream, and Genesis wanted them all.

She was trying on her third dress, when she heard the store door open, heavy footsteps entering.

Eliza smiled, "It looks amazing Gen–"

"Shh." Genesis snapped. She raised her palm to hush her friend, peering around the door to discover the familiar voices.

"I'm sorry sir, we can't help you." The receptionist spluttered.

"Quadrupedia." The male voice spat.

Genesis help back a gasp as she saw Jaspar standing over the young girl. He raised his gladio and plunged it through her chest. The blade glowed for a moment before it dimmed, the life leaving her eyes at the exact same time.

"Now, where is the girl?" He growled to the other woman.

Genesis turned to Eliza with a nod, before they sprang from the back room and into the lobby.

"Jaspar, do not do this." Genny hissed, "I'm about to marry your son, I do not want to kill you."

Jaspar smirked, "You think you're going to kill me do you? No my dear, I believe it won't happen that way."

Eliza let out a laugh, "Please. We have killed two of you already, we'll happily add to the collection."

"Eliza Kaimana." He said with a snarl, "You really think you're something don't you?"

Eliza grinned, "It's not a thought, but a fact."

The woman who worked in the store stared down at her now-dead colleague. "She's dead! Susie's dead. You killed her!"

Jaspar waved a dismissive hand, "She was a disease."

"She probably didn't even know she was an element!" Genesis cried, "She didn't even have her sculpes! She was practically mortal!"

Jaspar gave a snort, "Never mind."

"Put down the weapon." Eliza said calmly, "We *don't* want to hurt you."

"And I really like this dress, so if you ruin it, I will be mad." Genesis added, her lamina pointing forward.

Before another word was exchanged, Jaspar shot out his gladio like a flash, slicing into Genny's arm. She stared at the patch of growing red in the lace sleeve with anger, looking back up at him with a slight fire in her eyes. "I believe I did just specifically warn you about the dress."

"Well at least having you in a dress will probably make this easier." Jaspar retorted.

"You think a girl can't fight in a dress?" Genny said with a hint of amusement. She gathered up the length of her gown, before charging toward him.

Eliza came close behind, jumping up onto the counter and back-flipping onto his shoulders, "Not today you don't."

Jaspar slashed his gladio toward her, making her drop her blade and giving Genesis the opportunity to throw her blade into his leg. He let out a howl of pain, "You bitch!"

The store owner stood still in the corner, watching the havoc unfold ahead of her. She glanced down at the bleeding body of her friend, before taking the fallen lamina and starting toward the injured man.

As she reached his side, she raised the blade, "This is for Susie." She spat, implying her fallen friend. She brought the blade down, but not before Jaspar grabbed her wrist, twisting it to make her drop the weapon.

"You're coming with me." He smirked. He turned to Genesis and Eliza and winked, before disappearing in mid-air, taking both Susie and the store-owner with him.

Genesis turned to her friend, who had both hands upon her knees whilst regaining her breath.

"Eliza."

Eliza looked up, "We have to get to the boys."

"I need to take this dress off, let me change." Genny replied, "What are we going to do? Do we just shut the shop and leave?"

Eliza shrugged, "I guess so."

There was no blood were the dead girl's body lay. It was almost as if the last ten minutes had never happened.

Genesis headed out back to change, before returning to her friend and leaving the store quickly and unnoticed.

It had been five minutes, when they walked into Theo and Noah. The pair had both suit-bags slung over their shoulders and were laughing about something unknown to the girls.

"There they are." Theo said sweetly, "My beautiful fiancé, did you find a dress?"

Genesis said nothing in response, she grabbed Theo's wrist and dragged him toward the beachfront and out of the public eye.

"Is this the part where you call off our wedding because you can't find the right dress?" Theo said, half-heartedly.

"I will wear Margaret's dress." She said plainly.

Theo nodded. He glanced toward her arm, "Are you bleeding?"

Genesis pulled back instantly, "I'm fine. I really am."

"No you're not." Theo countered, "What happened?"

He called Noah and Eliza over, giving Noah the opportunity to heal her injury.

"It was your father." Genesis said solemnly.

He looked at her in confusion, shooting a glance at Eliza also. "Where?"

"He came into the store." Eliza explained, "He killed a young girl, she was quadrupedia, no sculpes. He took her body and the store owner's with him. He just disappeared, in thin-air."

"I believe that could be the workings of Seth." Genesis added, "Son of Charon. Ferryman of the dead, perhaps the dead girl was the key to alternate-worldly travel?"

"It's possible," Noah spoke up, finishing with Genesis arm, she thanked him before he continued, "If he has been with people of such authority, he may have learned a thing or two about his abilities."

Theo frowned, "Did he hurt you anymore?"

"No," Genesis said, brushing off his efforts to check her over, "I'm fine. Let's just get back. We have a wedding and a war to plan."

"Okay." Theo responded bluntly, he allowed Noah and Eliza to walk ahead so he could speak with his fiancé alone. "If you're going to wear Margaret's dress, I have an idea."

"Okay," Genesis said, "What is it?"

Theo went on to explain about a Pandoversian style marriage on Earth. The Elemental vows, the different wedding colours, the Pandoversian traditions. All in a normal mortal church.

"So you propose we use the Elemental vows as our own vows?" Genny questioned, taking everything in.

"I do. We can suggest we have written our own vows, although really we have not."

Genesis smiled, resting her head on his shoulder. She attempted to push aside all thoughts of Jaspar and how he killed a poor innocent girl, and all the thoughts of the upcoming battle. She was going to focus on the now – on her wedding day. "Sounds perfect."

Jaspar stood ahead of his army. Seth stood in the front row of the large crowd, his mouth drawn in a thin line.

"So she got away, again!" Jaspar howled in anger.

Seth shook his head as the crowd roared in annoyance, "Has she found my parents?"

Gregor waved a dismissive hand, "It doesn't matter anymore. They're no longer your family."

"She is due to marry Theodore, I believe that their wedding will be a suitable location to target all of the artillery at once." Jaspar added.

"In a church?" A voice came from the crowd.

"Yes, Ben." He replied, "Is that an issue?"

Ben shrugged, "I grew up on Earth, with a Christian family. It's a place of worship and respect, I don't think it would be fair to turn it into a bloodbath."

"Well isn't it fortunate I didn't ask for your opinion?"

Ben bowed his head in silence.

"Anyhow," Jaspar continued, "That is my plan. Those who stand against it can join our victims on the day. Any questions?"

Seth and the army stayed eerily silent.

"Very well, you're dismissed."

"He cannot get away with this any longer!" Claudia gasped. She had just been informed of the havoc at the bridal store. She, Katherine, Alexandrus, Sophia, Jax, Theo and Genesis were sat at the dining table.

"I can promise you he won't." Genesis interrupted. "Eliza and I had him until the store owner intervened," She sighed. "It's probably cost her life too."

"You tried." Katherine soothed, stroking her daughters hand.

"But you're okay." Jax spoke up, "That's what matters. He didn't succeed– yet again."

"I didn't get my dress either." Genny said with a light laugh, "But I have Margaret's."

She turned to Sophia, "You don't mind that, do you?"

Sophia smiled, "You're an element– you have every right to wear that dress."

Genesis gave a warm smile, "Thank you."

Alex turned his focus to Theo, "Did you get your suit and rings?"

Theo nodded with a large grin, "Yeah, they're great."

Genny smiled at them. All barbaric peril aside, she was happier than she'd ever been. She had her parents, her fiancé and the most incredible friends she could ask for.

What seemed like a perfect life, had more than enough trouble lurking in the shadows.

TWELVE

"ARE YOU HAVING A BACHELORETTE PARTY?" Sophia asked Genesis as they stood in the gardens.

"I hadn't really thought about it." Genny admitted, "I don't really know if it's fair to have one with all that's going on."

"I think you should." Claudia added.

Genesis pondered for a moment, "I don't know… What's Theo doing?"

"He probably doesn't know. I only found out about these celebrations earlier today from your mother. He may not know anything." Eliza smiled.

"I'll speak with him first." She replied, standing and going in search for her fiancé.

She found him in the attic. He was sat on an old dusty ottoman, his elbows on his knees and his chin rested on his palms. She stared silently for a moment, before making him aware of her presence.

"Hey." He mumbled, shuffling over to allow her to sit beside him.

"How are you?" She whispered, resting her head upon his shoulder. She noticed he was looking out of the window of the dormer. The stars were most coherent here, and at such height it was peaceful.

"I think," She began, "That when this is all over, we should have a loft conversion. We should make that into a door, with an open balcony-type roof top. So we could have a lovely view."

Theo nodded, not taking his eyes off of the window. "Sounds good."

"I would say to tell me what's up, but I guess it's useless when I already know."

This time he looked at her, "I'm sorry for moping, we should be looking forward to our wedding and–"

"Theo, stop." She silenced him, "You have every right to mope. You lost your mother, your father has turned against you, and you have had to move to a different world because of a war that you're going to have fight in."

"I guess you understand." He replied, "You thought you'd lost your parents, you had to move worlds, your brother turned against you, and now you're back home preparing to fight. I was born with the inevitability of battle, you weren't."

Genny sighed, "You're right in a way."

"I always am." He smirked.

She playfully punched his shoulder, "We're in this together– I guess that it'll be okay."

"It will be. Is everything okay anyway? Did you need something or you just wanted to see me?"

She smiled, "I wanted to see you. Although, I do have a question."

"Go for it."

"Are you going to have a bachelor party?"

Theo raised his eyebrow. "A-what-now?"

Genesis laughed for a moment, before realising, Elements had different traditions. Claudia and Eliza were aware of the situation, due to speaking to mortals. "It's a form of celebrations, a mortal celebration." She said softly.

"I don't understand–"

"Before a wedding, the groom gathers his friends, the bride hers, and they go out celebrating – either separately or together, whichever is preferred. It could be anything, most popular ways are to go to clubs, or bars. But you can literally go anywhere or do anything." She explained.

Theo looked perplexed, "What's a club?"

"It's a place where you kind of party. Loud music, alcohol, lights…" Genny realised that explaining mortal lifestyle to Theo was harder than she had ever anticipated.

"That sounds pretty fun." He admitted.

"But there's an issue." She continued, "Over here, you have to be twenty-one and over to go."

"Over here? On Earth?"

"America."

"Oh."

"But that's not an obstacle when you have the ability to transport anywhere, right?" She smirked. "I say we go to London and take all you elements to a nightclub, for the first time."

"Have you ever been?" He asked. Of course, she wasn't old enough when she was living in London.

"Once." She replied honestly, "When I had turned eighteen I flew over to London for a week to celebrate with family, an old school friend and I went."

"Was it fun?" He said, seeming highly interested.

"Very."

"Then let's go!" He grinned.

"Now?" Genesis said with slight amusement.

"Yeah!" Theo exclaimed, his mood had perked from before, and he was now stood, holding onto Genesis' hands and grinning from ear to ear.

"Okay then." Genny replied, "We'll go tell the others and get ready shall we?"

Theo nodded hastily, leading his fiancé back downstairs and to everyone else.

It was early afternoon. Genesis, Theo, Eliza, Elijah, Amethyst, Noah, Jax, Tom and Xavier were dressed up and ready to head to London.

"Okay Gen, do your bit." Eliza beamed, pulling her friend to her boyfriend's side.

Genesis took his hand in her own and closed her eyes, allowing him to replicate her memories of London into his own mind.

Soon after, he was ready, and everyone held onto his arm, ready to transport to London, England.

Upon arrival, it was almost eleven o'clock. The streets of Soho were crowded with tourists and locals. City workers headed into bars in their large crowds, laughing and joking with one another. The excitement of the weekend was in the atmosphere.

"This is amazing." Eliza said into Genesis ear.

Genny flashed her a smile, walking ahead with Xavier. "Tequilair?" He asked. She nodded, and they headed into the heart of London.

On arrival, the bouncer smiled at the pair, "Genesis, Xavier, long time no see."

The bouncer, Keith, had known Xavier previously, meaning they had all become acquainted.

"Keith?" Theo said distantly. He appeared at Genny's side, staring up at the man.

"Wait, what?" Genny replied, seeming baffled.

"Ah, Theo! How are you young man?" Keith replied, pulling the young boy in for a man-hug.

Xavier smirked, "I couldn't tell you this before but…" He pulled at Keith's sleeve, showing two triangular marks on his forearm.

"Demi-quadrupedia?" Genesis gasped, "Waterment and Earthment huh?"

Keith nodded, "Banishment. But my warrior training built me up a strong man, used my skills to become a security guard. At an Elemental club! The owner is a wonderful Airment fella, hence the creative name."

Xavier grinned and gave an approving nod, he was clearly still impressed by the fact he already knew.

"Oh my Zeus." Genny said with a slight laugh, "Whoever would have known." She added, looking up at the club with admiration.

"You would have, if you were aware." Theo said, not detecting her sarcasm.

"In you all go guys." Keith said cheerfully, lifting the red rope and allowing the group to enter the club.

Genesis gaped at her surroundings as the descended the stairs. She never noticed it when she visited before, but almost everyone had sculpes. "I didn't even know there were so many elements on Earth, let alone London."

Theo smiled, "That's just the half of it really. There's a lot of them out there that aren't aware of their abilities, a lot of them don't have their sculpes, and some are just simply banished."

"Amazing." She replied in a whisper. Her words disappeared under the sounds of the loud music, as she gestured her friends toward the bar.

"What can I get you my lady?" A tall gentlemen asked at the bar. He too, was an element. His firement branding stood out on his olive-toned skin.

"A blue lagoon please." Genny replied, as her friends gave their orders.

"That'll be £81.90 then please." The man chimed.

Genesis felt the lump in her throat that she got when she considered something impossible. Without remembering who she was here with. She turned to Theo as he raised his hand on the bar-top, producing a pile of fifty-pound notes.

"Thank you." He said unfazed.

"No problem." Theo chirped.

"You can't do that here, there's still mortals in the building." Genesis said agitatedly.

"Anyone here that is mortal is far too drunk to care." A voice said over Genny's shoulder. She turned to face a dark haired woman. She had piercings in every possible place. Her eyeliner was dark around her hazel eyes and her lips were red.

"Do mortals get drunk quicker?" Genny asked, looking around her awkwardly.

"Oh yeah." The girl replied, "Terribly. That guy over there, he's on his third tequila shot. Wasted. Whereas I've had my ninth and..." She raised what would be her tenth glass and knocked it back, "I'm feeling as fresh as a daisy."

Genesis gave a laugh, as the girl passed her a shot. "I see."

"To not being a lightweight."

Genesis raised her glass and took her drink, before Theo appeared at her side.

"Theodore Benedict?" The girl said in slight awe. She shot a look at Genny, "So you're Genesis, huh? I didn't recognise you."

"Yeah it's us." Theo said, extending his hand. "Nice to meet you."

She grinned, "And you, enjoy your night."

The couple turned back to their friends with a smile, "So," Said Genesis, "Who is ready to try and get drunk?"

"Challenge accepted!" Theo laughed, as they wandered into the crowds.

Despite the young woman's comment, Genesis found herself far drunk than she had ever been before. Her head was spinning, her legs felt like rubber and her sight was becoming a blur. She took hold of Theo's arm to steady herself, when she could just about make out the worried expression he wore.

"Why are you looking at me like that?" She giggled.

"Gen, are you okay?" He asked, gripping her shoulders.

"I thought that girl said that elements took longer to get drunk, I feel drunk. I'm not drunk though, I swear." She replied with a slur.

"Genesis." Said Theo, a growl lingering in his throat.

Genny pulled away, "Don't get angry with me."

Before he could say another word, she stomped off.

"Shit." He mumbled.

"Your girl seems quite the mess. Careful where she wanders off to, won't you?" The firement girl from earlier snickered.

"What do you mean?"

The girl gave a wicked grin, before turning on her heels and disappearing into the smoky dancefloor.

Theo placed his bottle on the bar and headed into the direction Genesis had gone, something wasn't quite right.

When he found her, she was laying on a leather seat. Her head rested beside the lap of a young man, who was giving a detailed explanation to his friend of what he was capable of doing to a young drunken element.

Theo marched forward, lifting her from her side and heaving her up. "Don't touch my fiancé or I'll make you regret it." He spat.

The boy laughed, "She came on to me."

"I swear by Zeus I will kill you."

Theo started at him, when an arm came in between the pair.

He looked up, to see a familiar face staring back at him. "Step away from her."

"Now now," The face said with a smirk, "That's no way to greet your father after such time, is it?"

THIRTEEN

"WHY ARE YOU HERE?" THEO SPAT.

A small smile played its way onto Jaspar's lips. "I heard my son was due to marry, I couldn't miss such an event, could I?"

"You have to leave."

Jaspar gave a hearty laugh. "I cannot. For you see, Seth is my only method of inter-world travel."

"How has he got such ability?" Theo questioned. "He is the son of Charon, ferryman of the dead–" He silenced for a moment in realisation. "He– You cannot kill anyone here. The majority of them are just innocent mortals!"

"Well they won't see what's coming then will they?" He replied with wit.

"Father you cannot." Theo growled. "I will allow you to leave unharmed with Tom's assistance and my vigilance, if you promise not to hurt anyone here."

Jaspar pondered, strolling slowly past his son in deep thought. "I guess that seems acceptable."

Theo released a breath he didn't realise he was holding.

"But–"

Theo scowled at him.

"I much prefer to do…" He turned to a young mortal girl, lamina in hand. "This."

He plunged the blade into her chest, the alchemical symbols glowing as the life withdrew from her.

Theo raged, jumping toward his father with his gladio outstretched before him. "I warned you."

He lunged forward, slashing the sword at his father's face with aggression.

"Now *now* Theodore, I told you, I'd like to watch the upcoming nuptials." Jaspar smirked.

"You arrive at my wedding and I'll make it your funeral." He spat.

"Such unnecessary fighting. I offered to spare you despite your *disease*."

Theo threw his head back in laughter, "You think for one moment I will allow you spare me and murder my friends and Genesis, you are wrong."

"I'll give you time to think." Jaspar smiled. "Before I go, would you prefer gift vouchers or an actual gift for your wedding present? I'm trying to understand these mortal ways, but it's really quite a task."

"I'd prefer your head on this end of a gladio." He replied sharply.

"Toodle pip!" Jaspar chirped, emphasising his hearty British accent.

Within seconds, he and the dead mortal girl vanished on the spot, Jaspar's little army going with them.

Theo dropped the gladio and ran to Genesis' side. "Gen, wake up."

She groaned, flickering her eyes open to look up at her love. "Theo?" She groaned. "Why do I feel like shit?"

Theo laughed, "Let's get you home."

She nodded effortlessly, allowing him to lift her into his arms and carry her to a quiet corner.

Their friends gathered beside them, Tom in the lead of the group, "Will she be okay to travel?"

Theo shrugged, turning to Noah, "Can you?"

Noah nodded, placing his hand on Genesis cheek. He closed his eyes and within moments she came to, her eyes pinging open with mild fury.

"When you do that," She began, "It leaves a horrible taste in my mouth. Like I've consumed a ghastly medicine, not the supernatural kind that you actually conjure up."

Noah chuckled, "Welcome back Gen."

Genesis shot him a glare, before pulling herself out of Theo's arms and landing swiftly on her feet. "Let's get out of here." She added, grabbing Tom's wrist and pulling him toward her. "Take us home."

He nodded in response to her command, allowing his friends to gather round and link arms. With a quick nod of his head, they transported back to Los Angeles.

"We need to be prepared." Genesis said loudly, taking leadership in the dining hall, alongside Theo and Eliza.

The rest of the group sat around the table, staring up at her with intrigued expressions.

"Eliza and I have already organised weaponry, how to keep it covered at all times."

"Like you'll have a lamina in a garter under your dress?" Tom questioned.

Genesis and Eliza nodded.

"Pardon me, Theo, Tom, Katherine and Alexandrus." Xavier said with a smile, before turning back to the two girls, "But that's quite sexy."

The room erupted into laughter, "I'll let you off, seeing as I agree." Theo chuckled.

"Super badass." Elijah grinned.

Eliza slapped the back of her brother's head playfully, causing him to rub at his scalp and wince.

"And being a mermaid came with some benefits." Amethyst smiled, standing from her seat and approaching the girls and Theo. She held up a small chiffon bag. "Black pearls, when consumed, whole or crushed, they become a deadly poison–"

"How can you expect us to get them to consume them though?" Jax questioned, raising his eyebrows apprehensively.

"*And* if you throw them at their feet, they can create a large cloud of poisonous gas, only harming the person closest, *a-k-a* the enemy." Amethyst finished.

"Oh." Said Jax.

"We have two days until the wedding. We will use this for extensive training and preparation." Genesis explained, "Boys, your suits have been tailored and altered to hold the weaponry you advance in. Girls, heeled boots to hold smaller weaponry and garters for the bigger blades.

Bouquet's also have hollow insides, use this to your advantage with anything you consider useful. Amethyst, we will use those pearls as jewellery. Disposable necklaces and bracelets will contain the pearls, making them accessible if necessary."

"And those with an arcus?" Felicity questioned.

Genny gave a wicked grin, "You'll like this."

She left the room for a moment, shortly returning with an arcus. "So as you are well aware, the arcus can fold, making it storable." She demonstrated with the weapon. "And with this." She picked up a fluffy shawl, "It has been adapted for the arrows and the arcus to fit in–" She pointed at a pocket on the inside of the shawl. "Here."

Felicity giggled, "The guys can't wear them?"

Eliza shook her head. "We've had some of them adapted into canes. With one click the arcus will expand into its normal shape. Again, the arrows will be in a hidden sheath."

"Cane?" Tom asked, "We'll look like old men."

"No," Sophia smiled, "You'll look like proper British Gentlemen. And with Genesis being from the lovely Britain, it wouldn't seem peculiar for her wedding to seem upmost British."

"Do we need to fake British accents?" Maggie questioned in her best attempted British accent.

"That will be your choice." Theo laughed.

"Oh this will be awesome, it'll be like James Bond." Elijah beamed, earning another smack from his twin.

Genesis smiled, turning to Amethyst who was preparing to ask a question.

"So when do we start training?" Amethyst asked.

Theo gave the group a look of appreciation, "As soon as you've finished your coffees – its game time."

Outside, Genesis stood facing Theo, her arms crossed over her chest and her expression that of deep thought.

"They're all extremely talented, I don't feel too worried." Theo admitted, staring out at the group of fighting elements, "Two days of this and my father and his army won't know what's hit him."

"We can't make them train intensively for two days, it'll weaken them and their abilities." Genesis stated. She spun at the mention of her name to see Felicity. "Everything okay?"

Her younger sister nodded, "I just wanted to let you know I'm going for a tea break."

Genny nodded, stroking the girls head as she passed.

"I always knew it. Like, deep down, I always knew." Smiled Theo.

"Knew what?"

"You and Felicity being sisters. You're too much alike to not be related in any way!"

Genesis chuckled, "I guess it's true. Would explain why I've always felt like I need to care for her."

"I'm glad you found your family, Gen." Theo replied solemnly.

She turned to face her fiancé, scanning his sombre expression. She reached out a hand and caressed his cheek. "I'm still so sorry."

"Don't apologise, it wasn't your fault–"

"But it was! Everything that has happened up until today has all stemmed from my arrival in Pandoverse. Now your mother is dead, Margaret is dead, your father and my brother have left us to be with the government and after everything I'm back on Earth anyway!" She snapped, tears springing from her eyes. "You never should have brought me to Pandoverse."

"Bringing you there was the greatest thing I could have done. It brought us together."

"But if you never brought me, Elizabeth would still be alive!"

"Don't say it like that."

"Like what, Theo?" Genesis sighed, "Like it's the truth?"

Theo groaned, "No. You're saying it like it could be a choice, would I rather have you here or my mother alive."

"If time-travel was possible, that would be a choice."

Theo shook his head, as much as he would do anything to have his mother back, alive and well, he wouldn't give up Genesis in a heartbeat. It would be an impossible choice if it were a possible situation. "We can't change a thing. If you didn't come to Pandoverse, you wouldn't have your family, or me."

"But I wouldn't have known any different, nor would've you! You'd not know Genesis Valencia, the pure-quadrupedia girl who is part of a prophecy, who was born to save an entire world, your world–"

"*Our* world."

"I would've continued on believing my parents were dead and that Seth was my only sibling. I would have ended up marrying a mortal, like myself, and that just would be life." She explained.

"Genesis." Theo said quietly, pulling her closer as she cried, "I can't change anything, but I know one thing for sure, having you marry me in two days is the greatest thing I could ever wish for. I would never change that, even if I could."

Genny nodded, "Two days."

"Two days."

FOURTEEN

SETH STOOD AHEAD OF A ROOM OF YOUNG elements, Jaspar at his side. "Elements," He boomed, "I assume you all understand why you are gathered here today?"

Elements from the ages of twelve to twenty stood facing him as he spoke, their bodies still and their expressions blank.

"Tomorrow is the day we finally defeat Genesis Valencia and Theodore Benedict. I will remind you that we are doing this to rid Pandoverse of those sort of elements, better known as, the *cursed*. If we fail, they will go forth and overrun Pandoverse. Guardians, this is for Pandoverse, for your children, for your grandchildren, for the future of Pandoverse. Is that clear?"

An eerie silence followed Seth's words, he scanned the room. "Is that clear?" He bellowed again, this time receiving a mumbled response. He turned his attention to an older boy in the corner, "Please wait behind. Everyone else, you are dismissed."

Jaspar and Seth waited for the room to clear before pulling the guardian forward.

"You understand what tomorrow will consist of?" Jaspar questioned.

"Yes." He replied.

"And it won't bother you, to kill Genesis and Theodore?" Asked Seth.

"No, it will not."

"Excellent," Jaspar smirked, "You too, may be dismissed, Anthony."

Genesis lay beside Theo, her head upon his chest, playing gently with the bed sheets. Her mind was a muddle, within twenty-four hours she would be married, and either dead or alive.

She lay awake, waiting for Theo to fall into a deep sleep, before sliding from beneath his arm and climbing out of bed. She silently wandered through the halls and down the stairs of the big farm house, grabbing a weapon before slipping out the back door into the huge gardens. Outside, the air was cool, she strolled to the swing and sat on the large seat, resting her head upon the rope. Her arcus rested again the tree trunk, at hand in case of an attack.

"Athena, some help right now, would be nice?" She said into the dark oblivion.

In a response, Genesis saw a flicker of movement further out in the garden. She reached for her Arcus, preparing an arrow in her bow.

"Who's there?" She called out.

A rustle followed from the bushes, but no one replied.

"Zeus pugnantem." She whispered, "Ignis." The point of the arrow lit up, flames dancing off the metal and giving a light glow, before dulling down, the power engulfed.

"Show yourself, or I will let this arrow fly." She commanded.

Again, no reply.

"Very well." She said smartly, releasing the arrow into the distance, watching the bushes go up in flames.

A figure ran forward screaming, "Put it out! I'm here to help, to warn you!"

Genesis cocked her head to one side before letting out a growl and leaping forward. She sprung at the figure, jumping onto their back and pushing them to the ground hard and fast. A vine crept out of the mud and wrapped itself around the figures wrists and ankles, shackling them down whilst Genesis extinguished the fire.

When she was done, she returned the face the intruder, tugging at their hair and pulling their head up to face her.

She released a gasp, "Oh my Zeus."

The following morning, Genesis woke with a groan. The events from the night before imprinted on her mind like an open wound, every thought caused pain.

She wandered into the kitchen, rubbing her temples as she begun to make a drink.

"Genesis Bella Valencia!" Katherine gasped, "Did you stay with Theo last night?"

"Mother, we are engaged, you know? It's not the worst thing–"

"But the night before your wedding! It's not traditional."

Genesis gave a hearty chuckle, "You know, we're having the least traditional wedding, don't you?"

"Being with the groom the night before the wedding is bad luck in mortal and Pandoversian tradition." Katherine explained.

"Mum, we don't need to worry about bad luck, we have an army of evil Pandoversian warriors coming to try and kill us today. We're entering a war zone today, and we might not come out of it."

"Xavier I need to speak with you." Genesis said briefly, pulling her friend to one side.

"Gen, shouldn't you be getting ready or something? I mean, Theo has already started on his hair, are you sure he isn't the bride?" Xavier chuckled, before noticing Genesis' expression and regaining a serious face. "Continue."

"Last night, I went for a walk outside, we had a visitor."

"Who?"

"Anthony."

Xavier stared blankly for a moment, before shaking his head, "What?"

"I don't know how he got here, but either way, he came to warn us." Genny explained, "He is working for the government."

"That traitor! That absolute–"

"Xavier!"

Xavier sighed, "Sorry, what did he say?"

"They've hired child guardians, to distract us." She said with a sombre expression, "They believe we can't bring ourselves to kill children."

"We can't!" Xavier replied, "This is absurd! Did he say much else?"

Genesis gave her friend a half-hearted smile, "That was it." She said, before going in search of a shower, and leaving Xavier to ponder over what was to come.

Genesis stepped out of the bathroom in just a towel wrapped around her torso, before she could do anything, Eliza and Felicity grabbed her hands, pulling her toward their room.

"What's this about?" She asked her friends, laughing as they locked the door.

"We have an early wedding gift, a family heirloom." Felicity explained, as Paisley appeared holding a long gift box.

"Right?" Genesis said inquisitively, staring at them with curiosity.

"Open it!" Eliza squeaked, taking the box from one friend to pass it to another.

"Okay, okay." Genny smiled, taking the box and pulling at the securing ribbon.

Inside was red silk, she lifted the material to reveal a pale pink stone, it was about eight inches long, and was almost shaped like a shark tooth.

"This is beautiful." Genesis admitted, although not entirely sure what it was.

"It's an intensifying stone." Eliza explained, "It's very rare, but your mother gave it to me to give to you before the wedding. It has been brought down in the family for years apparently. She used to wear it on a pendant, I think that broke off mind you, we'll have to buy a new chain…" She pondered, "It helps intensify your abilities."

"That sounds like something unrealistic. I vaguely remember it."

"Well it's not." Paisley added, "Another name for it is Athena's stone."

Genesis threw a look at her friend, "Athena's stone? The night I spoke with her, the night Elizabeth was killed, she mentioned a stone. Her words were 'find the stone and you'll triumph.'" She brushed her thumb over the edges on the stone, it was dangerously sharp.

"She thinks this is the key to us winning the war?" Felicity questioned her sister.

Genesis smiled, twiddling the stone in her hands "I think it may be of good use to us; that much I know."

Theo stood at the altar. He passed his cane to Elijah, nodding at the rest of the boys. They were ready.

The mellow sounds of the violin filled the air with classical sounds. Genesis appeared at the end of the aisle, her dress fit tightly around her chest, the rest flowing down her legs like a waterfall, trailing behind her beautifully. The lace sleeves of her gown contrasted against her fair skin, and her golden hair was pinned up in a royal yet messy fashion. She looked picturesque.

She had managed to get her hands on a white dress, rather than wear Margaret's. She chose to adorn it with silver crystals and jewellery. She also had a similar dress with gold detail for after the ceremony.

Theo's heart fluttered as she approached him, "Hey." She said softly. Quickly saying goodbye to Alex before turning back to him, "Ready to get married and kick ass?"

"Sounds romantic." He grinned.

Genesis took her place opposite him, he wore a silver suit, with a white shirt beneath it. His tie was yellow, to match the bridesmaids dresses. Yellow was Genny's favourite colour, as it reminded her of the sun and happiness. Theo was cynical about yellow ties and dresses but she managed to persuade him for the idea. He had a black shirt and golden tie to change into for afterward.

Despite everything, she tried to fulfil some of the Pandoversian tradition amongst the mortal tradition. She turned to Sophia with a nod of approval. Sophia, had chosen to be their minister, to spare questions regarding the traditions, and the bloody mess that was inevitable for the end of the event.

"Dearly beloved," Sophia began, "We are gathered here today to witness the holy matrimony of Theodore Jaspar Benedict and Genesis Bella Valencia."

Genesis noticed Theo tense at the mention of his fathers' name and gave his hand a comforting squeeze as Sophia continued.

"Due to the knowledge that today is not an ordinary wedding, I would like to grant the special couple the opportunity to read their own vows," She looked to Theo, "You may start."

Theo thanked her and turned to face his fiancé, he cleared his throat before beginning. "So this is the part where I'm supposed to read the Pandoversian vows we have rehearsed endlessly, but there's something short I must say before that."

Genesis gave him a puzzled look.

"Genesis," He said softly, "Today is not how you dreamed it would be, and it isn't how I did either. My mother isn't here, nor is my father, yet yours are back, with you. Your brother isn't supporting you here and my brother isn't alive, all due to the world we are from. Today should be hard for both of us, yet standing here, committing myself to you for eternity, is the easiest thing I have ever done."

A tear trailed down Genny's cheek as he began their vows.

"I, Theodore Jaspar Benedict, fere-quadrupedia, take you, Genesis Bella Valencia, pure-quadrupedia, to be my wife. My wife, my friend, my partner in battle. Until the waves wash over us, the air blows us apart, the fire burns us and the ground becomes our home, I will love you. I promise to protect you against the darkness and follow you into the light. I pledge my entirety to you, as your husband, for the rest of our lives. Please grant me my wish and become my wife."

Sophia spoke up through her tears, "Genesis, your turn."

"Well, I can't compete with that, so I'll just stick to what we practised." Genesis sighed, earning a laugh from her friends.

She spoke her vows with a wide grin.

"Well," Sophia smiled, "Do you, Theodore, take Genesis, to be your wife, to have and to hold, from this day forward, for better, for worse, for richer, for poorer, in sickness and in health, 'til death do you part?"

"I do." Theo grinned.

"And do you, Genesis take Theodore, to be your husband, to have and to hold, from this day forward, for better, for worse, for richer, for poorer, in sickness and in health, 'til death do you part?"

Genesis looked Theo direct in the eye, "I do."

Sophia looked pleased with herself, "You may now kiss the *warrior*."

Theo and Genny laughed for a moment before leaning into one another for a kiss.

As Genesis pulled back, she kept her face close to his, "Well we got to get married and nothing has happened, that's a good thing, right?"

"It's the best thing." He responded, placing a kiss on her head, "Now let's get back to the farmhouse before my father and his minions arrive, I don't fancy creating a bloodbath in a holy building."

Genesis laughed in agreement, before taking his hand and walking back down the aisle with her friends and family cheering them on.

Back at the farmhouse, Sally, one of the Artillery members, had set up food and drinks for everyone's arrival. Genesis only had those of her close friends and family at the actual ceremony, the others stayed behind, just in case.

"Congratulations!" Sally cheered as everyone walked in.

"Thanks Sal," Theo said, hugging the middle-aged woman without releasing Genesis' hand.

"Our little girl is married," Katherine smiled, "All grown up."

Alex placed an arm around his wife's shoulders, "We raised an incredible young girl."

"Young lady." She corrected.

"Everyone to the barn!" Sally requested at a shout, gesturing everyone outside.

The barn had been decorated for the occasion, fairy lights hung from the remaining beams and hay bales had been covered in wooden boards and table cloths to hold the food and beverages. A disco ball hunger on the centre beam, and the air was filled with sweet melodic sounds.

Theo led Genesis to the table, "Personalised glasses for us, who are they from?"

Genny shrugged, "Who knows? I like them though."

"Yeah, me too." He took the glasses and poured them both champagne, "To us."

"To us."

FIFTEEN

THE SCENE UNFOLDED QUICKLY.

Every guest in the barn lay unconscious on the floor – everyone except Genesis and Theo.

"This is some cruel joke, surely?" Genny squeaked, treading carefully over limbs and torsos.

"It can't have been the alcohol? We drank the same and the kids are unconscious too?" Theo replied, checking pulses.

She shrugged solemnly.

"It was the glasses." A voice boomed.

Theo and Genesis turned to face Jaspar, standing in the doorway and looking smug.

"I brought you your glasses as a wedding gift, I hope you liked them? I then laced every other glass in the barn with a drug created by illecebra poison.

I managed to poison all of your friends but keep you both awake, clever isn't it?" He continued, walking inside.

Genesis had to admit, it was a genius idea, but now she and Theo had to face this battle alone.

"It was hard, to recruit an army to fight against you." Jaspar spoke again, "Turns out, the majority of Pandoverse actually admire the pair of you! I admire you, really, you're both very brave, but slightly stupid. Theodore, I have given you endless opportunities to leave this girl and stand by me, yet here we are, on your wedding day, about to butt heads over her? Terrible, isn't it really?"

"I would chose her over you in every lifetime." Theo spat, standing protectively in front of his wife.

"I have learned to accept that, and I have learned to accept the fact that I must kill you. But anyway, as I was saying, recruiting was difficult." Jaspar waved a commanding hand to the outside of the barn, before turning back to the pair, "Then I managed to recruit an army that I knew you couldn't fight."

Just as Anthony had warned the night before, children came flooding into the barn, alongside many elements whose ages stopped at around twenty-one.

"This is sick." Genesis growled, "You can't force us to fight them, they don't know right from wrong!"

"Oh they do," Jaspar grinned, "I taught them."

Seth, Gregor, and two other Elders Genesis didn't know the names of, appeared at Jaspar's side.

"Seth, don't do this." Genesis mewled. She watched as her brother bent down to stroke their mother's hair, "We have the opportunity to be a family once again."

"I'm sorry Genny, it's what has to be done." He replied, standing back up and approaching her, "It's a shame, because I do love you dear sister, I wish you weren't the chosen one, as killing you will kill me too, but it's just how it has to be, I'm sure you understand that?"

"I don't understand you." She huffed, backing away from him.

"Not much to understand really." He responded.

Genesis' eyes flickered from her brother to Anthony, who looked ready for what they had to face. He gave her an encouraging nod.

"Very well," Genesis smiled, "Let's fight."

Katherine could feel Seth touch her, she could hear Genesis approve the battle and she could see Anthony Wentworth nod at her daughter approvingly. But she couldn't speak nor move any inch of her body – she was paralysed. Her eyes scanned the barn until they locked with Eliza's, she too, was paralysed. *I need to wake up*, she thought, *I need to help them*. But nothing she could do, helped her in any way. She wanted to sigh, but even that wasn't possible. She just closed her eyes and prayed that her daughter was stronger than she could ever be.

Genesis swiftly pulled the lamina from her garter, swinging it in her hand with ease before pointing it toward her brother.

Theo joined her side, holding his binarii with great strength, "It's sad that you've made us do this."

"Well, let's make it easy for you." Jaspar smirked, "Perhaps Seth, the Elders and I could battle you first, and if you win, then you can face the children?"

"You're delusional." Genny said bitterly, lunging at her father-in-law without hesitation.

Seth jumped forward, slashing his blade at his sister's face without a care, "Genesis, don't make this difficult, please."

"It won't be difficult if you understand that you're fighting two quadrupedia, we can outdo you without fail." She responded.

"May the better sibling win?"

Genesis launched at him once more, creating a deep gash in his chest. "And that's just a warm up." She said smugly.

Seth took her distraction to his advantage and knocked her lamina from her grip, knocking her back and holding his weapon to her throat.

"Nice try." She crooned, "But it's not enough."

With one swift movement, Seth flew back and crashed into the wall with a groan. "Told you." She huffed, sarcasm dripping in her words.

"Gen, look out!" Theo cried, as Elder Gregor sprung forward, two vines shooting from the ground and toward her legs.

Genesis reached down and pulled two una's from her boot, bringing them down on the vines gracefully. She took the opportunity to pull the arcus from her shawl and loading it with an arrow. "One step closer and I'll let it fly."

"Not today Miss Valencia." Gregor chuckled, a round wooden shield formed around his forearm, "Not today."

"Sorry, but I go by Benedict now." Said Genesis, "Zeus pugnantem, Ignis!" The arrow lit up as she released it from her bow, it sunk into Gregor's shield, igniting it along with his entire being.

She watched as the Elder screamed beneath the flames and fell to the floor in writhing pain.

The remaining Elders turned on her, all except Jaspar, who was still fighting with Theo.

"Step away from her." Anthony bellowed, "Step away from Genesis."

The Elders pivoted to face him, including Jaspar and Theo.

"What, in the name of Hades, are you doing?" Jaspar questioned the boy, wandering toward him in anger. "Stay true to your people, Wentworth."

"That, I can do." Anthony smiled, "GO!"

All at once, over half of the young elements in Jaspar's army advanced on their leaders, laminas blazing and arrows flying.

"What?" Theo whispered.

"Anthony came to visit me last night, he managed to turn many of the warrior's against Jaspar and his *clique*. They're on our side." Genesis said proudly.

"They're going to die."

"Not if we help them." Eliza said, approaching her friends, "I'm guessing they thought it would be over by now or they would have drugged us with something stronger."

Genesis looked around her, all her friends were waking up. She saw her mother, standing and staring at Seth in wretchedness.

"Mother," He said with despondency, "Mother I'm sorry. I thought I was doing the right thing."

"Seth, my boy." Katherine whined, stepping toward him, "You're on the wrong team here, join us."

Seth nodded, cradling his mother in a hug.

Genesis felt her heart swell.

"I'm sorry," Seth said sweetly, before reaching up to her head, and twisting her neck quickly.

The loud snap echoed in the barn, and everything slowed down at once. Genesis started toward her brother, Theo took a moment before realising what was happening, throwing an una at the boy.

"You bastard!" Genny screamed. She leapt up, shooting a surge of air at the ground, lifting herself upward and falling toward Seth with her lamina facing south.

Before he could register what was going on, her blade sliced through his chest at the speed of light and Theo's una had embedded into his skull. Genesis landed at a crouch, pulling her weapon from his torso, and watching as he crumpled to the ground. She didn't catch a chance to realise what she had done, or what her brother had done prior, before she was up and ready to fight once more.

She looked around at everyone, the children and the artillery were a mass of slashing laminas and flying hastams. All the faces were a blur amongst flames, vines and gushes of water.

"Genesis, I'm sorry this has happened!" Anthony called over to his friend, facing her with a solemn expression.

"It's not your fault. C'est la guerre." She remembered Margaret saying those exact words once before. Her heart shattered slightly at the realisation of the loss she had encountered over the past few years. "Shit happens." She added, trying to lighten the mood. It wasn't ideal, her mother and brother were dead at her feet.

But if she spoke gravely of the situation now, it would crush her and she couldn't afford to be weak at such a time. Weakness was for what followed the war, strength was for what it consisted of.

"Congratulations though, I'm so happy for you both." He said honestly, "You both deserve the world."

"Thank you Anthony." Genesis said sweetly. A light sparkled in his eyes as he smiled at her, before it suddenly extinguished. A reditum sliced open the side of his neck, causing him to choke on his blood and cough away his life. "Anthony!" Genny screamed, running to catch her friend as he fell to his knees.

He stared up at her as she embraced him "I've known Theo since I was a child," He said between splutters, "He's always shut away the world, he acted like no one, nothing, was worthy. Until he met you."

Genesis smiled through her tears as she tried to stop the bleeding, it was no use.

"Thank you Genesis Bella Benedict, for making my best friend the happiest man alive."

"I'm so sorry, this is my fault." She sniffed.

"Well I guess for what you've done for Theo, I owe you my life."

"Not literally, though." She laughed light-heartedly.

Anthony gave a weak chuckle, "Well, I didn't particularly mean literally either, but I guess life has its way. Zcus wouldn't sacrifice me unless I held a massive part in this. Protect my cousins, please. They are Quadrupedia, don't let them die."

"You created an army to save Pandoverse, you'll never be forgotten Anthony." Genny soothed. "And of course. Where are they, your cousins?

He didn't respond to that, he just went limp in her arms, staring up at the blood-splattered disco ball.

She laid him down and closed his eyes for one last time.

"That's it." Genesis growled, she stood up, Heading toward Jaspar and Cliffio, the Elder of fire. "First it was my parents, then it was Margaret, then it was Elizabeth, then my mother, then my brother and now Anthony." She stormed toward the two men, her eyes blazing with anger and hurt. "You crash my wedding day, you tore my family apart and you tried to take my husband from me?"

At this point, all the remaining elements paused their fights to watch in horror as Genesis screamed through her tears.

"I have done nothing, *nothing* to deserve this! I studied hard at school, I was always polite to my family at Christmas, I never swore at my parents, I didn't fritter away when my world had crumbled down, I worked hard. I have done everything right, I have done everything by the book. Yet here I am with my family and friends' blood on my hands, asking you, *why*?"

Jaspar went to respond, but was cut short by Genesis' wrapping a vine around his neck.

"I could burn you, I could drown you and I could blow you into dust, but I chose to choke you, to take your life slowly, the same way you've been taking mine. How? Why? Because I'm quadrupedia. I am *blessed* with all four abilities, not cursed. I am blessed and I am part of a prophecy and I am destined for great things.

You can take my life apart piece by piece, but you will never take me down." She watched with cruel pleasure as Jaspar's face turned blue as he choked. "I'm sorry Theo, and I'm sorry that I could never have a nice peaceful meal or anything with my father-in-law, but this is it."

And with that, she shot a fire-ball at his feet, Jaspar flashed her a quick smile, before he disappeared in thin air, the remainder of his army, and Elder Cliffio, going with him.

"Wait, what?" Said Genesis, "Where'd he– How?" She turned to where Seth's body lay, that too, was gone. "I had him!" She screamed, "I had him right there, I could have ended this!"

Theo said nothing, he just stared at Anthony's dead body, tears in his eyes.

"I could've ended this all! Make it all worth something, but– he just– he just disappeared!" She was crying now, "And he took my brother too! I can't even bury my own brother?" She looked at the scene in the barn. It was brutal, it was a bloodbath and it was haunting. "Theo?"

Theo wandered out into the mass of the bodies, in total, Jaspar brought approximately three-hundred warriors to the barn. Over half of them joined the Artillery in battle, the rest stayed loyal. Ahead of her, lay almost one hundred and twenty bodies, of elements between the ages of ten to thirty years old. Many of the older elements stuck by the Elders, true to their traditions. Amongst the bodies lay Katherine, Anthony, Sabrina, Jessabelle, Yale, Fabia, Lael, May, Konner, Harry, Crystal and Sally.

"Theo I'm sorry." Genny whispered, placing a hand upon his shoulder as he knelt beside his friend.

"No, don't be sorry." He said bravely, standing to take her hand, he looked over at Alex who sat sobbing whilst cradling Katherine's body.

"It's real this time, this time she won't reappear, I have to grieve all over again." She said quietly, "History repeats itself."

"I don't believe that." Theo replied, "Looking at history, no one that Zeus chose, ever made it as far as this, you've excelled. The prophecy stated many things, and you've done them all so far without a flicker of weakness. You're a true heroine."

Genesis smiled at him, it was a weak effort of a smile, but a smile, nonetheless.

"Gen?" Felicity whimpered at her side.

She had almost forgotten there were more to her family than herself and her mother. She knew she had to leave her father alone for now, but she entirely forgot about Felicity. Her little sister, her vulnerable little sister.

She said nothing, she just took the girl in her arms as they sobbed.

When she was Felicity's age, she dreamt of her wedding day. She dreamt of a shocking white dress, which hugged her figure in all the right places, with a flowing skirt to make her feel like a princess. She knew she wanted her hair in natural curls, a tiara keeping it in place. She wanted her bridesmaids in yellow and she wished for a string quartet to play as she walked the aisle to her husband-to-be. She wanted him to stand at the altar with his best man and her brother, she wanted her father to hand her over to him and sit with her mother, and the grooms parents, as they smiled and welcomed one another to the family.

She wanted endless amounts of people there to celebrate with her. She wanted her honeymoon in Italy. And so much of her dream had come true, she thought, staring down at her blood soaked and ripped dress.

Her friends stood in their yellow gowns, also gruesomely splattered. But Theo's parents weren't at the ceremony. Nor was her brother. She would be spending the next fortnight waiting to fight to the death for a world she never knew existed until a year and a half ago. Seth and her mother were killed at the reception. She killed him.

She killed her own brother, and she had to spend the rest of her life remembering that thought as though it was tattooed on her eyelids forever.

SIXTEEN

GENESIS STOOD BESIDE THEO AT THE BACK DOOR, looking out with a familiar pain in her chest.

"You ready?" He asked her, pulling her close and planting a kiss on her temple.

"Yes," Said Genny, "Yes, I'm ready."

They wandered into the back yard, in the centre situated a large, yet shallow, freshly-dug hole. The bodies of the dead warriors lay inside, all cleaned up and placed as though they were sleeping. Genesis peered over at her mother's body, beside Anthony's. It seemed as though they were fast asleep. She stared with anticipation at their chests, as to wait for the rise and the fall that their breathing created.

But it never came.

The lump in Genesis' throat grew in size, making her feel like she could choke on her own words the moment she spoke. Today, they were holding a funeral for the fallen.

Twelve warriors all lined up. Claudia had organised with Jax to communicate with the families of the other warriors back in Pandoverse, they sent the bodies back there so that they could say goodbye the way they wanted to. During this time, fortunately, Jaspar didn't disturb them at all. Claudia didn't take this a good sign of course, she knew what he was capable of– she had a few dozen bodies to prove it.

The rest of the Artillery gathered around the pit amongst Genesis and Theo. All dressed in four different colours. Genesis wore black. Theo had asked her earlier that morning why she hadn't gone with the Pandoversian colours. She said that four of those from the Artillery who were killed were quadrupedia, and her parents were practically mortal, so she chose the mortal tradition of black.

Quadrupedia didn't have set funeral wear, as they were never given any gift throughout life, let alone death. They were never given a farewell with a funeral, not until today.

It was Sophia and Jax who stood up to speak.

"Everyone," Jax greeted, "It is with a heavy heart to gather us all here today, to bid goodbye to our loved ones."

Genesis took Theo's hand and gave it a squeeze.

"With Genesis' request, we will grant whomever wishes, the chance to speak." Genesis had asked him this the day before. According to Pandoversian traditions, a funeral is brief and the only words spoken were those of the host.

Genesis chose to adapt those with mortal traditions. Giving everyone the opportunity to speak for the person they loved, and place something beside their body before they were committed, although none of the remaining Artillery wanted to do this, it was too hard for them. One member volunteered to speak for the others. Genesis would have spoken for them, but she never got the opportunity to get to know them enough to feel as though she gained the right. "Our first speaker, is Adorjan, on behalf of himself, Tiberius, Milo, Paignton, Lacey and Icarus."

Adorjan was twenty-five. He had long dirty-blonde hair, with brighter blonde natural hi-lights that Genesis had grown envious of. He had piercing blue waterment eyes and golden skin.

She realised he was quite handsome, his sculpted physique an exhibit of his extensive training. He wore his hair in a neat top-knot for the funeral. His facial hair had been trimmed and he looked smart. His suit was a shade of navy with intricate seashell designs along the jacket. In Pandoverse, Elements wore clothing the colour to represent the element of the deceased. The Artillery chose to wear their personal colours for the ceremony as those who were killed were of different elements. Icarus and Milo wore black, the same as Genesis, for they were Quadrupedia. As did Jax, Felicity and Xavier.

"I grew up in Nero alongside Yale. He was my best friend from a young age, and we did everything together. We got our first weapons together, our duplexes, everything. And it was May, who brought us to the Artillery." He said mournfully.

May had been his girlfriend of five years. She was pure-quadrupedia like Genesis, but she only ever got her Waterment sculpes as a child. "When she told me she was in danger, Yale and I swore to protect her. She said she had to leave, and that an army of Element's were waiting for her. Some, she said, were just like her, and that she needed to be with those like herself." He gave a slight laugh as though another memory had come to his mind, "I tried to stop her, but she was so stubborn, so instead I went with her, Yale by my side. She introduced me to Sally, an ex-government worker who had created the Artillery to fight back those who she knew were destroying Pandoverse.

At the time, there were almost fifty of us in the army. Sabrina, Harry, Jessabelle, Konner, Crystal, Lael and Fabia were amongst those who survived the escape from Pandoverse. When we passed the Fotia volcanoes, we all stayed quiet about those we had lost during the fight. Over the following years, I become best of friends with them all. And I owe them my life. Three days ago, they gave their lives to protect the remaining of the Artillery, including the newest recruits. But if it wasn't for Genesis' bravery, a lot more of us could be dead too. So I am grateful. I didn't know what I could leave with them, but I gathered their emblem's to place on their body." He looked at Jax inquisitively, "Is that okay?"

Jax nodded.

"To our warriors." Adorjan bellowed, raising his fist. Clasped in-between his fingers were ten rope necklaces, each one held a wooden pendant.

Genesis recognised the symbol instantly, for her parents wore the same. The same that Element's wore, a triangle with a cross in the centre. It represented the four elements together.

Genesis watched as Adorjan walked into the pit, placing the emblem's on his friend's rested bodies.

"Thank you Adorjan." Jax said sweetly, patting the boy's shoulder. "Next to speak is Genesis, on behalf of – well, everyone, really."

Genesis gave a half-hearted laugh before standing ahead of everyone.

She cleared her throat before beginning, "My wedding." She said simply. "Every little girl dreams of her wedding day, like it's the most important day of her life. I did too. I got to marry the love of my life, alongside my friends and my parents, whom just a year ago, I believed were dead." She gave Alex a comforting look. "When the ceremony was over, I felt relieved in a way, to know I managed to say my vows and marry Theo before I had to face a fight. When I saw Seth talking to my mother in the barn, for a moment, everything was okay.

I thought that he'd seen sense. When he cradled her I felt a pang in my chest. I felt gratitude which was soon replaced with regret. I don't regret killing my brother, for his actions were unforgiveable, but I will spend the rest of my life with his blood on my hands. No one should have to have that burden. But then again, no one should have to go about their life watching those they love, become victims of murder." A tear escaped her eye as she regained her posture to continue her speech. "I guess," She said with a rasp in her tone, "I guess I just wanted to apologise.

Before I came to Pandoverse, many of you were happy. You had all your loved ones, you had your lives and everything was okay. Not ideal, but okay. I had learned to live without my parents but with the pain that replaced them. I was due to go to college, to learn to become a teacher. I partied once a month with some friends who now think I've moved back to England. My brother would visit me every summer and we'd do things that brothers and sisters that love each other should do. But now, he's gone. And so is my mother, for real this time. And it's all my fault. So I am sorry. But, I swear by Zeus, that I will avenge their deaths and get well-deserved justice for all that has been done. I will fulfil my role in Zeus' prophecy and I will recreate Pandoverse as a peaceful place were my kind can live a long and happy life. And that is my vow to you all. Goodbye my mother, goodbye my friends, sleep tight and watch over us as the guardian angels we need."

Theo walked forward to hold Genesis as she began to sob. "It's okay, beautiful. It's okay."

She nodded, "I would like to leave something extraordinarily small with Katherine. It means a lot to us both. When she bought me my first guitar she gave me a yellow plectrum, 'your favourite colour, so bright and cheerful, just like you.' She had said. I was four. I never used it, I just kept it safe as a lucky treasure for years." She pulled a small yellow object from her pocket, "My luck has run out, but you may need it in your next life." She placed the item on her mother's hands as they lay across her stomach.

Theo stood were she left him, it was his turn. He was the last to speak. With Jax's approving nod, he begun.

"I'm going to keep this short and sweet. But for a long time, Anthony was my only friend. And I stayed by his side always. When we left Pandoverse to come here, I felt hurt to leave him behind, but we had to be weary of who we could trust. I could trust him, I always could, but I couldn't trust going to Aeras to bring him with us. His missing presence wouldn't go unnoticed. Genesis didn't tell me of how Anthony came to her the night before wedding. She only told Xavier her knowledge of the Elder's child army.

She shared with no one, her knowledge of his plans. They kept it safe from us to make sure the plan went ahead. And I respect that. I only wish that I could've seen him that night also, to get one final conversation with my best friend. Genesis said that he told her as he lay dying, that he owed her his life for making me happy. And I want him to know that she makes me happier than I could've ever asked. Now I owe him my life, for making an exceptional sacrifice. I owe you, and I will see you in the next life buddy." Theo finished with an expressionless face. He didn't leave an item for Anthony, he simply wandered back into the line of his friends and waited.

Jax stood back up, "And with that, I commit to Zeus, the bodies of our warriors, our champions. Those who sacrificed themselves in the name of the Gods. We shall see them once more, when Zeus grants us the chance to spend our next lives together, as he does with all those who are under his kingdom." Genesis watched as many of her friends, and Theo, placed their hands on their chests. Sophia shrugged at her, and they joined in, as Jax read the Pandoversian Prayer of Goodbye.

"You fought, you lived, you bore sculpes to prove your worth and pledged your worship to the Gods. Now we say our final farewell with sorrow. May the earth enclose you, the flames indulge you, the sea wash over you and the air keep you at our sides. May your legend live on with your children and may your name be remembered by those of Pandoverse. As Zeus takes you from us, we bid farewell one last time. Forever and Now. For Pandoverse."

"For Pandoverse." Everyone repeated.

Genesis watched in amazement as all her friends bowed their heads. Flowers grew in the pit, growing over the bodies and covering them in beautiful blends of whites, blues and pinks. Suddenly, the entire pit caught fire. Genny looked up at Jax, his hand was raised. She remembered discovering he was quadrupedia, and it made sense. The group turned on their heels and headed back inside the house whilst the flames continued on.

Around three hours later, Genesis wandered back outside. Everyone was inside, having drinks and celebrating the lives that were lost, recalling memories and looking through photographs.

Genny stood at the edge of the pit. Ash was all that was left of her mother and her friends. She raised her right hand, creating a wave of air to send the majority of the ashes flying off into the evening sky. It was a painted canvas. Blues, purples, pinks, oranges and yellows adorned the atmosphere. The sun was setting in the distance but the remaining light than shone from the large star reflected off of bits and pieces of the garden.

One bit in particular that caught Genesis' eye. She hopped into the pit, bending down the pick up the shiny object which lay hidden beneath some remaining ashes.

She let out a gasp in realisation. Her lucky plectrum, still intact and not even touched by the flames that burned there hours before.

She spun around and let out a scream.

SEVENTEEN

THEO RAN OUTSIDE AT THE SOUND OF SCREAMS.

"Genesis?" He called out, sprinting to her side as she lay crumpled her knees, in tears. "What's wrong? What happened?"

"Seth." She sniffed, "It was Seth."

He lift her hand to see what she had clutched in her palm. "How did this survive the fire?"

She shrugged lightly and looked into his eyes. The four colours in her irises sparkled with love and fear. He noticed that every time he stared into them, he fell deeper in love with her than before. And every time he wondered how that was possible.

"Seth is dead, Gen." He soothed, "You're seeing things."

"No, I'm not. He was here with Anthony."

Theo sighed, "Anthony and Seth aren't alive Genesis. You're bereft. You're hallucinating."

"Seth was here. He had fog around him and a stab wound in his chest were I killed him. He had hold of Anthony's collar, as though he was holding him into place. Anthony had a stab would too, but mostly he was blistering and charred. Almost as though he was dug from the fire and stayed alive." She explained her sighting.

"Genesis, listen to me. There's no way–"

"There's a way." Jax said, appearing behind them both alongside Claudia.

Theo shot him a look, as if to say 'I'm trying to comfort her, don't make it worse'.

"Seth is the son of Charon." Jax begun.

"*Was*." Theo corrected.

"He *was* the son of Charon. Hades could grant his soul the opportunity to see you, seeing as you're family. It's a rule in the underworld, you are granted one opportunity in the first twenty-eight days of death, to visit a loved one."

"Hardly loved." Genesis muttered.

Claudia placed a soothing hand on the young girl's shoulder, "He's trying to torment you. You must not let it get to you."

Genny gave her a half-hearted smile, to thank her for her kind words, before standing and heading back inside.

"I wish this could be over." Theo announced as he turned to follow.

"Don't we all?" Claudia added, receiving a thoughtful nod from Jax.

"We have one more shot." Cliffio explained to Jaspar, "*One*."

"Why one?" Jaspar asked in aggravation.

Cliffio huffed, "Because there's two of us left, and half an army! We're weak."

"We'll recruit more guardians. And we'll chose two more Elders." He smiled, "It's that easy."

"It's not that easy. You haven't got Seth, dead or alive, to help you transport back to Pandoverse this time if it all goes wrong. You narrowly escaped the girl before!" Cliffio exclaimed.

Jaspar chuckled, "Next time, it's her who'll need an escape route, not me. And we won't have traitors amongst us either." He said in reference to Anthony.

The bell of the Governing house chimed, breaking Jaspar from his conversation and leading him to the large doors.

Elder Ageas appeared looking his usual glum self, "A visitor, Sir. She wants to see you, urgently."

"Bring her forth." Jaspar sniped.

Ageas moved to one side, allowing the visitor and children into the hall.

"Ah," Jaspar grinned, "Adrianna Faolan and children. What a lovely surprise!"

Eliza came up with seemingly marvellous idea to hire a yacht.

Genesis sighed at the suggestion, "Don't be ridiculous!" She said.

"We can afford it." Argued Eliza, her arms folded across her front.

"We can, but it's too dangerous. What if Jaspar comes back?"

"Ah!" Eliza grinned, "But all that remains is the Earthment and the Firement. They wouldn't come after us in the middle of the Ocean! Too dangerous for *them*. The sea would be in our advantage!"

Theo spoke up next, "She has got a point."

"And we deserve a nice day out." Elijah had his input.

"And I deserve a honeymoon but I can't without the chance of being murdered." Genesis snapped. She looked around at her friends with a huff, "Very well, let's do it."

And so two hours later, they found themselves on a forty foot long yacht, in the middle of the North Pacific Ocean not far from the coast of Hilo, Hawaii.

"Are we allowed this far out? We're practically going to another country. Without passports." Genesis said anxiously, looking out at the islands ahead of her.

"We came from another world to Earth without a passport, we don't need one now." Xavier chuckled.

"You know what I meant. We could get into trouble?"

Everyone laughed at her, but it felt good. It was nice to hear laughter after such a tough time.

"Gen?" Theo said quietly, pulling her to one side.

"Hm?" She responded, "Everything okay?"

"I want you to forget about all the troubles we have going on right now, and answer me. Exclude my father and everything, okay?"

"Okay?"

"Do you want to honeymoon for two days in Honolulu?"

Genesis laughed, "I'd love to!"

"Really?"

"Yeah!" She smiled, "We will when this is over, yeah?"

Theo placed his palm to his forehead, "I mean now."

"Oh…" She looked over at her friends, father and sister. "We can't now. We can't leave them."

"I understand." He said solemnly.

"I'm sorry." She whispered, pulling him close, "After this is done, we'll come back here and go somewhere really exotic. Like, Bora Bora!"

"Bora– what?"

"It's in the French Polynesia."

Theo shook his head, "We've been to France– it wasn't *that* exotic?"

Genny snickered, "It's not in France. Never mind, I'll show you it one day."

Theo agreed, as they wandered back to the centre deck, where their friends began a barbecue.

Genesis looked over the railings in the turquoise ocean. It was so clear, she could see the fishes, the rays and the turtles. She could see her reflection also. She saw how different she looked from just a year ago. Her face was skinnier, yet her body was more muscular than before. She stared for a moment.

Suddenly, a body jumped up at her, grabbing her arm and pulling her in, giving her just enough time to use her ability to breathe.

She fell beneath the surface, struggling to release herself from someone's grip. Staring her in the face was the most evil being she had ever laid her eyes on. A mermaid. She knew instantly this one was old. Her sharp teeth and flawless skin said otherwise, but he anger and the evil in her eyes proved her real age.

"Let me go." Genesis said, pulling away with all her strength, it was no use.

"Never." The Mermaid spat; her fangs glistening under the light that bore through the sea.

"Jaspar sent you, didn't he?"

The Mermaid laughed, "He didn't send me." She gestured around her, "He sent us."

All around Genesis, she saw a dozen Mermaids and Merman, teeth pointed, eyes blazing with antagonism.

"So you're going to kill me?" She asked, feeling confident.

"We don't kill, we consume."

Genesis' confidence faltered at that moment, she hoped her friends would realise she had gone before she was turned into *earth* food.

With luck, they did just that. One by one, the Waterments of her group landed beside her, Laminas in hand. Theo, Felicity, Eliza, Elijah, Amethyst, Adorjan, Tiberius and Lacey.

"Leave now, or we'll kill you." Amethyst demanded.

One Merman swam forward to her, his eyes full of woe. "Amethyst?"

She spun to face him, "Tristan?"

Genesis looked over at Elijah, whose face was contorted with unease and jealously.

"Why are you here?" Amethyst questioned him, "On Earth?"

"I transported here after you disappeared." Tristan explained.

"I'm sorry." She looked over her shoulder, "You know, you have been immortal for less a time than I. We could change you back, you know? That's what happened to me?"

Tristan's face lit up with glee, "You could?"

"No need." The Mermaid, who still held Genesis' arm, growled. She threw a spear into Tristan's chest. "You can't bring back the dead, can you?"

Amethyst watched in terror as the body sunk to the bottom of the sea bed. "That's it." She darted forward, hacking her lamina at the clan leader.

Genesis pulled away fast and grabbed a blade from Theo, turning to the creatures to fight.

One by one they were killed by the Artillery, they were weaker than they seemed. All, except one.

"You cannot kill me." The leader snarled, "I am the strongest. Like a Wolf pack has an Alpha, a Mermaid clan has a leader, and that is me."

"For as long as they're underwater, they're strong." Theo whispered to Genny, who was conjuring up a fool-proof plan as he spoke.

She smirked at him in response, before speeding toward the Mermaid. She grabbed her arms, swimming toward the surface. The Mermaid tussled, trying to free herself, but Genesis didn't budge. She closed her eyes and allowed the water to carry them up and up, until they broke the surface and shot into the air like a bird. Genesis took the opportunity to react fast. She grabbed her lamina from her boot, and swung it in one swift movement. The Mermaid's head fell and rolled onto the deck of the yacht, landing at her father's feet.

Theo watched as the body landed back in the sea, sinking down. "That's my girl." He grinned, swimming up with his friends to the surface.

Back on board, Alexandrus grabbed Genesis by the shoulders and pulled her close, "For the love of Zeus, you near gave me a heart attack, Gen."

"Dad, I'm fine." Laughed Genesis, "Chopping off a Mermaid's head is quite… therapeutic." She teased.

Her friends turned to her with a look of confusion.

"It was a joke." She said simply, before picking up the head and holding it like a trophy. "Football anyone?"

No reply.

"Soccer, then. I get that American's call it soccer but I don't know about Pandoversians…"

"Something tells me," Maggie said, "That they have no idea what you're talking about."

Genesis rolled her eyes, "Honestly, it's like having a herd of children." She dropped the head and kicked it swiftly back into the ocean. "Whatever you have next, Jaspar," She shouted toward the sky, "Bring it on."

EIGHTEEN

"TODAY, I AM GOING TO TAKE A TRIP." GENESIS announced to her friends, as she paced around the living room. It had been a week since the boat trip, and everything had been ominously peaceful. No attacks, no ghosts, no deaths and no killer Mermaids either. She plopped herself down on Theo's lap, snatching the can of Coca-Cola from his hand to take a sip before returning it and addressing the group. He disregarded her actions and continued on with his drink. "I want to go to England."

"When you said trip, I thought you meant something gratifying." Xavier laughed, "Not England."

"What's wrong with England?" She asked, looking miffed.

Theo looked as though he was about to speak when Eliza interrupted, "Nothing is wrong with England sweetie. If you want to go, then we can all go. Right, Tom?"

Tom nodded, being their only method of transportation, it was almost mandatory for him to follow.

"I don't need you all to tag along, you know?" Said Genny, furrowing her eyebrows in disgust, "I'm a big girl now, I'm even married." She held up her left hand to boast her ring.

"Oh right," Theo replied, "And how do you expect to get there without Tom? Ignis can't fly all that way, and I'm pretty sure there isn't dragon pit stops across the globe."

"Oh ha ha. Theodore you're so funny!" Genny said sarcastically, spinning on his lap to face him. "But do you know what's funnier? This thing called an aeroplane, takes you places around the world." She stood up, "And as I have unlimited money, I can easily go on one." Theo shook his head at her and she smiled, "Perhaps I'll even fly business class."

"Okay, Genesis." He responded fleetingly.

She gave a fulfilled and complacent smile, before spinning on her heels and moseying upstairs.

When she was out of earshot, Amethyst looked over at Theo, "You're not going to let her take a plane, are you?"

"Of course not." Said Theo, "Not when we can get there in a split-second with Tom, if that's okay?"

Again, Tom nodded.

"Great." Theo slapped his friends shoulder appreciatively, "I'll go pack."

Eliza shrugged, "I guess we can't all go, who'll stay here to look after the house, and the duplexes?"

"The O.A can." Responded Elijah.

Felicity giggled.

"The…what?" Said Eliza with curiosity.

"The O.A" Felicity said, "Elijah, Amethyst and I came up with it earlier. Means 'Original Artillery'."

"That," Eliza smiled, "Might be the most ridiculous thing I have ever heard, but I'm with Theo on this, we need to pack." She took Tom's hand and led him to their room to start filling their luggage.

"Probably would've been fun to go on a plane, it's been such a long time since I've been on one." Xavier admitted, mostly to himself.

"When this is over, "Amethyst shouted, walking out with Elijah at her hills, "You can go on as many planes as you like!"

"She has a point." Felicity said earnestly, "I don't fancy Jaspar coming after us on one of those. Something about fighting demons and foolish Elder's at over thirty-thousand feet in the air, doesn't sit right with me."

Xavier smirked, ruffling her hair and walking out of the room.

"And then there were none." The young girl said to herself, before joining her friends in their departure's and going in search of her father.

Theo noticed that Genesis was acting strange. Not that he could blame her. Her mother had been murdered by her brother, whom then she murdered. He paused the thought, *murdered* sounded horrifying. He didn't see Genesis as a murderer, he saw her as a heroine, and they were the parallel.

He watched as his now-wife went about her business, taking clothing and underwear, shoes and toiletries, placing them all neatly in the suitcase. Her movements were fluent. He noticed that about her from the very first day he had met her. He wasn't sure if it was the natural Element inside of her, or the fact that she was just geologically graceful, but everything that she did, she made it look effortless. He remembered the pain on her face when she killed Seth, and how it only lasted a moment. But he saw it. It flashed across her expression *faster than thought or time,* before she was back up and ready, wearing her most valiant expression and preparing to get justice over what she had just witnessed and been a part of.

"So I roll them, so they fit in better. See? It was what my parents and I used to do before a holiday." Genesis said proudly.

Theo looked at her, oblivious to what she was on about, but he knew at that moment that he would be able to kill his father if it meant keeping her safe.

"Clever, isn't it?" She asked him.

He smiled, "Very. Very clever."

"Are we missing anything?" She asked, looking around the room in a fluster.

Theo opened his mouth to speak, closing it quickly as she spoke.

"Ah," She said, "I need to locate my phone charger…"

Again, Theo tried to speak, but this time chose to stay silent as Genesis ran riot around the room in search of a power lead.

Elder Cliffio stood parallel to Jaspar, his mouth set in a thin line. "It's just wrong." He spoke forcefully. "Too wrong."

Jaspar ignored him, bending down to the child's eye level. "Which one are you?"

The child looked frightened, his hands fluttering at his sides in anxiety. "I'm Tad, my brother is Tamas."

Jaspar shook his head, "Guardians!" A scurry of men appeared at Jaspar's side, "Dispose of this one. His mother doesn't know but this child is *quadrupedia*."

"That is enough!" Cliffio roared. "Send the poor child through the atrium and banish him to Earth to be with his father, but not kill him."

Tad stared up at Jaspar with big wide watery eyes. "But Tamas is my twin, we can't be apart."

Jaspar shrugged, "Banish them both then."

The guardians nodded, two of them taking the twins and heading out of the room.

Jaspar turned to Cliffio with a look of disgust, "Considering a change of sides, are we?"

"If you keep this up," Cliffio replied, "I'll banish myself."

"What do you suggest then, to win this war?"

"Take something precious from them. Something that they would have to return to Pandoverse to collect." Said Cliffio.

Jaspar gave an unnerving smile before walking out of the room, triumphantly.

Genesis arrived in the kitchen to be greeted by Xavier in an apron.

His now shoulder length hair, was tied in a messy top-knot, and his shirtsleeves were rolled up to his elbow. The apron, which was covered in tiny black paw prints and the words '*woof!*' was tied tightly around his waist. "What," Genesis asked, "On Earth are you doing?"

Xavier grinned, his face was splatted with casting sugar, but the dimples on his cheeks were still visible beneath the almost sheer coating of white powder. "I'm making cupcakes!"

"May I ask why?"

"Because," The boy begun, "We're going to London tomorrow, so we decided to take a trip to the beach today…" He paused to look at Genesis, whose expression was that of candid confusion. "And so Felicity suggested we had cupcakes."

"And here you are."

"Here I am."

Genesis shook her head and laughed, "You best clean that up before we go, mind you. You can't leave it messy, it won't be fair on the others." She dipped her finger in the bowl of icing and licked it off. "Mm, tasty." She shrugged, looking back over to Xavier, "How come we're going to the beach, anyway?"

"Because we're going to London for a seven days… we'll probably miss it."

"Seven days, not seven years. We spent most of our lives without a beach."

Xavier nodded slowly in agreement, as he pondered the thoughts. "Oh well. Do you fancy helping?"

Genesis shook her head, "It's fine, stick to your little bakery down Drury Lane." She began wandering off.

"That's the muffin man! Not a cupcake baker!" He called after her as she headed outside the large French doors.

"Same difference!" She shouted back before disappearing outside and leaving Xavier to his own devices.

Felicity sat outside on the lawn wearing a pale-yellow summer dress. Her bare feet dangling into the pond.

"Lucky there are no piranha's in there, hey." Genesis grinned, falling onto the grass bank beside her younger sister.

Felicity stared up at her with wide eyes.

"What's wrong?" Genesis crooned, "Have you been crying?"

The young girl nodded silently, staring back at the koi fish in the pond.

"If you don't want to talk about it–"

"I barely knew her."

Genesis looked stunned, "What?"

"Mum. I barely knew her." Felicity said with a sniff. "I was too young to remember her well when she and dad went away." She looked back at Genesis once more, "When we found them at the camp, I was so happy. I would have a mother to raise me. Now she's gone again."

Genesis looked down at her hands, she had stayed exceedingly strong, especially around Felicity. "She's still watching, she'll be proud of you."

Felicity threw her arms around Genny's waist, "At least I have you."

Genesis stayed motionless for a moment, shocked. She never realised it before, but she was the older sibling now, she had to care for Felicity. She placed a careful arm around her sister. "You'll always have me."

Two hours later, they were at the beach.

Genesis stood by the Rogers' beach shack beside Tom and Theo, "Okay," Genny said to Theo, as Tom he conversed with his mother and ordered the group some ice-cream and sodas. "Doesn't that seem sad to you?" She jerked her chin toward Felicity and her father as they sat looking out to sea. "If you see anyone else her age with their parents, they behave differently. I get she's been raised without parents and in a world where you hardly get a childhood, but it's sad."

Theo shrugged, "I haven't really known it any other way, so I wouldn't know. But I saw the photos of you at her age, you were always playing around. It seems so peculiar to see how different the two worlds are."

Genesis said nothing in response, he was right. It wasn't something she was used to, the lack of emotion that Element's show to their families. She wished Felicity and Alexandrus could attempt a mortal father-daughter relationship, it would seal part of the wound Felicity had gained when their mother was killed. It would help seal part of Genny's wound that she had from her mother, her brother and Margaret. She wanted to raise her own children as mortals. She wanted them to feel love.

"Gen?" Theo said loudly, snapping her attention back to him, "Could you help us?" He gestured to the cans of drink and small tubs of ice cream that Tom had ordered.

Genesis nodded, strategically balancing several cans in her grip, and two tubs of desert, before heading back toward the group.

Her quest was cut short, when she heard shouting from across the beach. A woman was screaming, at two children. Not an angry scream, or the type a parent would use when reprimanding their child. No, this was a fearful scream.

"His hand was just on fire! I saw it!" She screamed at the child, waving a shaky finger his way. "It's an animal! An animal!"

Genesis took a moment to register before realising. *Elements.*

She dropped the drinks and grabbed a man's lighter where he placed it on the counter beside his wallet. She sprinted toward the two young boys, who she noticed were twins, falling to her knees at their sides. "Good gracious!" She cried, pretending to take the lighter from the boy's hand, "Where on Pan–Earth, did you get this?" She waved the lighter in front of his face, "So careless. And never wander off like that again, both of you!"

The boys stared at her speechlessly.

She grabbed their hands and stood, "Now come along, we're going to pack our stuff up and return home. I can't have you wandering off, you're far too young." She turned to the petrified woman, "I'm so sorry. I've been scared out of my mind, looking for them. Thank you for bringing them to my attention."

The lady nodded silently before scurrying off.

As she was out of ear shot, she bent down to face the boys, "Hey, you're both from Pandoverse, right?"

They nodded.

"So am I, as are my friends. Could you tell me your names?"

The boy who had produced fire from his hand, spoke first. She noticed that he had green eyes. He was Earthment with Firement abilities. "I'm Tad, and this is Tamas."

Tamas gripped his brother's hand tightly and hid half behind him.

"Hey, it's okay. Who are you here with?" Genny soothed.

Tad spoke up once more, "No one. We were banwished."

Banwished?

"Banished." Tamas corrected shyly. "Our mama took us to Elder Jaspar and he sent us here for good."

Genesis felt a lump form in her throat and tears spill. "How old are you?"

"Two." They said in unison.

"And you were banished?"

They nodded.

She took a deep breath and blinked up at the sky. They were just babies, and they were *banished* to Earth. "Is it okay that you stay with me? I don't want you alone."

"Yes please." Tad said sweetly, "I'm hungry."

Genesis nodded through tears, "Sure, come with me." She took their hands once again and led them over to her friends, "Theo, we're leaving."

Alexandrus stood up, "What's this? Who are these children?"

Genesis stared at her father with tear-filled eyes, "I'll explain later, I just need to take them to the farm house." Alex didn't question his daughter, he simply nodded and moved aside to allow Theo to follow his wife to the truck.

Once they were settled in the Chevy, Theo drove off quickly, leaving the beach before speaking. "What on Pandoverse is going on? Why are there two children in the back of the truck?"

Genesis burst into tears, "They were banished by your father."

She saw as Theo's hands tightened their grip on the steering wheel, "He what?"

"Apparently their mother handed them over to him and he banished them, I think it's because one of them is quadrupedia."

Theo shook his head aggressively, "They're babies. Surely not?"

"I wish it wasn't true." She sniffed, reaching into her beach-bag for a tissue, "I really wish it wasn't. They were just sent to Earth alone. No parent, no guardian. We have to keep them."

"*Keep them*? Gen, they're not puppies." Theo said with a chuckle, "They have parents, we need to get them back to Pandoverse."

"We can't, Jaspar could kill them!" She held her breath, hoping they hadn't heard her say what she had said, "We can't risk it."

"Very well, we'll wait until the war is over, then we'll find their parents and take them home."

"What if their parents are… you know?"

Theo reached his hand and placed it on top of her own, "Then we'll have to create a plan B. I promise you Gen, we'll keep them both safe."

She smiled at him, her heart swelling with affection. "Thank you."

When they arrived back at the farmhouse, Genesis jumped out of the truck at lightning speed, swinging open the back door and helping Tamas out of the car, he reached his arms forward, wrapping them around her neck, "Carry?" He whimpered.

"Oh?" She said in shock, "Yes, of course." She held him as she swung the door shut and reached round the front of the truck. Theo stood there, holding Tad in the same way, he gave her a half smile before they headed inside.

"Jax, you home?" Theo shouted loudly into the hall. "We have a situation!"

Moments later, the Earthment rounded the corner from the kitchen at speed, "What's wrong?" He stopped in his tracks when he saw the children.

"Before you go into shock, let us explain. They were on the beach, they're Elements." Theo said briefly.

"They were banished here, we don't know where their parents are, just that their mother handed them over to Jaspar. That bitch." Genny huffed.

"We believe they were banished because Tamas is quadrupedia, although he has just green eyes. A bit like you really…" Theo trailed off as he looked from Tad to Jax. "Wait?"

"Daddy." Tad pointed.

Theo placed the little boy down, and Genesis did the same. Tad ran up to Jax, Tamas toddling behind cautiously.

"Oh my goodness." Genesis whispered, "They're Jax and Adrianna's children? But she said they were having a girl?" She thought back to her first visit to Gi.

Theo shook his head, "That's only what she hoped for. Unlike Earth, we don't have the equipment to discover things like the sex of an unborn child. She just guessed and probably wished."

Genesis nodded as she took it all in.

Jax cradled the boys in sobs, holding them close to his body as they wrapped their arms around his neck.

"Are you crying?" Theo asked Genny, looking over at her with a grin. "You're such a baby." He teased, pulling her close. "But I do love you."

"I love you." She said between sniffs.

He smiled and placed a kiss on her hair, but in the back of his mind, all he could think of was what he was going to do to his father when he got the chance.

NINETEEN

"WHY DO YOU THINK THAT JASPAR BANISHED THE kids to Los Angeles of all places?" Genny asked Theo as Ajordan drove them to LAX. They had to use the atrium there, as the one at the farm house was blocked for protection and they figured it would be easier to go about their trip to London Heathrow, rather than from Tom's ability and Genesis' memory. "Why here rather than anywhere else?"

"Perhaps he hoped that we'd find them, to upset us." Theo responded lugubriously.

"He did an excellent job." Eliza said from the back seat, "Everyone was freaked out from the entire situation." Genesis watched as she rested her head on Tom's shoulder. "And poor Jax, he was beside himself at the concept of his children being banished. How fortunate we did find them? Shame he chose to stay home mind you, although, it is understandable."

"They're definitely the cutest kids ever though." Amethyst said sweetly, "I love kids, I can't wait to have my own."

Elijah's eyes widened, but he kept quiet at his girlfriend's remark.

"We're here!" Adorjan said cheerfully.

Genesis reached over and gave him a big hug, "Thank you for the lift." She said politely, "See you in a week."

As she turned to leave, Ajordan grabbed her wrist, pulling her back, "Gen, be careful won't you. All of you."

Genesis smiled, "We'll be okay. Same goes for all of you back home, please call if anything happens?"

Ajordan nodded, "Of course. Have a great time!"

"Thank you! Bye for now!" Genesis called as she attempted to take her suitcase from Theo, "Theo I can take it, its fine."

"I'm being a gentleman, allow me." Theo countered.

Adorjan watched his friends walk into the airport, watching as a vision dome grew over them and they vanished out of his sight. But the nagging feeling in his stomach made him worry about their safety colossally.

On arrival in London, Theo called a cab to the hotel that they had booked. It was just around the block from Genesis' Aunt and Uncle's home, in Kensington.

"I'm going to miss the beach *so* bad." Eliza admitted, "I love the beach."

"Anyone would have thought you were brought up by the sea, Lize." Xavier laughed, "All I can think is, home sweet home."

"Will you be visiting your parents too, Xavier?" Felicity asked softly.

Xavier looked down at the young girl with an infectious grin, "Well of course!"

Genesis smiled at them, before Theo called the group to the road side to hop in the taxi.

Theo announced their hotel to the driver, whose expression turned to astonishment.

"Wow," He said, "You kids sure are lucky."

"Oh, we're far from lucky." Genesis admitted, "Just worked hard."

"You all seem so young though." The driver said honestly.

Theo laughed, "We are, just mature for our age."

"Except my little sister, she's just ten." Added Genesis.

"Well I won't be nosy, I'll just congratulate you on your successes." The driver said kindly, "And may your long lives be full of many more."

Genesis took Theo's hand in her own, she could only pray that their lives would be long and successful.

The hotel was beyond words. Genesis stood in the doorway for such time that Theo began to lose his patience, as she stared at their room in awe. "It's like the honeymoon we never got to have." She admitted, laying back on the queen-sized bed with a happy sigh. "What do you want for your birthday?"

Theo laughed, pulling the suitcase to one side and shutting the door, "I haven't thought about it."

"It's in two days. Can we throw a party?"

"Gen, it's not entirely the time for a party, is it now?"

Genesis shrugged, "We got married."

"But it's different now, your m–" His voice trailed off, he couldn't bring up the death of Katherine without feeling empty. He never got the opportunity to get to know her in the extent he would have liked, but she lived on in Genesis, therefore he knew she was a remarkable woman.

"We got married after Liz died." She replied quietly.

Theo said nothing, she was right, after all. He spent endless nights since his mother's death, wondering if there were anything he could do to make the pain vacillate.

The constant ache in his chest, it felt like his heart was yearning to grow and fill the void that was left inside it from her death. But it was an impossibility he had to apprehend. He thought, for some time, that Genesis was lucky. Disregarding the fact she had suffered, grieved and been bereft for many years, the parents she had learned to accept were dead, had return to her. But now he didn't have the same thoughts, at all. He watched Genesis' face when Seth killed their mother. He watched it when she killed Seth. He could see it, every day, like a haunting memory that kept replaying in her mind. It was visible in her eyes. The way she felt, the way she carried the weight of that burden on her shoulders like a ton of bricks. "I'm taking a shower." He said, placing quick kiss on Genesis' forehead and heading to the bathroom.

"May I join you?" She teased, wiggling her eyebrows playfully.

He hesitated. He wanted to be alone for a moment, but he would never be the husband to reject his wife's wishes.

"I'm kidding," Laughed Genesis, "I'm going to take a nap. Tomorrow will be hard for me and I want to be prepared." She rolled over and into a little ball. Theo loved the way she slept like that. She looked so small, so young and so fragile: like anything could hurt her or disturb her innocence. But he knew otherwise. He knew she saw the blood stains on the palms of her hands, he could tell by the way she washed them, as though she could physically see the blood of her brother on her skin, but once she was done, the panic would leave her eyes and she would return to reality as any normal soul.

It reminded him of Lady Macbeth, *A little water clears us of this deed*, just *far* less dramatic.

"Sleep tight." Was all he said, before he went in search for a shower.

Genesis rested her head on the pillow, closing her eyes in hopes of rest. She clutched the yellow plectrum, which she had created into a pendant, as though it would protect her from bad dreams, as though it was her guardian angel. But despite her hopes, every time she closed her eyes to sleep, she saw it.

She saw her mother's dead body, laying still on the ground. Beside her, lay Seth, his chest splayed with blood. Ahead of her lay Anthony, his lifeless body facing her, his eyes piercing her soul.

Across from him, lay Margaret, her body partially entwined with Elder Markos', whom she remembered so clearly. He was, after all, the first person she had ever killed. To her left, lay a pile of Guardians and Elders, their chests and heads bloody, some scolded, some whose skin had transfigured into a shade blue from suffocation or drowning. She would spin on her heels, to see what lay behind her. She would see Eliza, Elijah, Amethyst, Felicity, Tom, Xavier, Tiberius, Adorjan and Icarus. At their feet lay Sally, Sabrina, Harry, Konner, Milo, Jessabelle, Crystal, Yale, Paignton, Fabia, Lacey, Lael and May. Some who died on her wedding day, some who were still at home in Los Angeles.

Then she would look down at her own feet, where her father lay. His skin grey and his eyes without their usual spark. '*Daddy, wake up.*' She would whisper, but he would never wake up. Her sobs would be cut short from a familiar voice, *Theo*. There he stood, atop the pile of dead guardians, looking proud, looking humble. '*I love you Genesis and I thought you loved me too. But you didn't. If you did, you would have left a long time ago. You would have stopped the war. Instead you let them die, it's all your fault– you let us all die.*' His chest would slowly turn a deep shade of red, the colour running through his shirt, colouring his front with the image of a bloody flower. '*You let us all die.*' He repeated, before Genesis turned and ran, but she couldn't move. Alexandrus held her legs down. She looked over her shoulder at her mourning friends, '*Help me!*' she cried. '*It's too late.*' Eliza responded, '*And it's all your fault. You let us all die.*' Blood spilled from her mouth and eyes hauntingly, Elijah's the same.

Each and everyone one of her friends fell toward her, blood pouring from every orifice as they dragged her into the ground, all chanting the same words. '*It's all your fault, you let us all die.*'

Her cries brought Theo to her attention, he rushed to her side in a fluster. "Gen, what's wrong, are you alright?"

She shook as he pulled her close to his body. "It was just a bad dream," *The same bad dream I always have*, she wanted to say. "I'm okay."

Theo didn't loosen his hold as she curled into his side, her head on his shoulder, "I'll be there to protect you, I always will be, I promise."

But Theo, my love, she thought, *it isn't I, who needs protecting. It's you. I'll be the one who is the cause of your death and it'll be all my fault.*

I let you all die.

Theo waited until Genesis had fallen into a peaceful sleep, before he slipped away from her bedside and crept out of the room. It had passed midnight when she finally chose to sleep again, he waited for some time before feeling able to leave her side. He wandered the halls of the magnificent hotel until he reached the emergency stairwell, ascending the steps quickly but quietly until he reached the roof. He realised, that if he was Airment, the whole task would have been much easier. A quick vision dome and he could've climbed the side of the hotel like Spiderman.

When he reached the top he swung the door open to the fresh London air.

It was chilly, nothing compared to Los Angeles, or most of Pandoverse for that matter. London reminded him of Aeras, and Aeras reminded him of Anthony. He felt a twinge of guilt in his chest at the memory of his friend. When Anthony's uncle died, his legal guardian, Theo felt sympathetic of his friend, he had lost a lot of people and he couldn't begin to imagine what that felt like. When both boys were sixteen and had begun their most extensive training, the first time they saw one another since the death, Theo always stayed close to Anthony.

He felt the need to protect him, because he had lost so much. When Theo saw Anthony with the Guardian's alongside the Elders, he felt angry and betrayed, until Genesis cleared the air, then he felt a rush of relief– they could fight this war and he'd get his best friend back. But it didn't happen that way.

Theo sighed at the memory, it was still raw, as was the death of his mother. When he left her, he believed that she would be safe in Los Angeles and that it was he and his friends who were taking the big risk, he guessed that was his father's plan in the first place– to trick them.

"Theodore." A man's voice rumbled, Theo turned on the spot where he stood, by the edge of the roof top.

"You came." Theo replied, stepping toward the man.

"You summoned me, very smart, I'm proud."

By now, Theodore was face to face with his visitor, it felt warm now, as the heat radiated around them with a sun's glow. "Ares, please may I ask a favour?"

Ares smiled, "Of course my son, what can I do for you?"

Theo looked over his shoulder and then back at the God of War. "Is there any way I can speak to my mother one last time?"

Ares gave a pitiful sigh, "I'm sorry Theodore I can't do that for you, although I really wish that I could."

"Oh, right." He said, looking to the floor.

"But," Said Ares quickly, "I can allow you to speak with Anthony Rhys Wentworth? Is that of any value to you?"

Theo looked up at Ares in shock, how could he speak to Ant, but not Elizabeth? But he daren't to question a God. "It would mean a lot, thank you."

Ares placed a comforting hand on Theo's shoulder, "Give me a moment."

He vanished, taking the heat with him. Theo waited for a minute for his return, yet nothing happened. He sighed, strolling back to his original spot by the roof's edge before he felt the familiar heat once more. He turned and standing where Ares had once stood, was Anthony.

Theo said nothing at first, he stared emptily at his best friend.

"Theo, thank you so much for asking for me." Anthony said softly, walking forward, "I thought I'd never see any of you again."

Theo stuttered for a moment before he spoke, "I'm sorry."

"For what?"

"For allowing you to be killed, for not being there in your final moments."

Anthony gave a chuckle, "I know, Genesis held me, she's a beautiful girl, I considered dying in her arms a blessing."

Theo laughed at this, it was typical of his friend to acquire such attitude, despite the situation in hand. "I'm still sorry."

"Theo, remember when we were kids, we used to say how one day we'd be warriors, we'd work for the Government and be the best two Guardian's Pandoverse has ever possessed?"

Theo nodded.

"Well we were. Not the best two, because there's a load of us, and we didn't work for the Government, we were against them. But Theo, you and I, we are the warriors of Pandoverse, as is Genny and Eli and all of our friends. I accepted when we were just young children, that I could die young, a horrible death, but as long as I died fighting for the right thing, I'd be okay. When I got dragged into the Elder's plans, I panicked, what if they brainwashed me or I didn't get an army together and I was killed by the hands of one of you? I wouldn't have been fighting for what was right, that would be regretful, I would spend my entire afterlife regretting that. But that's not the case. I died fighting for the future of Pandoverse, I will always be glad it happened how it did. You need not apologise for my death, Theo, for I am not sorry it happened myself."

"We're going to win this." Theo said in response to Anthony's soliloquy, "I'm going to avenge your death, and my mothers. I will get revenge for the death of Katherine, Margaret and many more who were slain by my father's hand, or by his acquaintances.

I will fight alongside my wife and friends until it is over. If the war concludes with the Pandoversian streets made into rivers of blood, then so be it. We will win and we will do what is right, I promise you."

"When this is over, I would love that you re-marry Genesis. Have the wedding you wished for, you deserve to do it right."

Theo blushed, "I could've married her in the middle of a manure pile and it would've been right."

"I can't decipher whether or not that was cute or disgusting." Anthony chuckled, "I must go now Theo, but please be well, send my love."

"Wait." Theo said quickly, as Anthony turned away, "Why couldn't I see my mother?"

Ant looked over his shoulder at his friend with a shrug, "I spend my days amongst Evlo's City of Passed now, I haven't seen her yet, I'm not even sure she's there."

"Well whereas could she be, the underworld?"

As soon as Theo asked, he wished he hadn't the look on Anthony's ghostly face made him realise that could be a possibility. Elizabeth wasn't a bad person, by far, but if Hades had anything to do with it, she would be sat at his side begging him to go to heaven.

"Goodbye, Theo."

Theo gave a half smile as his friend vanished for the very last time. He waited for some time, wondering if Ares would return, but he never found out as a piercing scream cut through the night sky.

Genesis.

TWENTY

THE SOUND SENT CHILLS UP THEO'S SPINE.

Without hesitation he raced back down the stairwell, not even considering if he was making any sound. If anyone was still sleeping after Genesis' screams, he was sure his footsteps wouldn't wake them up. He spun at the foot of the stairs, sprinting into the corridor with his door-key in his hand, he was quick to unlock the door, running inside to find Genesis crumbled on the floor.

"For the love of Zeus, Gen? What happened?" He fell to his knees at her side, pulling her to him hastily.

She turned to face him and he had to stifle a scream of his own. The irises, which usually consisted of hazel, blue, green and grey, were white. Her pupil, which of course was black, was white. Her eyes were intensely blood shot. "Theo."

Theo cradled her face in his palms, "Genesis what is wrong? What is happening?"

In as quick as a flash, her eyes returned to normal, accompanied by fear and pain. "The children."

Theo gave her a questioning look, the only children in the Artillery were Felicity, Maggie, Milo, Tad and Tamas. All but Felicity were in Los Angeles. "What about them?"

"Maggie came to me in my dream, Jaspar has them, has them all."

Theo jumped up, pulling Genesis with him, Felicity was staying in Xavier's room and they hadn't heard from him. Either what she dreamt, was only just a dream, or something had happened to him, too.

They sprinted out of the door and through the corridor to Xavier's room, knocking hurriedly on the door. "Xavier, open up!" Theo shouted, knocking harder.

"Is everything okay?" A voice came from the shadows, it was the hotel security guard, looking confused. "I've heard screaming?"

"We need to get in here, to see our friend, pronto!" Theo cried, "Do you have a spare key?"

The security guard shook his head, "They're downstairs the spare keys, no one is there to give them to you, they're in the locked cupboard. I don't have the key for it I'm afraid, I would have to call the manager in."

Theo ran his hands through his hair with a heavy sigh. "What sort of lock?"

"I can't help you, sir, unless you believe your friend to be in danger."

"What sort of lock?" He asked again with a low growl threatening at the back of his throat.

The security guard shook his head, "Come with me."

Eliza pushed aggressively at the bedroom door, "It's locked!" She growled.

"Use the key." Tom said swiftly.

Eliza stopped what she was doing to glare at him, "Oh yeah, *sure*. How did I not think of using the freaking key?!"

"Sarcastic."

"No way."

Tom gave a grunt, before standing ahead of the door, "We're going to have to pay for damages." he said over his shoulder before throwing his hands against the door. The door flew off its hinges with a bang. "Probably could have transported to the other side of the door, you know, it's one of the things we are able to do, don't forget that."

Eliza rolled her eyes "I tried that, the room was protected. We're also going to be in a lot of trouble with the hotel for making so much noise." She admitted, waving her hands over the pair and creating a vision dome. "It's an expensive hotel, I would be exceptionally pissed off if my stay was disrupted by a bunch of kids causing havoc."

Tom gave a hearty laugh, "We'll leave a large tip to compensate." He said, as they set off in a jog toward Elijah and Amethyst's room.

They heard a lot of commotion before they reached the door, Amethyst was becoming aggravated by concept of being trapped.

"I can't break another door Lize, I'll be in so much trouble!" Tom said in a panic, "There must be another way."

"There is," Genesis replied, coming around the corner in a sprint. "Theo has gone with a security guard to get a spare key for Xavier's room, I think something has happened. Maggie came to me in my dream to warn me that all the children had been kidnapped by the Elders, I think Xavier might also be in trouble."

"I knew something was up when we heard you scream," Eliza explained, becoming flustered with anxiety, "How can we get into their room?"

"I've got this. Could one of you go see what's happening with Noah and Paisley, please?" Genesis smiled, "I'll be back in a bit."

Theo reached the front desk, the security guard, whose name he discovered was Greg, trailing behind him. In the journey downstairs, Theo had learned that Greg had come from a family of Elements, his Grandfather had been banished to Earth, like Margaret, sixty years earlier. Greg knew all about his family history, his family had been Earthments, but his Grandfather was demi-quadrupedia, thanks to his Earthment father and Airment mother.

"How can you get into this then?" Greg asked, patting his hand on the top of the small cupboard. It was made of a thin metal, the lock was fragile.

"I could smash it, but I don't think that'll be easy to explain in the morning." Theo laughed, he wiggled his fingers at the cupboard, and in a matter of moments it swung open.

"How?" Said Greg, his expression that of someone who was flabbergasted.

As Theo pulled the door open wide, they caught a glimpse of a green stem vanishing back into the bottom of the cupboard, "Earthment perks."

Greg nodded, utterly speechless, taking the reservation book off the desk and handing it to Theo quickly.

"It's key FORTY-SIX."

Greg bent down to become eye level with little shelves of key-cards, counting them as his eyes scanned the rows. "Got it!" He announced, closing the cupboard back up and heading out of the lobby with Theo at a fast pace.

When the pair reached Xavier's room, Theo snatched the key from Greg and unlocked the door without hesitation. As he peered inside, his worst fears were confirmed. Lying unconscious on the kitchen floor was Xavier, his face and torso bloody. Felicity was nowhere to be seen.

"Is he alive?" Greg asked nervously, "Do I need to call someone?"

Theo shook his head, "No, he's alive, just a little beaten, he'll be okay." He shook his friend by the shoulders, receiving just a groan as a response. "He'll be out for a while, but as long as someone stays with him, he'll be alright." He stood from Xavier's side, pulling the boy up and propping his body against the refrigerator door. "Could you stay with him for a moment? I'll go find the others." Greg gave a brief nod, before settling down beside the still-unconscious Xavier and watching as Theo ran off to help his friends.

Elijah sat at the kitchen table beside Amethyst, his jet black hair fallen messily into his eyes. He sat his chin upon his hands staring out at the room. He was a prisoner.

"It's going to be okay, Eliza said Genesis would get us out, I trust her." Amethyst soothed, rubbing her boyfriend's back.

"You heard them, they said Jaspar has the children. You know he's going to use them, as some sort of bargaining chip. If we surrender, they survive, if we fight– they die."

Amethyst shook her head lightly, "Eli, that won't happen, we won't let it. Theo is the strongest warrior in Pandoverse, his sister-in-law is at risk, do you think he'd let them get away with that?"

"It's his father." Elijah said blankly, "It's his father who is in control, of all of this. Can you imagine that? Knowing that the key to your happiness is to kill your own father?"

Amethyst bowed her head silently, not speaking any further.

"Amethyst?" Said Elijah, "Amethyst what's wrong?"

She sighed, looking back up at him with tear-filled eyes. "I planned my parent's murder."

Elijah sucked in a breath, saying nothing and allowing her to continue on.

"When they turned me, I hated them. I had learned to despise them for what they did to us and even more so after I had turned. They used to visit me at the beach once a week, every Thursday at midday. They would come to the water's edge and wait for me.

I had still not forgiven them, how could I? They had turned me into Pandoverse's most hated creature, I was going to live out the rest of my immortal life in Nero's ocean, I was mad. I would never marry, never have a family, and I would never just die. Only death could be placed upon me by murder. One day, it was mid-spring, I hatched a plan. I wasn't so far developed to have evil behaviours, but many of those I knew did.

I told my parents to meet me on Poseidon's Island, where you met me to bring me back and they came. When they arrived, two Mermen dragged them under, killed them almost instantly, they didn't even have time to consider the situation before they were beheaded and their corpses were left to float to the seabed. I was so mad at myself, I felt so twisted, so cruel," A lone tear escaped Amethyst's eye and Elijah was quick to wipe it away with his thumb, "I killed my parents because they were my enemy. It was horrible, but I felt it was necessary. I wanted justice for what they did to me and I got it in the worst way."

Elijah went to speak, to tell her it was okay, she did what they deserved, but he was cut short by a bang on the window. It was Genesis.

"I'd be grateful if you opened up," She said with a grin, "It's chilly out here."

Amethyst laughed as she spotted Noah and Paisley appear at Genny's side. "Hold on." She wandered to the window, pushing it open and allowing her friends inside. "Now you're in, how do you suspect you'll get out?"

Noah placed a hand on the door handle, leaning casually against the frame whilst the metal beneath his palm slowly melted. "Each room has been protected differently.

Genesis worked it out. I couldn't do this in mine and Paisley's room, yet I can in here." The door clicked open swiftly and Noah held up his palm, it was burnt, but slowly healing by itself.

"I figured if we couldn't use the doors, we could use the windows, I climbed to Noah and Paisleys room from the roof and then we came here." Genesis explained, "If Jaspar and his minions can't protect the entire room, more fool them. Plus, it was fun – I felt like Cat Woman."

"Who?" Elijah asked walking to the door as Noah exited.

Genesis just shook her head, heading out with Amethyst and Paisley following suit.

"Theo!" Tom screamed as he turned the corner, "Did you get in?"

Theo nodded, "He's unconscious, but alive."

"And Felicity?" Asked Eliza.

He looked down solemnly, "She's not here. She's missing."

"So Genesis was right?"

Theo looked over Eliza's shoulder as the rest of their friends appeared in the corridor, Genesis in the lead. "She's definitely not here?" She asked, fear, clear as day in her eyes.

"We'll save her, we'll save them all, I promise you." Theo crooned, reaching her side and planting an unblemished kiss on her forehead.

"I know, I'm just worried as to whether or not we'll get to them before it's too late." She admitted.

"Theo!" A voice came from down the hall, it was Greg. He sprinted toward the group in a fluster, "Theo, he's awake, Xavier's awake."

Xavier sat on the bed, his back rested against more cushions and pillows than he could count. By his side, holding his hand intensively, was Genesis. Her silky blonde hair was tied back into a messy bun, she wore no makeup, yet her lips and cheeks still were stained a pale pink. She wore a tank-top and a pair of cream bed-shorts with little black moustaches on them.

"Are you okay?" Genesis asked, her voice was etched with pain and fear, "What happened?"

"I'm sorry," Xavier mumbled, "I tried to protect her, I really did."

"I know," Genesis crooned, "I know you did. It'll be okay, we'll get her back and the others."

"The others?"

Theo appeared from the bathroom looking tired, "The children, all of them, my father has them."

Xavier shook his head in a panic, "No he can't."

"It's true," Amethyst said with a sigh. Her red hair fell down either side of her face in tousled waves, she too, looked exhausted. "Maggie came to Genesis in her dream, they've been taken."

"This is insane. This is one step too far." Xavier growled, "I'm sorry Theo, but when I get hold of him, I'm going to kill him, I swear to Zeus I will kill him."

One side of Theo's mouth twitched upward in a smile, "I'll be happy for you to do so, would save me from having to kill my own father. Despite everything, he is my father and I'm pretty sure that's some kind of sin."

"I'm pretty sure murder in general is a sin Theo, I wouldn't dwell on it too much." Elijah said matter-of-factly.

Theo shrugged.

"We need to get out of here, go to my Aunt and Uncle's home, tell them the situation, maybe they can return to Los Angeles with us and help?" Genesis suggested.

Theo placed a hand on her shoulder and looked her in the eyes, "Do you really want to bring anyone else into this war, Gen?"

She looked away with a sigh, she didn't know what to do. She didn't know what was right or wrong anymore, just that she wanted this to be over.

"It'll be alright. We'll win this war and everything can go back to normal."

Genesis shook her head dismissively, "It won't be normal, neither of us have a mother nor a brother and your father will be gone too. Theo, when you are different, normality is non-existent. Even this trip couldn't be normal. We seldom get time away from all the hustle and bustle of being an Element and it still ends in havoc."

Tom walked over to the couple, excusing himself for interrupting, "Did you want to return home to L.A? Say the word and I'll take us all home."

"Half the hotel is awake from all the events of the night, we've drawn so much unwanted attention." Eliza added, chewing the inside of her cheek anxiously.

"I can help." Amethyst said, pulling away from her conversation with Paisley to promote her abilities, "I will need Genesis' help mind you, or Xavier."

"You need an airment?" Theo asked, his words sounding relatively bitter, he had always been covetous of others with his missing ability.

Amethyst agreed, "I have something in my bag back in my room, it's a vial of powder, I kept quite a few lotions and potions from my time as a Mermaid, it is memory-erasing."

"Like what was used on myself and Felicity by our parents?"

"Yes."

"So why do you need Xavier and I?"

Amethyst went on to explain her plan of spreading the memory-erasing powder through the ventilation system of the hotel. Elijah then explained how they could leave a note for the manager, saying they left through the night due to a family emergency. The only problem left was to fix the damages.

Greg, who had kept quiet the entire time, finally spoke up. "I'll deal with the damages. I'll change your details in the system so no one knew it was you. When the powder takes effect, no one will remember I was working tonight, I'll act as though I'm oblivious, I've got your back."

Theo clapped him on the back, "You're a great lad, thank you."

"Gregory, when this is all over, we will have reign over Pandoverse, I want you and your family to know that you'll be more than welcome to return if you wanted to." Genesis added, giving the guard a swift hug, "Thank you for all your help tonight."

"Thank you."

"Right," Said Noah, quickly and loudly, "Let's get Genesis, Tom and Xavier to the ventilation room downstairs.

Elijah and Theo, we'll get everyone's stuff together, meet back here in half an hour.

Ladies, go with Tom, Xavier and Gen, stay unseen. If anyone see's you placing unknown powder in the vents, you could end up in serious trouble."

Genesis laughed, "It's a plan, let's go!"

The ventilation room was dull, dark and dingy, despite the entire hotel being outrageously spotless, this room was not. It was full, floor to ceiling, with giant air conditioning units and heating systems. "Where do we even start?" Genesis said, turning to face her friends with a look of confusion.

Amethyst wandered for a moment, looking for the ideal place for them to concoct their plan. "Here will be perfect." She motioned toward one of the larger units with a big pipe attaching it to the wall. "You know how to create a temporary gap in the metal, don't you?"

Genesis thought back to the first time she learned such trick. In the disabled restroom, beside Margaret's office. Theo explained how to create the space and she did so, watching as Markos threatened Marge, advising her of her early death. Genny shuddered at the thought, "Let's do this." She said, placing her hands on the pipe. It was cold, icy cold. A space appeared between her palms, and Amethyst was quick to pour the vial of powder into the pipe. Xavier placed a hand over the gap and the powder flew into the depth of the pipe flawlessly.

"Well that was a lot easier than I expected." Xavier admitted, "You said it would be tricky."

Amethyst grinned at him, "That was the easy part, the hard part is getting the others and getting out of here before the powder gets into the air and we lose our memories too."

Xavier stood up straight, his face that of shock, "Well let's hurry!"

They all sprinted out of the ventilation room, heading back to the meeting point they had previously arranged with the others. Genesis felt an uneasy feeling in the back of her mind, she stopped in the hall, looking over her shoulder in anxiety. "Something isn't right, I'll meet you outside in ten minutes."

Amethyst pulled at her friend's wrist, "Gen, you mustn't wander. If you get caught the gases from the powder will make you forget the past day, you can't risk that– it will slow us all down."

"I'll be fine." Genesis said sternly, pulling her wrist free, "I'll see you very soon."

Tom shook his head, "I'll go with her," He planted a quick kiss on Eliza's head before chasing Genesis down the corridor and into the darkness.

Xavier sighed, "Let's go, I trust them to be back in time."

Amethyst hesitated for a moment, the niggling feeling in her stomach made her want to go after the pair, but she knew she had to let them be.

Genesis reached the roof top with little air in her lungs. "Someone's up here." She said to Tom, as he appeared at her side, bent over himself as he gasped for breath. "Someone untrustworthy."

"How do you know this?" He questioned, straightening himself up and looking around.

"I just know." Genesis pulled an una from her boot as she trod lightly toward the roof's centre.

A familiar feeling passed through her, like the chills received from a winter's day. The fair hairs on the back of her neck stood to attention and goose bumps made their way onto her skin. Her stomach churned and her heart fluttered as she turned back to her friend. "Tom, move slowly." She whispered.

Tom furrowed his eyebrows in confusion.

"Don't make any sudden movements, okay?"

He swung round to see what she was looking at as the air filled with a screech.

"Illecebra." Genesis spat.

Tom pulled a lamina from his belt, swinging it at the demon and separating its head from its body. It disintegrated in the early morning air, leaving no trace. "What is that? I have never seen one of those ones before."

"You and I both, but I don't like the look of him either."

Tom ran to stand beside Genesis, as more illecebra appeared from the shadows, "Some of them have wings." He squeaked as they gained on them both. "There's so many."

"There's too many, I don't think we can fight them all." Genesis admitted. Both Tom and herself were relatively new to the world of demon fighting, despite their strength, they had many weaknesses.

"What should we do?"

Genesis looked over at the edge of the building, "Can you transport us in mid-air?"

"I think so."

"Then we're going to jump off the building."

Tom stared at her wide-eyed, "I said I think so, I'm not certain."

"Well I'd rather die by becoming a human pancake on the streets of London, than be eaten alive by illecebra, wouldn't you? I'll take my chances."

Tom didn't give her a response, he just took her hand and began to run, slashing his lamina in all directions. Genesis pulled her free hand back and threw the una into the forehead of one demon, reaching to grab the blade out of thin air as she passed the disappearing body of the illecebra. She missed, leaving the blade to clatter onto the floor. She didn't have time to go back for it as they reached the roof edge quicker than anticipated. They leapt up onto the wall, then in one swift motion, they dropped and soared toward the ground.

"Where are they?" Theo snapped when Eliza, Amethyst, Xavier and Paisley arrived back at the room.

"They ran off." Eliza said calmly, "Well, correction, Genesis ran off. Tom refused to allow her to go anywhere alone."

"Wow," Said Theo as he rolled his eyes, "Running off at dangerous times sure doesn't sound like a Genesis thing to do!" Sarcasm dripped from his voice. "Any idea where they went?" He pulled out his phone and began to dial.

"I think they headed to the stairwell, so I'm going to say the roof." Amethyst added as she rummaged through one of her bags.

"She behaved like she could sense something," Paisley said further, "I'm not sure what."

Theo shook his head with a sigh, "Xavier, you and I will go to the roof, the rest of you should get outside before the ventilation system turns on and we're wiped of our memories." He turned away to make a call, leaving the others to all abide with a few groans and sighs, taking all the bags and luggage and heading to the elevators.

Theo clipped on his weapons belt, Xavier doing the same, as they sheathed a variety of weapons that they pulled from their bags moments before. "Ready?" Xavier nodded and the pair headed out of the room and up the stairs at a sprint.

A while later, they reached the top. Theo shot out a hand to stop Xavier before they stepped out. "There's demonic energy up here."

Xavier looked over at him in confusion, "Illecebra? On a hotel's roof? On Earth?"

Theo nodded and pulled out his binarii from its scabbard. The pair stepped outside onto the rooftop apprehensively, their eyes darting around in all directions. "They're not up here. Nor are any illecebra."

Xavier, who was a little way ahead of Theo, turned back to his friend with a look of sheer panic. He held up an una blade, the metal winking in the moonlight. "They were up here. So were the illecebra, but where they are now? I have no idea."

Tom held Genesis' hand tightly, growing vex as he tried to transport them safely to the ground. It was no use, they were going to die.

Genesis realised this as she looked over at him, she shot out her free hand creating a rush of wind to slow their fall yet it wasn't enough. Her abilities seemed weaker. It was their parachute– but it wouldn't save them.

"It won't work!" Tom screamed through the sound of rushing air in his ears, "I don't know why it won't work!"

Genesis closed her eyes to blink back tears, they were going to die. In a matter of half a minute, they would hit the floor, still at a deadly speed. They would be dead as their bodies came into the contact with the concrete. "I'm sorry." She said in a mild shout, "This is my fault."

"You were right. I'd rather die this way, than be mauled to death by some reptilian demon." Tom replied, looking anxiously at the ground as it grew closer. "Thank you for being my friend." He added.

Genesis smiled despite herself, "Thank y–"

Her words were cut short as their bodies smack into the solidness beneath them.

TWENTY ONE

IT WAS DARK FOR A MOMENT, QUIET AND THE AIR had been knocked from Genesis' lungs. This was it, she thought. This was her final moments before she died. Her sight had gone, her hearing, soon her sense of feeling would leave too, then she would drift off to sleep and her body would grow cold. She could still feel Tom's hand in her own and the only sound she could hear was the wind in her ears. The wind which muffled the sounds of a recognisable voice. Uncle Richard.

Genesis pleaded for her eyes to open, but they just wouldn't. Her body had gone into shock, her limbs were numb and her torso felt cold. But hearing her Uncle meant that she was still alive. She begged her body to move in any way, but she could only just stretch her fingers to feel what was beneath them, scales. She was on a dragon.

Finally, her eyes peeled open ever so slightly, as she took in her surroundings. She was laying over the back of a dragon, alongside Tom, whose eyes remained closed. Behind her, sat her Uncle Richard, he sung loudly to himself over the sounds of the early morning London Traffic.

She pushed herself up slightly, carefully assuring she didn't sleep from the dragon's back and turned to face him, "Uncle Richard?"

"Ah, Genesis! You're awake, thank Zeus. You were just metres from the ground you know. How fortunate that the roads were clear, would have given anyone a heart attack to see a dragon gliding across the pavement. What were you thinking, jumping from a building? You're an element, not a pixie. You can't fly!"

Genesis forced a small smile, "It was either that or be killed by illecebra."

"And you chose to try your luck at *not* becoming a pizza base outside the hotel's front gates? I thought you were a mighty fighter, Genny."

"There were too many of them. And I used the term, pancake, but pizza sounds more appetising."

"Why did you jump?" Richard asked once more, growing concerned.

"Tom is the son of Hermes, he can transport us anywhere he knows. We figured he could do it mid-air, land us safely to the ground, but it didn't work." She explained as they flew over Hyde Park. The sky was becoming lighter as the sun rose. She could see Big Ben in the distance, situated ahead of a pink and orange sky.

"It wouldn't work, of course not. Fear is the strongest emotion, fear overrides everything, including adrenaline and determination. He was frightened, his abilities were at a minimal."

"That's why I couldn't slow us down much." She said, mostly to herself, looking beneath them at the Princess Diana Memorial Fountain. "I honestly believed at that moment I would die. I thought to myself, this is it, this is the end. I have been married all-but five minutes and I'm going to die."

Richard laughed lightly, "Speaking of marriage, what happened to mine and your Aunt Jemima's invites to the wedding?"

Genesis stared at him awkwardly, she hadn't invited anyone to her wedding, just those who were there already.

"Aren't you going to ask me how I ended up here, anyway?" He said, thankfully changing the subject.

"I was going to briefly mention it."

"Well, your lovely Theodore called me, he said he believed you were in danger. I got on Rex and flew over as quickly as I could and fortunately for you, not a second later. If I'm not the coolest Uncle ever, I don't know what I am." He said with a childish grin, "I'm your favourite Uncle, right?"

"You're my only Uncle."

"Excellent."

Rex curved right over the Serpentine Lake, heading back toward the hotel to Genesis' friends.

"My sister was kidnapped." Genesis said in realisation, the adrenaline had worn off and she remembered the reason she was in the situation all together.

She looked up at Richard, remembering that her secret sibling may not have been known to her father's brother.

"Theo told me. I also know about Felicity."

Genny frowned, "You knew I had a sister but did not care to tell me? Does that mean you knew my parents were alive too?"

"Well you found out both of those things before I did, so I didn't care to bring it up." Said Richard with a smile, "Your father called me after you found them all and brought them back to Los Angeles. He also called me regarding Katherine. Gen, I am truly sorry for your loss."

She looked down at her hands, "I've lost her once before."

"But this is different, this time she's not coming back."

"She wasn't coming back last time!" Genesis snapped, causing Tom to stir. She saw Richard wince at her tone, "I'm sorry. I just– everyone says that. But it's true, last time she wasn't coming back. I didn't spend each day after she had gone expecting her to return. She was dead, I believed she was dead! I mourned as though she was dead and never returning to me, *ever*. Then by some miracle, she is alive again. She's standing ahead of me, watching me say my wedding vows. She is holding me when I cry over everything I had been bottling up since the last time I saw her." Genesis allowed tears to escape her eyes as she continued talking, "We caught up on all the lost time. For years, I had no mother. My mother was dead. I would go to Margaret often, when I needed a shoulder to cry on, or a mother to talk to.

Then I would go home and be the mother, I would cook, clean, do laundry. Everything a mother does for her child when they are only just a child. I was my own mother and a child. I learned to live without her, even though the pain of their death was etched into my heart like a poisoned tattoo. I mourned for her already, she was dead. She wasn't coming back and this time she isn't either!"

Richard stayed quiet. Tom had woken half way through Genesis' monologue and was staring at her in painful awe.

"My mother is dead, my brother is dead, my guardian is dead and so are some of my friends. Just four years ago, I had only five friends to care for, one of which had abandoned me when I moved to L.A, and another who nearly died himself tonight because of me.

My parents were alive, my brother was a medical student who loved his sister and parents dearly, I had my entire life planned out and everyone that mattered, was alive. What has happened to me?"

She flinched as Tom placed a hand on her shoulder. He knew what was going on, she thought, if she could hear whilst she was unconscious, he must have been able to as well.

"You're growing up." Richard said mournfully, "Everything changes as you grow up."

"No Uncle Richard, not this much. I've suffered for so long." She traced a finger over her sculpes that adorned her arm.

"When my parents died, I became extremely depressed. I wanted to help people who suffered too, when I grew up. I wanted to help them get through the tough times, let them know that other people understand even the darkest of thoughts and that they can speak to those people and befriend them, have them for support when the going gets tough. I wanted to help children who had suffered great loss, like myself. That's what I wanted to do in life. But now I cannot. My dreams are shattered, my world is torn and I'm flying over Kensington Gardens on a dragon." She laughed through her tears, "I want everything to be okay again."

"It'll never be okay again," Richard said soothingly, "But it will get better, I promise you. When this is over, you can live your dream, you can just do it with a pet wolf and the ability to shoot fire from your palms."

Again, Genesis laughed. She had grown strong in time and she was proud of her achievements, she would continue to grow and achieve in time, with Theo and her friends by her side.

"There they are." Tom said, speaking for the first time, "But it's practically broad daylight, how can we get to them now?"

"I'll drop you off, get ready." Richard said, he placed a kiss on Genesis' head. "Please be safe, Gen. And please come visit us soon."

"Thank you, for saving us." She smiled, giving her Uncle a warm hug, "You really are the best Uncle."

"Oh I know." He winked.

"How are we going to do this?" Tom asked as Rex hovered over the hotel.

"The way Element's do everything." She smiled, looking over at Richard proudly. With a swift movement, she encased herself and Tom in a vision dome, allowing them to go unseen as she used the wind to drop them safely to the floor.

Upon landing, she broke the dome, allowing the pair to become seen once more. A young male jogger, passed them, screeching in fright as they mystically appeared in thin-air.

"Ta-da!" She cried, taking a bow.

Tom laughed at her acting skills, "I'm hoping it's early enough that he'll believe that."

"You and I both." She countered, rounding the corner to find the rest of the group.

Theo noticed them first, pushing apologetically past Elijah and Xavier as he made his way to his wife in a fluster. "God, Gen, I thought you were dead!"

"I'm not a pizza base." She mumbled into his shoulder, "I'm sorry I frightened you."

Theo dismissed her pizza comment and held her tightly, "Don't ever do anything stupid again."

She pulled back, looking up at him with a singular raised brow.

"Well at least not without me to protect you."

Genesis grinned, "Protect me? If you and I had a fight, I would whoop your ass, Benedict." She said with an imitated American accent.

Theo shook his head, "Not a chance– *Benedict*."

"Ugh, I definitely should have kept my surname."

"Excuse me?"

She winked at him, "Maybe I'll go by Genesis Bella Valencia-Benedict."

"Well of course, if you want the world's most ridiculous name." Theo said sarcastically.

"I was named Genesis, I think I won that title a couple of decades ago."

"You have an answer for everything, don't you?"

"And that's why you love me."

"Oh of course."

Tom and Eliza appeared at the pair's side, "Are you ready?" Tom asked, "We should get going."

Genesis nodded, "We need to get to Pandoverse."

"Gen," Theo sighed, taking her hand in his own, "I want to save Felicity as much as you do, but you need to understand we can't just go rushing in."

"They could kill her? And the others?"

"Theo's right," Eliza said solemnly, "We need to return to the others in Los Angeles, then make a plan. If we rush in, we could cause more damage than it's worth."

Genesis felt her throat close up and her eyes blur, "I'm scared for her, she's the only sibling I have."

Tom rubbed Genesis arm comfortingly, "It'll be okay. I promise you."

She nodded, heading to her friends as they grouped up and transported back to California.

Felicity waited until the final guardian left the cell, before she made a move. She reached under the back of her shirt, pulling a blade from the high-waist weapon belt. It was hidden under her clothes. It carried a vast amount of weaponry, all sheathed for her safety and able to remain unseen. Tad and Tamas were huddled together in the corner, whimpering, whilst Maggie tried to comfort them.

Although Maggie was the eldest, Felicity was the strongest. She realised that she had the responsibility of getting them out safely. Milo, who was only eight, was sat in the opposite corner. He was quiet, he always had been, but now especially so.

"You know," Felicity said to Maggie in a hushed tone, "If you were only six months older, they wouldn't have taken you."

"How do you know that?" Maggie asked, turning from the twins and looking up at Felicity with big blue eyes.

"In six months, you'll be fifteen, that's the age that Elements leave school."

"But I don't even go to school anymore, neither do you?"

"Correct," Felicity said with a smile, "But Jaspar wouldn't have seen you as a child. He'd see you as a graduate, which is practically an adult to Pandoversians, you'd not have been kidnapped."

Maggie shook her head, "It doesn't matter. I'm here now." She wandered over to Milo cautiously, "You and I have to keep these three safe. You know that right?"

"I know."

"Hey Milo," Maggie crooned, crouching to be at the boy's eye level, "We're going to get you out of here, I promise. It'll be okay." She ruffled his hair and walked back over to Felicity who was watching the cell door anxiously, "Who are his parents anyway, I heard that Sally looked after him."

"His parents died a fear years before Sally took him to the artillery." Felicity recalled, "He is fere-quadrupedia.

I remember his family living in Tampou, his father was killed first, during an ambush, then his mother. Sally took him in and raised him until she was killed. The poor boy has no one now, he rarely speaks to anyone back at the house because he's scared to be close to anyone. In case they get killed too. He spends most of his time wandering around the grounds aimlessly, he doesn't really have a set guardian. He's like a stray wolf, no family, no nothing."

Maggie looked over her shoulder at Milo, he was staring at them eagerly. "He seems so fragile."

"He is. When I was his age, Genesis had saved me from almost being killed."

"By Elders?"

Felicity nodded and began to recall the memories of the day at the school.

"Did you know that you were related to her then? Did you have any idea?" Maggie said inquisitively, "You're both so much alike."

"Not at all, I just believed it was fate that she saved me, like she was meant to be in my life as my role model or something."

"Genesis is an incredible girl, she'll be here soon to save us, with Theo."

Felicity noticed the dreamy look in Maggie's eyes. It was understandable however, Theo was exceedingly attractive.

The cell door burst open, causing Milo to leap up and run into the girl's arms, Tad and Tamas following. Felicity slipped her lamina into the back of her jeans, unseen yet easily accessible. She and Maggie stood forward, blocking the younger children like a human shield. "Who's there?" She asked loudly, standing solidly without any fear.

A woman stepped into the cell, "I want my children."

Felicity knew immediately who she was, Adrianna Faolan.

"He banished them without any warning, I did not know, I want them back, I want to take them home." Adrianna cried.

Felicity shook her head, "Tad is quadrupedia, you can't have him; you despise him."

"No!" Adrianna sobbed, "I do not! He is my little boy, I cannot despise the one I love."

"You dislike Theo, he is your cousin."

"I do not dislike Theo, I love Theo. I love all of my family, even Jax. I know his secret, I have always known his secret. I didn't tell him, because I hated that he was quadrupedia, but I still loved him. I don't agree that this world should be full of difference, but it is and it effects my husband and one of my sons. I love them, I love them all!"

Felicity shook her head, "You brought your children to Jaspar– you knew his capabilities, what if he killed them? It would have been all your fault!"

Adrianna shrank back in fear and pain. "I didn't hand them over! They knocked me unconscious, they took the twins and when I came to, I was back home. I was so scared!" The words stung her like illecebra poison, so Felicity continued.

"You made a vow to love Jax despite anything. You brought two children into the world and vowed to love them too. Yet you pushed your husband away and you brought your children to a homicidal old man! What were you thinking?

Did you think, because you are his niece, that he'd make an exception? That he'd spare your children if they weren't wanted? He killed his wife and is trying to kill his own son!"

"Elizabeth is dead?" Adrianna said in shock, "Aunt Liz, is dead?"

"Not just dead, she was murdered. She was slain by the hand of your Uncle Jaspar, the man whom you gave your innocent little children too. The man who banished them to Earth without warning and guardian. They were just placed on a beach in Los Angeles with nowhere to go. They're only two years old!"

"I didn't know."

"Oh, of course you didn't. They trusted you, you are their mother. They believed you'd protect them but instead you handed them to the cruellest man in all of Earth and Pandoverse combined to their deaths!" Felicity was crying now, without any knowledge as to why. She was hurting. Jaspar had been the reason Seth killed her mother before she got to know her. The reason Genesis had to kill Seth.

The Elder's destroyed her home and tried to kill her too and her sister, her brother-in-law and her friends. She was mad, so mad that she would kill him herself given the opportunity.

"Please don't shout." Adrianna whispered, "Please hush."

"Why?" Felicity asked with a huff, "Don't you want Uncle Jaspar knowing you actually give a damn about a cursed child?"

"No." She replied, "I don't want him knowing I'm here to save them."

Felicity stared at her in shock, *save them*?

"I can help you both too, if you let me."

The young girl raised an eyebrow, but it was Milo who spoke, reaching through the shadows, staying still half-hidden by the girls. "How do we know we can trust you?"

"You don't," Adrianna admitted, "But if you don't let me help you, Jaspar is going to kill you."

Jax was beside himself, understandably. As was Sophia. "I thought they were safe." He cried, as Genesis made him a cup of coffee. "They were all playing outside, Ajordan was keeping watch. I heard some screams and ran outside to see him unconscious and bloody on the patio. The children were gone, all gone. I shouted for help and began to search around the house and gardens for the kids, but I couldn't find them anywhere. It was then that I realised they had been taken. There was only one person, sick enough to take four innocent children, Jaspar."

"I hate to say this, but on Earth, there's a lot of sick people. It's the sad truth, everywhere has bad guys." Alexandrus commented, leaning against the counter. He wore loose fitted jeans at a red and grey chequered shirt. Genesis looked over at her father with a sense of comfort. He looked relaxed, even though his youngest daughter was missing, his eldest son was dead and as was his wife, he was doing okay.

"But you know it was Jaspar, right?"

He nodded.

"I don't get why." Genesis admitted, "Why take the kids, they're the innocent ones."

"And the ones that'll push us over the edge." Said Theo as he entered the room quietly,

"On our wedding day, they used young Elements to fight us. Why? Because they believed that we couldn't fight children. Again, they're using the element of youngsters to make us panic."

Genesis bit her lips together, "Is it wrong to want to laugh at your pun?"

Theo shot her a look. "If we run into the Governing Parts, all guns blazing, they will have us where they want us, to their advantage. We need to be more prepared, this is a big war we're waging, not a street fight."

Genny tilted her head to look at Theo, "When did you become so mortal?"

Again, he glared at her, making her hold her hands up defensively.

"So what you to propose?" Jax asked calmly. He had stopped crying now, fortunately for everyone else, and was sipping his coffee gently.

"We can't go into the Governing Parts."

Genesis shook her head angrily, "We have too, how else will we save them?"

"We won't." It was Alexandrus who spoke this time, staring intently at his son-in-law, "We won't save them."

Genesis frowned at her father, "Dad, seriously, Felicity is in there!"

"And she is strong, so strong." He said, "Just like you. In fact, she's a better fighter than you, she's been doing it her entire life."

"And whose fault is that." She replied, rolling her eyes.

"What I'm saying is, Theo has thought this through and he's right."

Genesis looked at Theo, who was standing and smiling rather smugly.

"We can't go in to get them, but they can get themselves out."

"They're just kids. Only Felicity knows how to fight."

"And she's pure-quadrupedia," Theo smiled, "She can do it, I know she can."

"And in the meantime?" Genny asked, raking her fingers through her long blonde hair.

"In the meantime we go to Pandoverse." Theo said swiftly.

"But you just said–"

"I said not to go into the Governing Parts, but if we stay undercover we'll be okay. They expect us to storm in, rescuing the children and being defenceless in their kingdom. If we sneak in, avoid them entirely, we can use it to our advantage."

"Attack without expectation." Alexandrus grinned, "I like the way you think." He placed a kiss on his daughters head, before heading out of the room, "You picked a good man, Gen!" He called out to her before he left.

Genesis dismissed his comment to prevent inflating Theo's ego any further. "So we go into Pandoverse, we prepare to attack, then what?"

"No." Theo corrected, "We go into Pandoverse, we build up our army and then we advance on the Governing Parts. Then we attack."

"And if we win?"

Theo noticed Jax had left the room also, leaving just himself and Genesis alone.

"If we win," He smirked, walking over to her and placing his hands smoothly around her waist. She wore a cropped blouse and denim shorts, leaving her mid-torso bare. His fingers light against her skin, created a warm sensation into her stomach, she leaned into him instinctively. "If we win, I am going to take you on the greatest honeymoon you could wish for."

"Is that a promise?"

He placed a kiss on her lips and smiled against them, "It's a vow."

TWENTY TWO

FELICITY STARED OPENED MOUTHED AT ADRIANNA, "How do you know?"

Adrianna looked over her shoulder cautiously before stepping forward, "He believes I'm on his side."

"Because you are!" Felicity screeched, throwing her hands in the air with exhaustion, "You hate my kind!"

She tried to hush the young girl. "Your kind is my kind, Felicity! We're all Elements, some are just slightly different."

"And by different you mean cursed."

"That's not what I meant."

Felicity frowned, "If we leave with you now and you betray us at all–"

"We will kill you" Maggie added, "And we will take the twins back to Los Angeles to Jax, away from Pandoverse."

"I swear, I am on your side." Adrianna said adamantly.

Felicity and Maggie exchanged a look, "Very well." Said Felicity, "But I have my eye on you, one false move and you're dead."

"I am privileged to be standing in front of Pandoverse's future greatest warrior." Adrianna complimented, "Maggie, would you carry Tamas for me? I'll take Tad." She looked over to Milo.

"Milo can take Tamas, Felicity and I will be on hand to fight." Maggie said proudly.

"I would like to help." Adrianna admitted, "If anything happens, I will fight."

"Holding a child?" Felicity asked with a raised eyebrow, "Seems irresponsible."

"I know how to get by."

Felicity nodded.

"Let's go."

The group started out of the cell, Felicity taking in the sight around her. Dead guardians, dotted around the hall. "What on Pandoverse, did you do?"

Adrianna looked at the young girl with a grin, "Did you honestly think they just let me walk in there?"

Felicity smirked, perhaps she was trustworthy after all.

Genesis sat with her feet dipped into the ocean. It was three in the morning, the beach was practically empty; so she drove there with the twins, Tom and Xavier. Some space behind her, Eliza and Elijah were running laps of the area of beach they were situated on.

She watched them in amazement, growing up in Nero meant they were used to only ever walking and running on sand. They ran on sand effortlessly, yet Genesis could just about walk without twisting an ankle. None of them could sleep. In the morning, they were due to return to Pandoverse, to recruit an army and fight Jaspar and the government. It was the moment that they had all been waiting for and it was just around the corner. For millenniums, the Gods had wanted someone to defeat the Elders and no one had ever gotten as far as Genesis. But there was still the chance it could end too soon, she could mess everything up.

Tom sat back beside her, Xavier at his side, as they brought over some drinks. Tom had access to his family's shack at all hours, which was fortunate for them.

"We should head back soon, get some sleep before we head off." Xavier commented, sitting down in the sand and handed Genesis a cold refreshment. "We're going to be useless, tired."

Genesis nodded, taking a sip of her drink and looking out to sea. She remembered the first time she had sat at the beach, two days after moving to Los Angeles.

"It's a beautiful view, I think you'll like it here." Katherine said softly, "A family friend owns the little hut there too, they sell great milkshakes."

Genesis looked up at her mother with a sigh, "Is that a hint that you're going to buy me a milkshake?"

"Yes, I will buy you a milkshake."

The young girl grinned, standing up from the sand and heading to the hut. Seth soon appeared at her side. He was shirtless and his blonde hair was tousled from the sea air. "You know mum's going to kill you when she sees your tattoo." She said, pointing to her brother's arm.

"Its fine, she's seen them before."

Genesis shook her head, taking long strides to keep up with her brother. "When are you going back to London?"

"When the summer is up, around mid-September." Seth responded, grinning down at her.

They reached the hut and Genesis caught sight of a young boy, around her age, behind the counter. He looked like Xavier and it made her heart hurt. She missed him. Katherine paid the lady, who she guessed by the distinctive grey eyes, she was a relative. "Genesis, this is Ava Rogers and her son, Tom."

Genesis made eye contact with Tom for a moment, before looking at his mother, "Pleasure to meet you."

Genesis didn't say anything more when Tom passed her a large milkshake, "Strawberry?" He asked, she just nodded.

She noticed on Ava's arm, a tattoo, similar to Seth's. Perhaps it was a fashion statement, more than anything.

Later that day, she visited the hut once more with Seth, this time for a Slurpee. *Tom handed her the blue ice refreshment, staring at her wordlessly.*

"Is there a problem?"

He shook his head, "I'm sorry, I just noticed your eyes."

"Heterochromia." She said exhaustedly, like she was used to having to explain.

227

"Is that what it is?" He asked. She noticed Seth in the reflection of the glass-front refrigerator in the hut, he waved his hand by his neck, as it to tell him to cut it out. Tom looked from Seth, to his mother, who was giving him a peculiar look.

Genesis opened her mouth to speak when Seth interrupted, "She has amazing eyes, I know." He placed an arm around her shoulders, pulling her close, "She got the beauty: I got the brains."

She wanted to argue that she too, was intelligent, but it was useless, he was already walking them away. She stayed silent after that, just enjoying her dessert and the late afternoon Californian sun.

Genesis felt the tears trickle down her cheeks, they were warm against the coolness of her skin. Even in California, it got cooler at night.

"Gen, are you okay?" Tom asked, looking at her with concern.

No, no I'm not okay. My mother is dead and I killed my own brother, she wanted to say. "I'm fine, just overwhelmed by the series of events, you could say." Tom and Xavier pulled their friend in for a hug, soon followed by Eliza and Elijah.

"I don't know why we're hugging, but I'm getting involved." Eliza said cheerfully as she knelt down to their level to wrap her arms around her friends.

Genesis leaned into Xavier, for he was closest, and for a moment it felt like home, like ***normality***.

Theo wandered into the back yard, it was cool out. He couldn't sleep and Genesis wasn't around, she left a note telling him of her whereabouts, in case he awoke, so he wasn't worried.

He hadn't actually expected her to sleep. After all, in the morning she was going to face the biggest challenge of her life. In the morning he was taking the first step toward killing his own father. Genesis understood him, she had killed Seth for killing their mother. He was to kill Jaspar, for killing Elizabeth. He would get justice for all the Elders had done, all those they had killed, for all the hurt they had caused not just himself, but for Genesis. No matter what, he would protect her, physically and emotionally. As of midnight, it became his birthday, and here he was, preparing to go home to Pandoverse, to kill his father.

His thoughts were cut short by a rustle in the tress, "Who's there?" He called out, pulling up a patio paving stone and taking a lamina from the secret compartment, "Show yourselves."

"Put the blade down." A female voice muttered.

"Who are you?"

"A goddess." The girl smirked, walking toward him smugly.

"Don't flatter yourself." Theo huffed.

"Oh I'm not. My name is Athena, Goddess of wisdom and battle strategy. You may also know me as your wife's mentor… well, one of two, the other one lacks significance."

"I do not." Another voice countered. Unlike Athena, with her bright blonde hair and piercing blue eyes, the other woman had jet black hair and green eyes. "Hecate, Goddess of magic, sorcery, witchcraft, trivial knowledge and necromancy."

"Well thank Zeus she didn't give you an entire list." Athena said sarcastically, "If you're going to be like that, I'm the Goddess of wisdom, strategic warfare, courage, the arts, strength–"

"I get the point." Theo said, a little too bluntly, "Genesis isn't here."

Both Goddesses turned to look at him, "She's not?" They said in unison.

Theo shook his head, "She's down the beach with some of the others. Is there an issue? It makes me uneasy that you're both here."

"Well you're quite the charmer." Said Hecate indignantly, earning a glare from the other Goddess.

"When will she return?" Athena asked politely.

"God knows." He replied.

"Actually," Athena said earnestly, with a tilt of her head, "I do not know."

"You're welcome to wait around for her."

"Well, duh." Hecate said with an eye roll.

"Is she usually this rude?" Theo asked, raising an eyebrow.

"Yes."

"No."

"Right."

Athena clapped her hands together, "Let's get to know you whilst we wait! Ares won't give us any of the inside scoop on you, he says you're his Element, no one else's." She gave a sigh, "Yet everyone is allowed to know about Genesis."

"You make us sound like we're pets."

"Well you're not, no one keeps humans for pets. As a matter of fact, I have an owl."

Theo didn't question her erratic behaviour, "What did you want to know?"

"Well, for starts, happy birthday."

"Thanks."

"Now, tell me about how you knew you were in love with Genesis?"

"Oh boy," Hecate groaned, "You've been spending far too much time with Aphrodite."

"Aren't you meant to be old?" Theo asked, looking between them both, "I mean you're ancient Gods and Goddesses, surely you should be grey and wrinkly?"

Hecate snorted.

"I drink from the fountain of youth," Athena admits, "We all do. It makes my skin silky smooth."

"Well that makes sense, I met Ares the other night and he looked like a Calvin Klein model." Theo replied, growing knowledgeable of mortal terms and ways.

"A what?"

"Never mind."

"We should just go." Hecate said loudly, inspecting a flower, "We have no reason to be here."

"Don't you need to see Genesis?" Asked Theo.

"We don't need to, no. We wanted to. We were both bored and Hecate wanted to meet her in person. So we came here." Athena said quickly.

"At three in the morning?"

"Is that the time? We don't really keep track of time in Evlogimenos, we don't sleep either. Well we do, I mean, we don't have to, but we do, because being a God is exhausting." She replied, dramatically throwing the back of her hand across her forehead.

Theo threw his head in his hands with a deep exhale, "Of course, I can imagine being treated like royalty all day each day could become tiring."

"I have to cook my own food, you know." Athena huffed.

Theo shook his head, "I'm too tired for this."

"Well then, Theodore, you shouldn't have been awake when we came here, now you must stay awake until we leave."

"I do?"

"It's kind of rude to dismiss a God, so I'd suggest you grab some matchsticks to hold your eyes open, with Athena here, it's going to be a long night." Hecate groaned, taking a seat on the lawn chair.

"Neither of you dress like Goddesses." He stated. He imagined they'd be in long tunics, or at least gowns. Yet Athena wore a floral romper and Hecate wore black skinny jeans and a t-shirt. "Nor did Ares, he wore sweatpants when I last saw him."

"That's his usual attire, yes." Athena replied, seeming agitated, "I wish he'd dress more appropriately when visiting Earth."

"He's your brother, isn't he?"

"Kind of."

Theo was aware of the stories, how Athena sprouted from Zeus' forehead, all grown up and prepared to fight a war. He was curious as to whether or not the stories were true, but he felt uncomfortable asking about it. "I fell in love with Genesis the moment I broke into her home." He said suddenly, in response to Athena's earlier question.

Athena, and even Hecate, both moved closer to the boy excitedly, "I love a good love story." Athena squealed, listening intently as Theo explained his story.

Genesis climbed the back gate gingerly, swinging her legs over the metal bars and jumping down onto the dry dirt.

She wanted to sneak inside and not to wake Theo, he needed the sleep. Yet again, so did she.

She wandered quietly down the side alley and round into the main garden, preparing to clamber up the trellis and through the window. Her plan was to surprise him with breakfast when he woke up, in attempts to make his birthday a little less barbaric. Her plan was ruin however, when she stopped at the corner, as she heard voices, all too familiar voices.

"Athena?" She grinned, running over to the Goddess and embracing her in a hug, "It's so great to see you." To her right was Theo, she gave him an odd look. To her left, was another woman, she had not met before. "Hello," She smiled, extending her hand for the girl to shake, "I'm Genesis, nice to meet you."

"I'm Hecate." She replied swiftly, shaking Genny's hand, "It's even nicer to finally meet you."

"Oh– holy crap." Genesis said quickly, curtsying at the Goddess.

"Oh, please, don't." Hecate said humbly.

"See, I didn't even get this greeting." Athena said to Theo, who was staring at Genesis' with an unknown expression, "The girl is far too intimidating."

"No, I'm just far more vital than you." Hecate smirked.

"You mean more imperative." Athena rolled her eyes.

Genesis allowed the Goddesses to dispute between themselves, as she headed to Theo. "Is everything okay?"

Theo nodded, "How was the beach?"

"Yeah it was nice, relaxing. Did they wake you?"

He shook his head hastily, "Oh no, no they didn't. I was awake anyway."

"Scary, isn't it?"

"Quite."

"Happy Birthday."

"Thank you, although it's not particularly 'happy'."

Genesis stood ahead of him, looking briefly over her shoulder at the Goddesses, who were still in the midst of countering one another's opinions.

"You look like them." Theo said honestly, causing her to look back at him once more, "Athena and Hecate."

"How so?"

"You look like a Goddess."

Genesis gave a light chuckle, "You don't have to flatter me to such – we're already married."

"No, I mean it. You look like you could be a Goddess."

She shook her head, "I'm far from a Goddess, Theo."

"You're not understanding me." He said politely, "I meant it, literally. You walk like they do, with upmost elegance and you have some sort of aura around you, like you glow."

Genesis bit her lip and blushed, "You're lacking sleep, Theodore."

He didn't fight back, he just smiled, as the Goddesses returned to their side expeditiously.

"I sense someone is coming." Athena announced, "Be prepared."

Genesis and Theo exchanged looks.

A light flashed in the trees and a figure emerged, *Ares*.

"Oh look," Hecate said sarcastically, "Family reunion."

"What, on Evlo, are you doing here?" Said Athena, aggravation etched into her tone, "On Earth?"

"I could ask you the same question?" Ares responded wittily.

"I'm visiting Genesis."

"I'm visiting Theo."

"And I'm so done with your bullshit." Hecate added. She turned to Theo and Genny, "All they do is fight."

"Do not!" Athena and Ares choroused.

Hecate rolled her eyes and shook her head, "I'm going to make some coffee, is that okay?"

"You drink coffee?" Genesis asked, sounding perplexed.

"Oh it's like the sandwich conversation all over again," Theo replied with a groan, remembering a similar conversation with the twins back in Nero.

"I don't want to know what you're on about." Hecate directed at Theo, she turned back to Genesis, "But yes, I drink coffee. I'm still a human being."

"Kind of." Genny replied.

Hecate sighed and headed to the kitchen, leaving the pair to their own devices as their mentor fought.

Finally, after around ten minutes, Athena returned to them, seeming pleased. "I apologise," She huffed, "My so-called brother can be quite the ass."

Genesis raised an eyebrow. Every seemingly mortal thing that a non-mortal did, was a huge shock to her. From eating sandwiches, drinking coffee and using minor profanities.

"Anyhow, he came to wish you luck Theodore, so I guess I shall do the same." She took both of their hands in her own, "Tomorrow, is the beginning of the most anticipated yet treacherous step of your journey."

"Thankfully the last step." Theo laughed.

Athena looked at him with an unreadable expression, before continuing. "I know this has been hard for you. I never wished for either of you to suffer great losses throughout this war and I'm sorry that you had to do so. You have excelled anyone in history and even if you failed after this point, we would never forget you all. Our hearts are with you the entire way, we vow. We will watch over you, as we cannot be there ourselves. We wish we could. You have both lost and earned vastly over the past two years and we are ever so proud of you." She looked at Genesis with a smile, "I was so concerned when Theo first came to you, I knew you fell in love with him on the spot, I was worried your emotions would get in the way, but you proved me wrong, I am proud."

Theo looked at his wife, "You fell in love with me straight away?"

She said nothing.

"Don't let anything falter you now." Athena added, as Ares appeared at her side.

"Theodore," He smiled, "As of tomorrow, you will be on the journey to destroy your father, I'm sorry it had to be him and you, I'm sorry that he fell for Hades' trap. I have faith in you. I have faith in you all. All of us from Evlogimenos have faith in you."

"Thank you." Theo replied sweetly. Genesis gave Athena a hug farewell. "We'll see you when the war is done."

Both Gods nodded, being joined by Hecate and preparing to depart.

"Athena." Genesis said quickly, catching the Goddess' attention, "I have a question."

"Fire away."

She gave a nervous smile, "What ever happened to Olympus?"

"Oh you want that story?"

Genny nodded.

Athena looked at Hecate, "This is your expertise."

Hecate grinned, she must've finally felt like she was involved. "Very well, I shall tell you the story."

TWENTY THREE

"IT WAS SO LONG AGO, I'M SURPRISED I CAN remember, but I was at the heart of it all, therefore I guess, it's unforgettable. It started, when I was visiting Olympus– to see Athena, in fact. We had spoken a few times about mentoring Pandoversians, creating stronger warriors. She knew I wanted to be free from Hades and his shady followers, she was the only one who knew- or so I thought. I was sat with Athena having a glass of wine, courtesy of Dionysus. We were discussing our plans, alone, when what we believe to be an earthquake of sorts, tore through Olympus. Athena stared at me. Of course, it couldn't be an earthquake, not in Olympus? It was so vastly protected by the Gods, it wouldn't, *couldn't* happen. We got up and ran to Amphitrite, she was not at her palace that day, so we figured we could ask her if Poseidon was okay. After all, he was the only God who could create Earthquakes. She said it wasn't him. Athena and I stared at one another anxiously for a moment, before politely dismissing ourselves from the Sea Goddess and going in search for answers. It was then, we saw it.

"Standing at the foot of Zeus' palace was his not-so-lovely brother, Hades. I stopped in my tracks, I had snuck to Olympus to see Athena and if I got caught, he would most likely kill me. I had been the bad guy for so long. Well, the assumed 'bad guy'. I was previously a necromancer. I worked with dark magic, it was a surprise that any one trusted me in Olympus, including Zeus, who allowed me in for a visit.

Hades spotted me and began to head our way. His eyes were full of anger, his face flushed, his eyebrows furrowed and his mouth was set in thin line. Athena stood ahead of me, blocking me from him. 'Whatever it is you want, you can discuss with me.' She said adamantly.

"By this point, all the fuss had brought Zeus and Hera outside to see what was going on. Zeus came down the stairs hastily, heading toward his brother in a huff. 'What are you after, brother? Why have you come?'

'I want Hecate, returned to her rightly place, immediately.' Hades responded.

'She has every right to be here. You claimed her many years ago without giving her the opportunity to be anywhere else.'

'She works with dark magic. She spent enough time away from the Underworld, but it is where she belongs, she chose to be there.'

At this point, I was angry. 'I chose to be there to help Persephone, I didn't choose to be there because of you!'

Hades smirked, 'Well now you are a citizen of the Underworld, no take-backs.'

I wouldn't stand for that. And apparently, neither would Zeus. 'If she wants to join us in Olympus, she may.'

'No, she may not!' Hades roared. The ground shook once again.

Athena came forth, her eyes blazing with annoyance, 'You cannot take claim over her– she is a human-being. She has every right to stay in Olympus.'

'Athena, please stay out of this.' Zeus responded, being the responsible father he was.

'She isn't a human, she's a Goddess of *my* Underworld!' Hades cried.

'Technically not,' Athena added. 'She doesn't belong anywhere. She chooses to live wherever.' She turned back to Zeus, 'She has a choice, right?'

Zeus nodded turning to Hades, 'As your leader, I demand you to allow her the right to stay where she chooses.'

Hades, Zeus and Athena all turned to look at me.

I smiled, 'I'd like to live in Olympus.'

Hades laughed, 'Very well, witch, stay in Olympus.'

'I will. Until Olympus falls, I shall live here.'

The look on Hades face should have been a big enough warning, 'Oh,' He said, 'One day, it shall fall.'

And with that, he disappeared, leaving no trace or evidence of his visit.

"The next few years were hard, of course. Despite everything, at this point, Athena and I didn't really see eye to eye.

I didn't, and kind of still don't, see eye to eye with anyone, really. She despised me, a lot of the Gods did. They were civil enough, after Zeus told them that they had to respect me as a Goddess and make me feel welcome. But I never felt welcome. I didn't care that I was hated, mind you. But that was only the beginning of it.

"Two years after that visit, I still hadn't been back to the Underworld.

When Persephone came to visit Demeter, she came alone, without my assistance. I visited her to apologise, explaining the risk that would come if I returned there to help. Thankfully, she understood. It was on a Sunday, when Zeus came to visit me with Athena. It was, and still is, unlike Zeus to leave the palace unless something calamitous is happening. I knew instantaneously that something had happened.

'Hades has issued an attack on Olympus. He wants a war, because of you.'

I stared at him in shock, I didn't want to return to the Underworld at any cost, but I knew the right thing to do. 'Let me return. It's for the best'

Zeus shook his head, 'We shan't let you leave. You will stay, for you live here now. It will be okay. Olympus is too strong to fall in the hands of my brother, please do not worry.' As he walked away, I heard Athena say that I should go back. It wasn't out of spite, or dislike. It was because she was truly fretful. Not for me, not for her, but for Olympus.

"And she was right, of course. By that evening, we found out the nature of Hades' war. He had brought in new allies. The Titans. Soon, the streets of Olympus were flooded with Titans and the Underworld Gods and Goddesses.

Creatures that were conjured up by Hades hand in the fire, tearing down our homes.

Yet no one attacked us. We prepared to fight them, as anyone would in battle. Yet they never even touched a hair on our heads.

We watched in shock as they tore apart our beloved and ancient city and left us standing there without even a scratch. The creatures that Hades had created, however, were ready. If anyone chose to fight them, they wouldn't stand a chance. We couldn't risk it. All we could do is sit and watch Olympus burn and fall.

"When it was over, the following morning, there was nothing left: no buildings, no pathways, no palace, no ocean, nothing. Zeus went insane, swearing revenge on his brother and the Titans. In time, we learned that Hades had offered the Titans a gift for their services, and that gift, was Olympus. Nothing was left standing, but that didn't faze them. Despite Zeus over throwing them millenniums before, they had returned to get back what was theirs.

"We realised we couldn't fight, this time, they had the upper hand. We travelled far and wide until we found a new location for us to live in. Somewhere bigger, better and safer than Olympus, somewhere so special, that if Hades tried his luck once more, this time he wouldn't succeed. We felt blessed that we had found this place, blessed that we had found a second chance, after all that had happened. No mortal would ever know the stories that followed our mythology, but we were safe, and that's what mattered. We were safe, secured and blessed to still be alive. So we called our new home, Evlogimenos.

"It wasn't much difference from Olympus really. It had the similar styled buildings and lakes and mountains. It was a nice place to live, we were happy.

Meanwhile, the Titans were parading around Olympus with pride, Hades backing their every move. It was okay, though. We were safe, for now. Hades then chose to take his power elsewhere– to Pandoverse. Then known as Stoicheío. He poisoned the minds of the governing leaders, making them believe that his brother's creation, of Quadrupedia, was a curse sent to plague Pandoverse. Zeus was mortified, so he created his ultimate warrior, to defeat the Elders. He spoke with us all, asking us to mentor Pandoversians until they were ready to defeat Hades' army. Numerous failures made us begin to believe it was over, we would never have Olympus back and Hades' would overrule us: always. Any future was soon seemingly diminished when Genesis' parents chose to raise her on Earth, unaware of her roots. When she was brought to Pandoverse for the first time, there was a celebration across all of Evlogimenos. For the first time in so long, there was hope. We threw a party in her honour. With the prayers and wishes that she would be the one. And now we're only days away from finding out."

TWENTY FOUR

FELICITY STOOD AT THE CORNER OF THE HALL, HER back to Adrianna and the others. "It's clear." She said quietly, before side stepping into the corridor and jogging to the next corner. The dungeons of the Governing Hall were a labyrinth. There were corners and multiple turn-offs everywhere. All the young girl had to rely on, was her senses and Adrianna.

"I think it's this right." The twins' mother commented, jerking her chin in the direction of another corridor. "Then it's another right, a left and then up the ladder."

"And you're sure that's the route?" Felicity asked, looking around and giving the group the all clear.

"Positive. We can get out of there and then we'll find the others before we can come back and destroy Jaspar, for good."

Felicity grinned, excited at the possibility. "Let's go."

They headed East: to a corridor longer than imaginable. It stretched out for what seemed like a mile.

Adrianna gave her a comforting smile, "It takes us from one end of the Governing Hall to about thirty-yards from the other. The secret exit isn't close to the building, it's far away enough to get out safely."

"We have to do this quick." Maggie added, "If they realise we're gone it's only a matter of time they're flooding these passages to find us."

Tad groaned into his mothers' shoulder.

"It's okay baby; we'll be out soon." She crooned. "Mummy will take care of you."

Felicity's chest burned for a moment. She wished that Katherine would round the corner, weapon in hand, to protect her. But she knew it was an impossibility. She wished Genesis would show up too, she felt sick with fear. She wanted this to be over. She wanted her sister. "Not too far." She smiled at the other kids, "Just be quiet though, yeah?"

Tad, Tamas and Milo nodded. Maggie tousled Milo's hair playfully, "You're all doing great."

They continued down the length of the corridor. Far ahead a patch of light was visible. "That's the exit." Adrianna explained, "It's an open doorway. It just leads onto the outskirts of the Governing Parts.

"That explains it." Maggie said, earning a questionable look from the others, "It explains why my legs hurt– we're going uphill."

Felicity and Adrianna nodded in understanding, and continued forward with as much speed as they could muster. The walls were damp and a foul smell came from different directions.

"Old sewage-systems." Adrianna explained, as if reading her mind.

Felicity gave a simple 'ah', in response.

As they neared the light, the smell seemed to grow faint. Either that, or they had grown used to the stench. The passageways became warmer, as the heat radiated through the doorway from the strong, searing, Pandoversian sun. Felicity could see the green of the grass and trees already. She could hear the distant woodnote of the Clidaro, the Pandoversian bird that closely resembled a love bird.

"It's so close." Maggie grinned, "I can't wait to see light again."

They reached the exit. It was sloped upward, meaning to get out you would need to almost crawl. Adrianna went first, then Tad, Tamas, Milo and Maggie. Felicity tailed the group, keeping a watchful eye over her shoulder. When she saw Maggie's feet disappear into the sunlight, she followed. Crawling out with the hilt of her Lamina between her teeth. As she reached the top, she sheathed her blade and turned to her friends, "Oh thank Zeus' we got out."

An unnerving smile greeted her, blue eyes glaring her way. She saw five guardians, four of which held onto her friends. The last one staring at her too. She looked back at Jaspar, "You will regret this, I promise you."

Jaspar grinned. It wasn't a playful grin, but a sickly grin. The grin of an evil man with malevolent tendencies. "Oh I doubt I will, Miss Valencia. Do I call you that now? Or do I stick with Reynolds? After all, with your mother dead and your filthy sister married to my son, you are the last female Valencia?"

Felicity turned to Adrianna, who mouthed the words *run*.

She looked back at the Elder with a grimace. "I go by Valencia."

"How sweet!" He cheered, clapping his hands together in a mocking manner.

Felicity waited no longer before she threw up her hands, creating a partially-clear wall, like a force field. She turned on her heels and sprinted, reaching for the lamina in her belt and pulling it free. Her long legs struck out ahead of her, taking longer strides and making the space between herself and Jaspar augment. She ran and ran and ran.

A shot of air knocked into her back with so much pressure her vision blurred. She fell to the floor in agony, crawling forward as though she could get away. Jaspar, and his airment Guardian, appeared at her side. She rolled to face them, keeping her lamina in hand, twisted beneath her torso. She looked up at the pair, her chest heaving as it gathered any oxygen it could congregate.

"Oh dear," Jaspar said with a tone of faux concern, "I'm starting to believe your sister might not be the one I should be worried about."

She saw as the guardian raised his hand again and everything, went black.

Ares appeared at his sisters' side, looking pleased. It was now just past eight in the morning, and Genesis and Theo hadn't slept a wink – still.

"Are you both ready?" The God of War asked the pair.

Athena and Hecate looked anxious. They understood what would happen in the next day or two and they were clearly concerned.

Genesis, however, was not. She knew what was in store for her and her friends. Her entire life had changed drastically in a matter of years– whatever happened in the next few days, wouldn't make a difference. Regardless of the outcome, it would become easier for her. Jaspar lives: she is dead, yet free from his power. Jaspar dies: she is free also – and alive. Either way, she would be at liberty.

Theo took her hand in his own, "We're ready."

As if on cue, the rest of the Artillery came from the house, out onto the lawn with admiring expressions at the Gods.

"It's such an honour." Said Eliza, slightly awe-struck.

Athena waved her hand dismissively, "Please, treat us as your equals."

"Are you all stocked up?" Theo asked Tom as he and Genesis headed inside briefly.

Tom nodded, "I placed your weapons on your bed."

Theo thanked his friend as he followed Genny upstairs and into their room. Laid across the bed were four Laminas, an Arcus, two sets of arrows, and a Militum, a Binarii, two Gladios, three hastams and several Unas.

Genesis gave a big sigh, "Well, thank Zeus I'm not taking my clutch bag to fit all of these in."

Theo shot her a side look.

"Shall I grab a couple of extras, for Felicity and Maggie?"

"I've already done that." Sophia said from the doorway. "I've packed some weapons for them both."

Genesis flashed her a small smile, "They're going to be okay. You know that, right?"

Sophia nodded, "Felicity is an incredible warrior, I'm sure she's protecting them all."

"If I could be half the warrior my little sister is, I know that the next few days would end well."

"They will, I'm sure." Said Sophia, "In fact, we were discussing yesterday… What happens after the war?"

Genesis looked at Theo, who shrugged, "It's your prophecy; it's your call."

"You can't behave so casually over the fate of an entire World, can you?"

He grinned playfully, "I'd elect you as the new leader of Pandoverse."

"The idea is to rid of leadership and be a free world."

"We can't just be free, that would be more dangerous than living under a Government!"

Sophia shook her head quickly, "He's right. We can't live in total freedom. I think you ruling would be a good idea. We could go from having Elders, to having a Monarch. After all, you are the chosen one."

Genny stared blankly as Sophia departed the room. She *was* the chosen one. To win this war, she would have to call the shots.

Back outside, the Artillery stood in chatter as they waited to leave for Pandoverse, the trio of Gods watching over them.

Genesis headed into the small crowd and toward Athena, who seemed pleased with her return, "Genesis, is everything okay?"

Genny nodded, "I just need to address everyone with the plan before we leave. It can't hurt to be extra safe."

Athena kissed Genesis' cheek, "That's why you're the chosen one." She turned to the group, "Elements, listen up. Genesis is going to go through the plan with you one final time before you leave. Listen very carefully, one mistake could cost not only your life, but someone else's. Remember, the future of Pandoverse is in your hands." Athena moved away, leaving Genesis alone.

Genesis stepped up onto the small patio wall, so she could see all her friends clearly. "Artillery." She began. "I want to make this quick so we can get going. The plan is as follows: when we reach Pandoverse, we are going straight to Tampou. There is nothing there but ruins now and that is where we will live for the next two days. Throughout the two days, a small handful of us will visit each town, recruiting who we can, without causing any havoc or a stir. Once we have recruited, we give them orders. We tell them to be in Tampou for Tuesday at sun-down, and from there we will spend one last night preparing for battle. On Wednesday, we will march into the Governing parts as an army and bombard the Guardians first. Then, with my go ahead, we will begin on the Elders. We will discuss the matters of post-war, after it is over and won. Any questions?" She looked to Theo, whose expression was that of annoyance. Something had bothered him, she wasn't sure of what.

No one asked any further questions, they all just stared blankly.

"Very well then," She looked over to the Gods with a grin, "Let's go kick ass!"

The Artillery cheered wildly turning toward the Gods.

Hecate raised both hands in a swift, circular motion and a black hole appeared. "To Tampou." She smiled.

Again, they cheered. Before all huddling together and making their way into the darkness. Athena gave a curt nod to Theo, as though approving something unspoken – at least to Genesis' awareness.

Genesis stepped off the wall and approached Theo, "You ready?"

He looked down at her blankly, "Let's go."

She didn't question his behaviour, he was on his way to kill his father– she knew he wouldn't be happy. She just took his hand and they stepped into the black hole, together.

Jaspar stood at the doorway to the cell. His hands behind his back, his right hand holding his left wrist. He looked like an army sergeant, Adrianna thought. She wished that they had made it out. They would be on Earth by now, she could explain herself to Jax and her mother. It would be okay. Instead, she was locked back in a dirty cell all alone. The Guardians first took the twins and Milo into one cell. She kicked and screamed, daring to use her abilities to fight back, but it was no use. Every vine was burned, any leaves were blown away and any dirt was dampened.

Secondly, they took Maggie into a separate cell, the Guardian enjoyed this. He mentioned something about the weakling and the 'unbranded' one of the group. He underestimated her. Thirdly, they locked away Felicity. She too, put up a fight. Adrianna couldn't believe how powerful she was at such a young age. She was a true fighter, and hopefully Genesis was too. Lastly, she was locked up. Jaspar ordered her into the largest cell and they threw her in. She landed on the cold, damp floor with a thud and swore she heard a bone crack. Jaspar didn't leave straight away, he stood at the door and watched her whilst she struggled to regain the wind in her lungs that had been previously knocked out. Once she was okay, he spoke.

"Adrianna. Oh my sweet, sweet Adrianna. First my wife, then my son, then my sister and now my niece." For a moment, she believe she saw a wash of real pain pass his face, but it was gone too soon to be authentic. "Well, you know what they say? You can pick your friends but you sure can't pick your family."

"Choose." Adrianna mumbled.

Jaspar, who had begun pacing back and forth, stopped to look at her. "Pardon?"

"It's choose." She remembered the quote from a book Theo had lent her once. He admitted it was a favourite of his and that she should read it, she was ever so glad that she had. "You can choose your friends, but you sure can't choose your family." In response to his confused expression, she added, "Harper Lee, To Kill a Mockingbird."

"Did you learn that from my son, by any chance?"
She nodded.

"Of course. Being so invested in Mortals makes you weak, doesn't it. Makes you a sucker for sappy poetry and English novels"

"To Kill a Mockingbird is American."

"Do you have an answer to everything?"

"Pretty much, learnt that from your son too."

"Yet you despise him."

"I love Theodore, he is my cousin."

"Your mother was adopted."

"He's still my cousin, and I love him."

"He's Quadrupedia!"

"Because you made him that way!" Adrianna screamed.

"I don't like the thought of it as much as you, but its life. Get over it. There was a time on Earth when people despised others because of their skin tone, or their sexuality. Quadrupedia is the same. It bothers me, because it isn't something that's tradition to Pandoverse. But I am learning to move on from that. My husband is Quadrupedia, my son is Quadrupedia. Your daughter-in-law is too!"

"She is not my daughter-in-law."

"Oh, but she is! She married Theo!"

"Without my blessing!"

"Get over it! She and Theo are happy, how could you even think about jeopardising that? What made you so bitter, Jaspar? What happened to my fun, loving Uncle? The one who used to take me to lunch with his children every Sunday? The one who took me to Earth for the first time? Where did he go? What changed him?"

"Nothing. I have always been this way."

"You married someone of a different Element! You have *not* always been this way! You never would have married Liz and had two children if you despised the outcome!"

"I fell in love with Elizabeth before I knew she was an Airment."

"How is that possible?"

"I saw her from afar, she was mystical. I fell in love with her there and then."

"You could have walked away as soon as you knew."

"I couldn't, because I loved her."

"Like Theo loves Genesis?"

"That's entirely different. That's just lust. I loved Elizabeth."

"That doesn't matter."

"How doesn't it?" Jaspar growled, "Because Jax walked away from you? Because maybe he actually had stopped loving you, you know?"

Adrianna wanted to hurt him, but she hadn't the energy to do so. "He walked away from me because he loved me. Because he loved my family and friends and Pandoverse. He did what was best."

"To turn against *me*?"

"You make it sound like it's the wrong thing to do."

"It is."

"It is *not*. You banished my children to Earth! If Genesis hadn't of been down the beach to find them, Zeus knows what could have happened!"

"Do not use that man's name in my kingdom!"

"Kingdom? Really? This isn't your kingdom, Jaspar. This isn't your kingdom, your throne, your realm or your time. You're making a mistake."

"I'm protecting Pandoverse from evil."

"No, you are not. You are an Elder, and an Elder is what killed your son."

Jaspar's face turned red with anger, "Quinten was killed by illecebra! Not an Elder!"

"You're so naïve! It was a Governing member! They killed him in cold blood, not a demon, an Element, and why? Well, you know why, don't you, *Uncle*." Adrianna said the last word as though it was bitter tasting and revolting. "Tell me again, what changed you?"

Jaspar shook his head, "Don't do this Adrianna, you will regret it."

"You're going to kill me anyway, aren't you? So tell me. It was Quinten wasn't it. Why was it Quinten? Because he too, was Quadrupedia? You were so mad at him for being murdered, not the Elder, *him*. You blamed him for it, because of his abilities. You decided to turn against all Quadrupedia at that point also, because it was his fault, wasn't it?"

"Stop it."

"It was poor little Quinten's fault. He had that God damn disease, Quadrupedia, and that got him killed. But instead of avenging his death by hating the Government, you burrowed yourself into them more and more. Until finally, here we are, Head Elder. You now have control over who kills who. But you're still so mad, so why not kill more Quadrupedia, why not start a war! Not even a civil war, because you don't see yourselves as equals with that kind, do you? No. you think you're superior.

You know how I know this? Because no matter what happens, who you have to kill, you won't allow anyone to kill Theo. You blame Quadrupedia for Quinten's death, so you want them all dead. But you become Head Elder so that you can keep Theo safe. But, plot twist, Theo would rather die than be by your side. He will sacrifice himself for his friends, and most of all, for Genesis. So why do you keep trying? Why not give this all up, right here, right now? Oh yes. That's right. Because who's fault is it that you're like this? Poor, innocent, blameless, little Quinten. It's all his fault."

"I said stop!" Jaspar roared with aggression.

He ran at Adrianna, grabbing her neck in his hand and holding her up, "You need to learn to keep that filthy mouth of yours shut or I'll kill your boys in front of you and that is a promise. You have two days until your execution, then my army and I are headed to Earth to destroy those you're protecting so badly." He turned to head out of the room, but not before peering back over his shoulder with a sickly smile, "And you were wrong, Theo is the one I'm going to kill first."

TWENTY FIVE

TAMPOU WAS COMPLETELY DIFFERENT THAN THEO remembered it.

It was all dust and stones now, although it wasn't much before, either. The buildings that were left originally, were almost all gone. Turned into ashes, alongside people, duplexes and more. Every step he took, he stepped on a stone or a human bone. His stomach churned menacingly at the sight. In the distance, he saw Xavier stare emptily at the structure of what once was a house. He didn't even need to ask, to know that was his old home. The place that Volant, his Owl, was killed. He looked over at Genesis, who was comforting her father. He listened intently.

"It was a good friend of mine and your mother. We grew up with her. She was fere-quadrupedia. That's who was looking after her, not really an Aunt."

"She raised her well."

"But she was killed, by the hands of the Government. The people we spent centuries believing were the good guys, in all of this."

"It'll be over soon. We might not bring back those we loved, but we can avenge their deaths entirely."

Theo felt an uneasy feeling in his stomach. Around him, stood the beginning of an army. An army whose soul-purpose was to kill his father. He knew it had to be done, it was the prophecy, after all. Yet it still bothered him. He saw the anger in Genesis' eyes at the thought of him. He also saw the gleam in her eyes at the thought of killing him. As though she would enjoy it. He couldn't blame her, for all Jaspar had done. But he only had one wish, if she wants to kill his father, make it quick. He didn't want to watch him suffer.

He knew his mother was killed by his father's hand. He knew he was banished to Earth by his father's hand. He knew that all the tragedies surrounding him, were by his father, or those alike. It had to be done, but he would not be the one to do it. He could not live like Genesis, with the blood of a relative on his hands. He could not do it, despite how deserving it may be. He would rather lock him up and throw away the key than kill him. But he knew that he wouldn't have a say in that. When Genesis addressed the Artillery before leaving Earth, there was a spark in her eyes. The same spark she had when he and Sophia had mentioned electing her as the Monarch of Pandoverse. He was worried. Power was a dangerous thing, especially in the hands of someone as strong and vengeful as Genesis.

His thoughts soon came to an abrupt halt, as he watched Genesis' body go limp and collapse to the floor.

Maggie closed her eyes and willed herself to see. Who could she reach? It was daytime, no one would be sleeping. She longed to reach Sophia, or even Genesis.

Genesis.

She knew that Genesis had the ability of visions. She just had to get inside one. She wasn't even sure it was possible. She was the daughter of Morpheus, the God of Dreams. Dreams were something you encountered when you were sleeping. The chances of any of the group sleeping during the day, was unlikely. Yet she tried. She tried until finally, she got what she wanted.

Genesis.

Everything she saw seemed blurry, but Genesis was clear. "Gen?"

Genny looked up at the young girl, "How on Earth did you do that?" She rubbed her elbows, they were bleeding. "You made me drift out of consciousness!"

Maggie grimaced, "I'm sorry! I didn't know it would work that way. Are you hurt?"

"I think I fell before anyone could catch me, but I'll be alright. Just try not to do this again, next time, it could be on the battle field."

"Again, I am sorry."

"Is everything okay, anyway? Why did you need me?" Genesis paused for a moment in recognition, "Of course everything isn't okay. I didn't mean that in a stupid way. What's happening?"

"Adrianna is with us. Well, she's in another cell."

"What? But she is working for the Government, is she not?"

Maggie shook her head.

"Well that's a massive change in events, one that will please Jax and Claudia, I am sure. What else? How's my sister?"

"Felicity is fine. She almost got away."

Genny grinned, "Sounds like her, what happened?"

Maggie went on to explain the events of the almost-escape. How they reached the exit before being captured, and how Jaspar caught up with Felicity after she made a run for it.

"She's so silly, taking a risk like that, it could have gotten her killed. It could have gotten you all killed!"

"It has."

Genesis paled, "It– what?"

"Our execution is in two days' time. Then they are coming to you, to Earth. To kill you."

"Can you keep a secret?"

Maggie nodded.

"They can't come to us on Earth, when we're already on our way to them."

Theo cradled Genesis in his arms, "Wake up. Gen, please, wake up!"

She groaned, and a smile spread upon her lips. Soon after, her eyes fluttered open, her multi-coloured irises staring straight into Theo's eyes. "Hey handsome."

"What on Pandoverse was that about, Genesis?" He snapped, "You scared the crap out of all of us!"

"I'm alive, aren't I? Or did no one actually bother to check my pulse whilst I was out?" She sat up and away from him, analysing the injury to her elbows, "Oo, that's definitely going to scar."

"Of course we checked your pulse. How are you so calm about this? You just fainted? I thought, for a moment, you had been shot or something."

Genesis gave him a side glance as she rubbed at her elbow, "Do I look like I've been shot?"

Theo was growing impatient with her now, he waved his hands in the air defensively and turned away, "Whatever."

This made Genny jump up and trot to his side, "What's gotten into you? Stop being so grumpy all the time. I was just messing around, no big deal. You know, if you–"

"Stop, okay. Just stop." He said aggressively, turning to her with an unfamiliar anger in his eyes, "I can't do this anymore!"

A lump formed in Genesis' throat, "Do what? Us?"

Theo sighed in response.

"You don't want to be with me anymore?"

"I do."

"Then what is it!" She was shouting now. Her throat burned with emotional pain and tears bit at her cheeks. "Tell me! What is wrong?"

Theo shook his head, "I threw a blade at Seth, when he killed your mother."

"I know." She said bluntly, "I saw it. Just like my vision." She recalled the vision from the night she and her brother ran away back to Earth. Just before he tried to get her killed by Elder Maximus.

"Yet you still stabbed him."

"He killed my mother."

"He is– *was* your brother. You still wanted to kill him?"

"I was half way there before you got him, I couldn't have stopped if I wanted too."

"You're not getting the point," He groaned, "You *wanted* to kill him?"

"Well yes. He tried to kill me, he tried to kill us all. He killed my mum–"

"Do you feel guilty?"

Genesis exhaled deeply, "Theo, I do. Yet, I don't. I saw him murder my mother, just weeks after I got her back in my life. We didn't even get the chance to make up for lost time: to catch up. He just twisted her neck like she was a rag doll. Snapped her bones like she was a twig. Like she was an object without meaning. Because that's what she was to him, that's what I was too. An object without meaning. A big old nothing.

I loved Seth with all my heart, even after he tried to kill me. But in that moment, as I saw her body fall to the floor, all the love was gone. I had no other choice. I acted in her defence. It was defence for a defenceless woman. How long had you wanted to kill him, Theo, for all he had done?"

Theo stared blankly, "I still want to kill him, even though he is already very much dead."

"Exactly."

"And you want to kill my father."

"Yet you don't."

Theo looked down at his shoes, tears filling his eyes.

"Then don't kill him…"

He looked up at her, feeling hopeful. She was understanding him, she was going to reason with the idea, he thought.

She placed a hand on his cheek. "…I'll do it."

Felicity stared out of the small window of her cell door. Each door was marked with a different symbol: one for air, one for water, one for fire, one for earth and one, for all four, the cross. That was what was on her door, the symbol for all four elements. She first thought it was a way of labelling her. Like an illuminated sign saying: 'Hey! Look! This one's *cursed*!' Within an hour of being in the cell she discovered the real meaning. It wasn't a sign to say she was Quadrupedia, it was a theoretical slap in the face, saying: 'How unlucky, this door is protected, your powers can't save you now!'

No matter what she tried, she was trapped. She tried to flush the door open: nothing. Burning the hinges until they had melted: nothing. Creating a minor earthquake that would crack the walls and free her: nothing. A surge of air, strong enough to break the door open: of course, nothing.

A Guardian had been by to inform her of what was to happen over the period of the next two days. She would be entitled to rations of food: bread, cold-chicken and a fruit of her choice, an apple. The fruit was her breakfast, accompanied by a glass of pomegranate juice (the most common fruit in all of Pandoverse). Her lunch was two thin slices of bread, wholegrain, with a sliver of margarine on the top, and a glass of water. Her dinner was two chicken sandwiches, with another glass of water. She also got three glasses of water between meals.

When she asked the Guardian why they were feeding and nourishing her, he simply stated, 'you must look well, for your execution. We cannot allow you to die before we get the chance to kill you'. *Excellent*, she thought, they're just going to parade our deaths in front of all of Pandoverse and make an example out of us: *you rebel, we'll kill you*.

By nightfall, or at least what she assumed as nightfall by counting the minutes after her dinner ration, a different Guardian appeared at her cell, with her fifth glass of water for the day. He was around her age, which was upsetting. He was being lured into Guardiancy before he had even finished school.

He appeared at her window, his face peering through it, all one foot squared of it. She stared at him directly, eye to eye. His eyes were a daunting shade of grey, but she couldn't help but notice the miniscule fragment of blue beside the iris. It was barely noticeable, probably not noticeable to many mortals or elements. But she spent her life amongst Quadrupedia, she could sense one from a mile away. He had dark brown hair, which was almost back, and a chiselled jaw. He stared emptily at Felicity, saying not a word.

"Are you going to give me my water or just stand there?" She asked, raising an eyebrow impatiently.

"My apologies," The young Guardian said quickly, stuttering on his words in the hurry. He handed her a glass and she took it, none so eagerly.

She half expected him to leave afterward, yet he stayed. "You can go, I probably won't drink this all at once so I can't return the glass yet."

"You look like her." He said straightly.

"Like who?"

"Genesis Valen– Benedict? Or is it Valencia?"

Felicity wasn't too sure what Genesis went by: Valencia, Benedict, or both. "She is my sister. Of course I look like her."

"You carry yourself the same. When they brought you in, after they captured you outside, you didn't falter. You held your head up high as you allowed them to march you inside the cells. It was brave of you."

Felicity gave a snort, "It wasn't brave. It was logical. I had tried to fight back, but look where that got me."

"I'd like to come in."

Her eyes widened in shock, "In– in here?"

He nodded.

"Why?"

"So we can talk. I have been designated to guard you, I'd like to sit with you for my shift, is that okay?"

Felicity stared at him in confusion, before giving a brief nod and stepping aside as he unlocked the door. In that moment, she could have escaped. She could have gotten past him and out of that door before he had even realised she was gone, she knew she was capable of that. She could have killed him, if she had needed to. But she didn't. She just patiently waited as he stepped inside and locked the door behind him. It was locked by a large brass key, which hung on a large ring on his Guardian suit. She could take the keys and knock him out, escape and release her friends in the process– but for some reason, she didn't.

He wandered inside the cell and sat down on the bench, she soon followed. "So, you're pure, huh?"

Felicity kept her eyes locked on him, "Why do you trust me? I could have easily killed you and escaped."

"But you didn't, and I know why."

Her expression questioned him further.

"You trust me, I'm just like you." He gestured to his fore arm, where she saw the two symbols for air and water.

"You brought me water." She begins, "I don't need it."

"I know that. If you get thirsty, you can get water yourself."

She nodded slowly, "When did you become a Guardian?" She changed the subject again, trying learn all she could in a hurry, in case he got caught.

"Not that long ago," He said honestly, "around a month ago. I was pulled from school to do it, I had excellent grades in Physical Training."

"So did I, but I wasn't pulled from school. I was just pulled aside to be killed, if Genesis hadn't of saved me, I would be dead right now. Which makes me question you. I was almost killed for being different, yet you are working for Jaspar, how so?"

"Elder Jaspar said I was a sufficient addition to the army, especially at such time. There was a catch, of course."

Felicity was confused as to why he was being so open with her, she was a prisoner, yet he spoke to her like he was a friend. "What was the catch?"

He sighed, looking down at his gloved hands, "I will have to give up one of my abilities. Through illecebra treatment. I have a week to choose which ability to keep, and then I go for the procedure."

The words such as treatment, and procedure, made it sound as though it was something medical, a method or a cure. It wasn't, it was twisted. "You don't want to, do you?"

The Guardian shook his head, "Honestly, no. But if I don't, I might be executed myself."

"And if you do, you may die from the poison, or be left entirely mortal?"

The boy gave her a half-hearted smile, "I wish there was another way."

Felicity didn't know what came over her in that moment, but she surprisingly told him the biggest secret of them all. The secret that could cost her, and her friends, their lives. "My friends are forming an army, I'm not sure when they're coming to Pandoverse, but they will be here, you can join us. Fight against the Government, you can keep your abilities." She paused, "You know it's the right thing to do."

Shockingly, he took her hand in his own, "Will they come, within the next two days? Before your execution?"

"I hope so."

"Theo Benedict, Elder Jaspar's son, he and your sister will rule Pandoverse one day, I am sure of it."

"You mean, you're against Jaspar too?"

"Of course. He believes that Quadrupedia cannot coexist amongst normal Elements, although we all are of the same kind. I wouldn't be here if it were not for the fact he had threatened my family if I did not join him. I have a younger brother, his name is Eadric. He is only five years old. I must protect him, and my mother."

"And your father?"

"He was once a Guardian too, he was killed by an illecebra demon. His brother and his sister-in-law were killed too. Left my cousin an orphan. My father left the family home to live in the Governing parts alongside Jaspar, to care for my cousin. He was killed by a demon at the boundaries of the Valle-Mortis, my cousin returned to Aeras. I thought he was here, I thought he would help me escape to Earth, to the Artillery. He knew Theo, you know. But he isn't here, I believe he is dead."

The story sounded familiar, Felicity thought, too familiar. "You never told me your name?"

The boy seemed perplexed at how she had bypassed everything he said before. "Zaire, Zaire Ra Wentworth."

"You're Anthony's cousin?"

His eyes lit up. It was easy to see the emotion his expression held: *hope*. "You know him? Is he alive? He's with them, isn't he? The Artillery, he's okay?"

Felicity felt a lump form in her throat. She had to now break to the poor young Guardian that the cousin, the one person he pleaded to see, was dead. She stared silently for a moment, trying to find the right words. Yet it soon seemed that she needn't say anything at all.

"He's dead, isn't he?"

"I'm sorry." She whimpered.

"Were you there? How did it happen? Please tell me he did not die in vain?" His eyes searched hers for a moment, wandering as though they could pick up the answers in her face.

He did die in vain, that was the problem. At least, for now. "He was killed, by Jaspar. He arrived in Los Angeles alongside the Governing Army. He had gathered an army of his own within the Guardians. He turned them to our side. There was a large battle, yet he died in my sisters arms."

"And the battle wasn't won, was it?"

"Almost, Genesis had Jaspar at her fingertips, but he managed to portal back to Pandoverse before she could kill him."

Zaire said, "He had pledged his allegiance to Hades and the Titans. They granted him the ability to transport, with Seth as an ally, if there was anyone dead around him."

"But Seth was dead too?"

"It was his final journey, he no longer has that power."

Felicity smiled, it was a good thing, that he no longer had that ability. "It's going to be okay, in the end."

"How do you know?"

"I just know. I know Theo, and I know my sister. It will be okay."

A flicker of hope and joy passed Zaire's eyes in a moment, "May I help you, Felicity?"

Felicity cocked her head to the side inquisitively.

"Is there any favour, I can do for you, without Jaspar knowing? In return for your acceptance of me. For allowing me the opportunity to join you and your friends."

"There are a couple of things, actually." She admitted, "Firstly, I need you to get a message to Maggie and Adrianna.

Tell them you're on our side, that you and I have spoken, and that you're going to help us."

"Help you, how?"

"That's my second favour," She continued, "I need you to find out who is truly a follower of Jaspar, and who is only here for reasons alike to yours. Create an army amongst an army, like Anthony did. The Artillery are going to grow their own army before the war, with your help, we'll be unstoppable."

"And how do you know that they'll arrive in time, the Artillery, before Jaspar comes to kill you and the others?" He was standing now, the darkness of his Guardian cape like wings in the shadows.

Felicity looked at Zaire with a warm feeling spreading in her chest, "Just trust me, I know."

The Artillery had made camp in the stairwell of a small abandoned building. Genesis had volunteered to take first watch, whilst she was still running on adrenaline and coffee. It was Xavier, Icarus and Ajordan, who had chosen to watch alongside her, to as much as Theo's disgust. Genesis was grateful though, as Theo still hadn't moved on from whatever was bothering him, and she didn't need his negativity at such time. The building wasn't intact, the walls had crumbled, the glass in the window shattered. It was just a skeleton of what once was, with a roof on top.

There was a total of eight floors, each floor contained approximately six apartments, (which were really just one room with a small bathroom attached), and stairwells on the end of each corridor. The group were clustered in the fifth floor stairwell, Adorjan and Icarus guarding them from either side.

Xavier and Genesis were told to watch from the outside, and that was when she decided to watch from the roof.

She gestured Xavier to the opposite end of the corridor, it had a large hole in the wall, where a window would have been. "Can you climb?"

Xavier furrowed his eyebrows at her, "Can *I* climb? Genesis, you're the one who's new to all this," He closed his eyes and shook his head lightly, "How are you so fearless?"

When he opened his eyes she had already gone. The only thing he saw was her foot disappearing at the top of the used-to-be window. He quickly checked his weaponry, before pulling himself out and climbing up behind her. He couldn't quite believe how agile she was, like she had been doing this her entire life. Her feet found chips in the concrete and rebar rods that stuck out perilously from the walls, without hesitation. He tried to recall any time she learned to rock climb or anything similar, but nothing came to mind. Without looking down at the ground that was so far below, he scrambled up, latching onto anything he could use to pull himself up.

When he had reached the top, Genesis was sat waiting with a smile. "Finally." She grinned.

"Why?" Xavier asked bluntly, "Why did we have to do that?"

"Is there an easier way?"

"Yes it's called not scaling the side of a eight story building."

Genesis shrugged, pulling herself back onto her feet, "Better view from here though. You certainly can't see much from inside a stair well, can you?"

"Very well." Xavier replied, standing beside her, "So what now?"

Genny smiled, "Now we just wait out the next two hours and kill anyone if they try to kill us."

"I remember the days when you were so sweet and innocent." He mocked, rolling his eyes.

"I've never been sweet and innocent!" She shoved him playfully.

"Hm," He replied, "I guess not."

Genesis looked at him briefly, before climbing onto a metal box that sat centre of the roof, checking its stability before she did so. "So what's the deal, with Pandoverse?"

"I think you ought to have figured that out by now." Xavier chuckled, sitting beside his friend.

She gave him a sideward glance, "What I *mean* is, why does it have electricity, and many modern day pleasures, yet they don't have cars?"

Xavier gestured to the view ahead of them, "Do you see any point, in cars? Everything is practically in walking distance. Although, they have them in the Governing Parts, for learning and travel past the boundaries on patrol. Only the army drive, or those in the Governing families – hence Theo."

She nodded slowly, looking out at the world in front of her. She felt Xavier staring at her contently, "I wanted to be there, you know." He said suddenly, pulling her from her thoughts.

"Pardon?"

He shook his head, his golden hair (which had now grown to just below his shoulder), fell partially in front of his eyes. "When your parents… died. Well, when you believe that they had."

She stared at him, giving him a look with a raised brow that suggested he continued.

"When I had heard, I was in Pandoverse at the time. I felt my whole world crumble. They were like my second-parents, growing up, and even with all that time apart after you moved to Los Angeles, I still mourned for them. I mourned for you. My parents never really explained as to why I couldn't contact you, or see you. I just knew it was something regarding being an Element.

I hated it. But I understood." He paused for a moment, sucking in lung full of air and deeply exhaling, "There was one point– I think it was your first Christmas without your parents that I wanted to come see you. I almost broke my promise to my family to sneak to California and visit you, to see if you were okay. Your brother was in Pandoverse, working, and your Aunt and Uncle were still in London. I felt so much pain for you, thinking of you on your own. Your first Christmas as an orphan: alone."

"I wasn't alone," Genesis interrupted, "I spent it with Margaret, Sophia and Maggie."

"I didn't know that at the time." Xavier admitted, "I didn't know much, to be fair. I just knew that I had, in your eyes, abandoned you… and I hated myself for that." He took her hand in his own. "We grew up together, you were my best friend, my sister, the one person I couldn't bear to live without. By the time you left for the states…" He trailed off, looking at her with eyes full of pain.

"Go on."

"I was in love with you."

The words felt like a blow to the heart to Genesis, she spent all her time with Xavier before she had left, wishing she could tell him how she felt. She wasn't too sure if it was love, but it was something. When she left for America and he made no attempt to contact her, she felt lost and empty. Her entire world was shattered.

"I'm sorry." She muttered, "I didn't know."

"When I took you out for dinner, when I first saw you in Pandoverse, it wasn't to act on those previous feelings. It was to see if they were still existed, which I guess they weren't. I will always love you, Genesis, just not in that way." He smiled, "And seeing you with Theo makes me happy. You two are made for one another."

Despite her unconditional love for Theo, she couldn't help but feel a pang of sadness at his words.

"But," He said cheerfully, "Moving on from the sad stuff, we should discuss some things."

"Such as?"

"Such as when this is all over, and you and Theo have a proper wedding, what is the deal? I wanna hear it, all the details."

"You want to hear the details of a wedding? Isn't that the job of a female best friend?" She giggled, leaning back on her palms and staring up at the stars.

"Yes." Xavier concedes, "But we have another hour and forty-two minutes until the rotation of whose on watch… so I'll have to do."

Genesis didn't question him further before rallying off her dream wedding plans and praying, deep inside, that she would have the opportunity to bring them to life.

TWENTY SIX

THEO AND HIS GROUP WERE THE LAST TO KEEP watch.

He was alongside Amethyst, sat in the hole in the wall, their legs swinging over the edge in unison. Not too far behind, were Eliza and Lacey, guarding their sleeping friends. Theo looked over his shoulder at them, he could see Genesis between Tom and Xavier, snuggled into her friends; she was *safe*. All he cared about, for years, was himself. He didn't care for any others. He had fooled around with girls throughout Pandoverse but never stayed with them, he didn't do commitment. The only friends he made, besides Anthony, lived in different towns, he barely saw them. And when Anthony left, he was alone. The only person he had ever cared for was his little brother, Quinten. When he was killed, Theo turned cold. Cold against his parents, cold against his friends, cold against the world. Now he had lost his parents, he could lose his friends and he might even lose his world. But none of that mattered right now, as he looked over at the young blonde, fast asleep. Her head was on Xavier's shoulder, Tom's head was upon hers. They had all huddled together: to keep warm, to keep safe and to be comfortable. But they were safe. Genesis was *safe*.

"Do you ever wonder what your life would be like, if you were mortal?" Amethyst asked, breaking the silence.

He turned to face her. Her red hair was flowing across her face like fire. He shrugged. "I don't really know. I guess, I'd probably have joined the army or something?"

"That's what you think now, because you've learned to fight your entire life, but I think, personally you'd be a police officer or something. Maybe a fireman."

Theo chuckled lightly, "So I'd be an authority figure, in a uniform, who does potentially life-risking activities for his job and works in a team… sounds similar to being in the army here, really."

"It's anything but similar."

"Same concepts."

"Okay, well, perhaps a teacher then?"

"I hate children."

"A scientist?"

"I suck at science."

"A rich boy who doesn't have to work a day in his life because of his family fortunes?"

Theo grinned, "Now *that*, sounds more like it." He pondered for a moment, "What about you, what do you think you'd have done?"

"Me?" She stared outward in thought, looking across at the Pandoversian stars. The constellations were different there than on Earth, a different galaxy, she presumed. "I think I'd be a lawyer, or something."

"Why? You can do that here?"

"I just guess it's what I excel at. I wanted to be one before, but the whole mermaid thing kind of stopped that." She laughed, "Okay, so. What do you think your life would be like if Genesis never came to Pandoverse?"

The thought felt like a stab in the chest for Theo. He had never really thought about it at all. His rarely even thought about his life before Genesis, let alone without her completely. He thought carefully about what he believed it would be like, and what he would prefer it to have been like. "Well, horrible." He admitted, receiving a side grin from Amethyst, "I mean, my dad is a bit of an asshole, so I doubt it would have been great."

This earned a laugh from her.

"But in all honestly, I don't know. Actually, no, I do know." He squinted his eyes, as if he was trying to see it himself. "My parents would still be together, my father would be an Elder and I would probably be a Guardian, training to be higher up in the ranks. Eventually, he'd probably strip me of my abilities, all but water: like him, so I could take his place when he dies. Within the next year I would be married to one of the young girls from the Governing Parts, no one half as beautiful as Genny. I would probably be considering a family soon too, because, as you know, that's just how it is here." He paused. Amethyst noticed he had chewed his bottom lip anxiously, so much so, that it had begun to bleed. "I'd visit Earth," He resumed, his voice carried away in the winds of Tampou, his words sounding lost in thought. "And I'd see her. I'd have my wife with me, we'd be doing a routine visit: Governing orders, and I'd see her.

On the beach, probably hanging out with Tom, or her other friends from the local college. She'd be a teacher, I think, and she'd be on her day off, it would be a Saturday.

I would watch her cross the beach, on the arm of another man, she would be smiling. Her body would be bare of any marks. No sculpes, no scars. She would look up at this man and kiss him, the way I kiss my wife, but it would hurt me. I would not know her, she would no know me, but it would hurt. Because I would know, in that moment, that she was my missing piece, the one I could not live without, even though I had lived so far without her. I would feel complete, once again. For the first time in a long time. She would complete me." He stared at Amethyst, "I couldn't do that though, I couldn't live in world where Genesis wasn't mine."

Amethyst had teared up at some point during his speech, and she was now wiping her eyes with the cuffs of Elijah's sweatshirt.

"I'm sorry," Theo mumbled, "I rambled on. Caught in the moment."

Amethyst placed a comforting hand on his bicep, "It is fine. I admire you for how much you love Genesis." She removed her hand and placed it carefully in her lap. "When you brought her to Nero, when you all made me human again, I saw it in your eyes. I was so shocked, I had always known you as quite the player– no offence."

He raised his hands as if to say, 'none taken, I know I was!'

"I saw the twinkle in your eye when she spoke, when she moved or did anything.

You watched her like a hawk, like your eyes were glued to her soul and you couldn't look away without ripping your sight away painfully. It was tragically beautiful."

"I hope she feels the same way." He admitted.

"She married you, didn't she? At just twenty years old."

He nodded. She was right, Genesis did marry him at such a young age. It was nothing to him, Pandoversian tradition was to marry young. But to her, someone who had grown up around mortal traditions, it was huge. "What do you think your life would be like without her?"

"Well, firstly. I'd have one less incredible friend. And secondly? It would be kinda wet. Very wet. And long, too. Immortal kind of long."

Theo placed his hands on his face to muffle his laughter.

"But I'm glad she is here, she is going to change the world."

Theo stared ahead of him as the sun began to rise. Today, they would start the first leg of their battle: developing an army. As of today, regardless of the outcome, Amethyst was right.

Genesis was going to change the world.

"What's beyond the water?"

Amethyst gave him a questioning sideward glance.

"In Nero, the ocean, it must end somewhere, right? Where does it end? On Earth, the ocean connects different countries, what's beyond our sea?"

"Nothing." She replied straightly, "Nothing we're aware of, anyway. You can only swim so far out, and there's an invisible barrier, preventing you from going any further.

Rumour has it that Zeus placed in there centuries ago, it prevents anyone from going farther out to sea… you can't see beyond the barrier either, it makes everything distort."

"Wow." He replied, furrowing his eyebrows in confusion. He pondered for a while, his mind contemplating thoughts and wondering what was beyond the barrier. What was Zeus hiding?

"Hey, Theo." Amethyst said at barely a whisper. "What's up?"

The young girl smiled at him, "I have an idea."

Felicity woke to the sound of her cell door closing, Zaire wandering inside. "Morning!" He said cheerfully.

She glared up at him from the corner of the room that she had slept upon. "Morning." She grumbled.

"You're happy." He replied sarcastically, placing a tray of food in front of her, "I tried getting you extra but Jaspar has eyes everywhere."

"I'm getting killed tomorrow, I'm sorry I'm not back-flipping off the walls." She looked at the tray, "Thank you anyway."

"No problem."

A moment of silence passed before Zaire spoke once more.

"I have ten people."

Felicity looked up at him from her breakfast.

"To join the Artillery, ten people I know of. They're now searching themselves amongst the Governing Army for more Guardians who want in."

"Just be careful, if you trust the wrong person, it could cost you your life."

Zaire gave her a comforting smile, "It's so sad. We should be friends, at school, in classes together. Enjoying our childhood. Instead, you're the prisoner and I'm the Guardian of you. It's not right, it seems so… messed up."

Felicity gave a light chuckle, "Everything about Pandoverse is messed up. Spend a year on Earth and you'd wish you were mortal."

"Do you?"

"Sorry?"

"Do you wish you were mortal?"

"Well I wouldn't be facing the death penalty if I was." She laughed, "I would be living in London, with my family. They would all be alive… and my brother wouldn't be the person he was."

Zaire sat beside her as she ate, bending his knees and resting his arms upon them with a deep exhale. "I would have a full family too. I have no idea where we'd be living though."

"I reckon somewhere like Georgia or something."

He raised an eyebrow at her.

"It's a state." She explained, "In America."

He's expression didn't falter.

"On Earth?" Felicity shook her head, "Oh, never mind."

Zaire gave her a lopsided grin, "How's your breakfast?"

"I'm not particularly a fan of pomegranate but other than that, it's fine."

"I was going to get you an apple, but another Guardian took that for Adrianna."

"Well at least the good fruit isn't going to waste." She stared at the cell door, "How's the kids?"

"They're scared, understandably, but they're doing okay, so is Maggie."

She went to speak further when a sound disrupted her thoughts. "Zaire, get up, quick, someone is coming."

Zaire jumped up at ran to the door, but not before Jaspar's face appeared on the other side.

"Wentworth, what are you doing in here?" He growled, sending a glare at Felicity who was quick to return the gesture.

"I'm so sorry, Elder Jaspar, I was just brining Felicity her breakfast."

As to emphasise the point, Felicity held up her glass and half eaten pomegranate.

"You left the prison kitchens a while ago, how long did this task take you? Do I need to reassign something with stronger capabilities?" Jaspar said with a huff, "What was *really* going on?"

Panic flared up inside Zaire. If Jaspar found out the truth, he would be joining Felicity and the others on the execution line the following day.

"It was my fault." Felicity said loudly from her corner, "I wanted to talk to him, after all, he is my assigned Guardian."

Jaspar seemed unimpressed, making Felicity speak further.

"I was sleeping, so he had to bring my food in and leave it for me, which woke me. As he was leaving, I called him back, I just wanted to know my friends were okay. Then I asked him about his life before being a Guardian, I was just trying to make a conversation. Seeing as you plan to murder me tomorrow, I figured I could make some sort of small talk prior to my death."

Zaire stared at her wide eyed, mouthing a 'thank you', she just smiled.

"Very well, Felicity." Said Jaspar, "That is a fair and valid point. I have decided to bring your friends to your cell for today, in respect for your last today. The Guardian's will bring them in the hour." He turned away from her and to Zaire. "Wentworth, you will be the in-cell Guardian. You will monitor what they do and say, making sure that they do nothing stupid, of course. The others will guard the halls."

"Of course Elder Jaspar, I will do as you please."

Jaspar nodded, flicking his eyes to Felicity, "Enjoy your breakfast." And with that, he walked away.

Zaire turned to Felicity, as if to speak, but she waved a dismissive hand. It was risky for them to speak further, they would have to be discreet. Or tomorrow would become a whole lot messier.

When Genesis woke, Theo wasn't around. She stretched beside Xavier with a groan, looking at her friends all huddled in the stairwell. The twins, she noticed, were also gone. Lacey, who was guarding with Eliza, had returned to the group, yet no one else.

"Morning." Xavier smiled, sitting up straight beside her.

"Morning," She paused, looking out down the corridor, "Where's the others?"

Xavier just shrugged in response.

Genesis went to respond when Elijah and Eliza came charging in, their faces flustered and seemingly anxious. Elijah's eyes scanned the group, until they landed on Genesis.

"Is everything okay?" She asked, standing up and heading his way, "You look concerned."

He shook his head and handed her a piece of paper, folded into a small square. She instantly knew it was from Theo. He always over folded paper, into the smallest little square possible, it was a habit of his.

An uneasy feeling spread in her stomach as she plucked the paper from his grip and began unfolding to read what Theo had left for her. The look in Elijah's eyes told her that it involved Amethyst too. She became panicked.

Gen,

I'm sorry I didn't wake you to talk you through this, but Amethyst and I have some things we need to do. Keep searching and recruiting. The battle is in one day, please be safe until then. And be careful when it begins. I have faith in you, we all do. Make sure you lead the Artillery to victory, won't you? I love you. I will see you soon,

Theo

"Do you have any idea where they've gone?" Genesis said, barely at a whisper.

Elijah shook his head, "This was all that was left. Not even a note from Amethyst. At least we know they're not dead or kidnapped though, that's one thing."

"But still, do they just expect us to go on without them?" Asked Eliza.

"I think so." Genny replied, "Why have they gone? Is this the coward's way out? Is that it? Are they going to leave until this is over?

284

It wouldn't surprise me, I know Theo is uneasy without the whole concept, it is his father after all."

"Then why would Amethyst go with him? She is the daughter of Artemis, she's a hunter, not a coward." Elijah admitted, "It makes no sense."

"It's whatever." Genesis huffed, "We can do this without them. I don't need him by my side *all* the time anyway."

"Gen…" Eliza reached for her friend, but she was shrugged off as Genesis walked away. "Eli, where on Pandoverse have they gone? They can't just walk out now, not when we have to face the Government tomorrow!" She said to her brother, her tone laced with fear and panic.

"I don't know." He mumbled, "But Genesis is right, we'll just have to do this without them."

Zaire brought Adrianna in first, before leaving to fetch the children. As soon as he closed the cell door, Felicity ran into her arms.

"Hey, are you okay?" Adrianna crooned, stroking the young girl's hair.

"I never thought, when we first were captured, that I'd say this… but I missed you."

Adrianna laughed, crouching to her eye-level. "We'll get out of here, I promise. Soon we shall be alfresco."

"I know."

"I mean it, tomorrow, we'll escape."

"Keep it down," Zaire hushed, "What if someone else came in?"

Adrianna stared at the young boy with wide eyes.

"It's okay." He comforted, brushing the twins forward to their mother, as Maggie ran to Felicity's side, Milo close behind. "I'm on your team. I have my army ready and waiting for tomorrow morning."

"How is that going, by the way?" Felicity asked, hugging her friend before standing before the young Guardian.

"There are more than four hundred Guardian's in the Governing Parts alone, it was risky, finding out who to trust. So far I have gathered over half of them to be on our side."

"How do you know they're trustworthy?" Maggie questioned, earning an agreeable nod from the others.

"I don't. I just know that if they go against us, they'll be killed. We're going to triumph, we're going to win."

Felicity smiled, an unnerving and twisted smile as she realised that this time, they would become the champions.

TWENTY SEVEN

FIRST STOP: GI.

Genesis scaled the trunk of the large tree in Gi, also known as the Wise Tree or the Lucky tree. It was the centre point of the town, a large oak with a trunk the diameter of a small car. It stood almost sixty-five feet tall, with branches stemming out metres from the trunk, aggrandising the tree and creating a seemingly endless shade.

She soon reached the top, her vision dome protecting her from everyone around her, including her friends. Half of the Artillery were secretly scrutinising the town, looking for potential candidates for their army for the upcoming battle.

Genesis had insisted since the morning, that she wasn't affected by Theo and Amethyst's disappearance, and she was sure her friends believed her. Yet she didn't believe herself, and now she was climbing a gargantuan tree for a high vantage point to see if she could look out for her husband and her friend.

For years, Genesis had never been fazed by heights. She was always the first to suggest a roller coaster, or sit by the window on the plane. Yet as she sat, tucked in the joining between the branch and the trunk of the Wise Tree, she felt nauseas. The leaves beneath her blurred her vision at the scene below. Leaving her only to see outward rather than down. Although the sea of green was vertiginous. She waved a free hand to remove the vision dome from around her, clearing her view from the slight haze the dome bestowed.

A rustling in the leaves caught her attention, as a figure appeared.

She pulled a lamina from her belt, preparing to fight, if necessary. Within a moment, Noah appeared, his long blond hair pulled back into a bun, wisps of it flying across his face. He held an acutam between his teeth, its blade coated in green foliage where he had used it to steady his climb.

"Noah?!" She said breathlessly, "Why on Pandoverse are you up here? You gave me a fright, I could have fallen."

"I'm sorry, Gen." Noah replied with a slight chuckle, "I was growing worried about you, you wandered off a while ago without returning."

"How did you know I was here?"

"Luna."

Genesis spoke an 'ah' and nodded her head. Of course, her wolf duplex would have directed her friend to her. She would have been concerned too. She thanked Zeus that Ignis hadn't grown concerned and flown up to her, making her positon obvious to everyone in and around Gi.

"Why are you up here?"

Genesis looked over at the son of Asclepius, wondering what excuse she could give. The look in his eyes told her than he wouldn't believe anything but the truth. "I wanted to see Pandoverse, one last time, like it is."

Noah's eyebrows knitted together as he studied her face, trying to discover whether she spoke the truth or a lie. "Like it is?"

"Uh-huh." Genny mumbled, looking back out at the view, "Peaceful. Besides the odd Guardian walking the perimeters of each town, its calm. As of tomorrow, this entire world may as well become a bloodbath."

"Agreed." Noah replied, sitting in the acute meander of an opposing branch, "It could get messy. Pais and I will be on hand to help our warriors though, we will rescue and protect as many as we can."

Genesis nodded. "How many do you think there'll be?"

"Well, Eliza and Elijah have managed so far to gather a dozen Pandoversians, that's just in the first half an hour in Gi. We have still a lot of the town to search, and three more towns to visit."

"Not the Governing Parts?"

"We think it's too risky."

"Noah," Genny sighed, pushing a lock of her hair behind her ear, "Some of Pandoverse's best warriors are in the Governing Parts, it's a huge risk to take to not visit and attempt to recruit."

"It's a huge risk to take to visit where Elder Jaspar and his army are too. We need to stay alive until tomorrow, not put our lives on the line before."

Genesis shudder at his choice of words. *Elder* Jaspar. The fact his title made him one of the most important Elements in all of Pandoverse, an authority figure, yet he was deceitful, evil and working toward his own personal execution from his daughter-in-law. "It's risky, I agree, but I think it would be worth it."

"Genesis." Noah said, his tone laced with aggravation, "I've been in Pandoverse my entire life. So, trust me when I tell you that it's not a smart move.

The vast majority of Element's living in the Governing Parts are loyal to the Elders. The likelihood of us being caught within the first five minutes of being there, is around twelve to one. Each family *at least* has one person who will turn any one of us in if they saw us, let alone if we were trying to create an army against their leaders. I see your point, Genesis, I really do. But it would be so reckless to try it."

This time, Genesis didn't fight her case any further. She just stayed silent. Theo would know what to say or do right now, something she admired him for: always knowing what to say. He would probably understand both her and Noah's points and take them both into consideration.

It wouldn't surprise her in the slightest if he snuck into the Governing Parts without going noticed and recruited those he knew were safe. After all, he grew up in that town. *That's it*.

"I know where Theo is." She said quickly, placing a vision dome over Noah and then herself. She reached out a hand, a vine appearing on the branch momentarily, and smiled. "I know where both he and Amethyst are."

Before Noah could question her any further, she jumped from the highest point of the tree top and swung to the ground like Tarzan. He gave a sigh as he began to climb down the sixty foot tall trunk, one loitering step at a time.

By the time the group had left Gi, it was midday. They had recruited thirty-one Elements who had returned to Tampou with Adorjan and Lacey, leaving the others to move on to their next town: Nero.

Elijah took lead as their group wandered under a selection of vision domes, heading into the centre of Nero. Xavier stayed close to Genesis, along with Jax, who was humming an unfamiliar tune.

"We're going to so short of time." Xavier mumbled, shielding his eyes from the sun with a single hand, "Its passing midday and we're just onto our second town out of two."

"We should suggest we split up." Genesis said honestly, looking for an opportunity to get to the Governing parts, from there she would find Theo, she was sure of it. Of course, she couldn't admit this to anyone, it would make it obvious she was bothered by Theo's disappearance. So far, she had put on a front that told them otherwise.

"We can't split up Genesis, it's too dangerous."

Genny sighed, there was no point arguing without installing a growing suspicion. She would have to get away on her own terms.

Elijah came to a sudden halt, listing off duties to each Element: where to go, who to trust, where to meet up after they'd followed their instruction. He was splitting up the group.

Genesis bounced from one foot to another with anticipation, she could get free, find Theo.

"Gen, you, Xavier and Noah will go there together." Elijah commanded.

Genesis shot a questioning look at her friends, she had no idea of the plan– she only caught the latter of Elijah's order.

"Let's go!" Noah chimed, hooking an arm through hers and smiling at her with a mischievous gleam in his eye.

Xavier caught on, hooking his arm through the other as the pair chaperoned her in a direction she was unaware of.

"Where are we going?" Genesis asked, whilst attempting to free her arms from their stronghold.

"To do what we have been asked to do." Xavier said swiftly, "To recruit soldiers."

"Any reason you're holding onto me like I'm a convict?"

"Because you practically are one."

Genesis glared at him and gave a huff. She *had* to get away.

After a brief walk, they arrived at a housing complex, similar to the one that the twins live in.

"So the plan is, we will go to the following houses," He pointed at a selection of white walled homes in the complex, "As they're the ones Elijah said would join us." Noah explained.

Genesis bit her lip and nodded. "Like door to door salesmen."

"Exactly." Xavier replied, "But there's an issue."

"Me."

"Kind of." He said awkwardly, rubbing the back of his neck, "You and Theo are the most wanted Elements in all of Pandoverse right now, we can't risk them seeing you. You need to stay under the dome."

Genesis smiled sweetly, as soon as they left the dome, they would no longer be able to see her; she could get away. "Very well."

Noah and Xavier exchanged glances before searching the area. When they knew it was safe, they stepped aside, Xavier allowing them out of the dome and leaving Genesis inside. "Stay here." He insisted.

Genesis nodded, not that he could see, as the pair walked off. Once they were out of sight, she turned on her heels and headed south, to the Governing Parts, to *Theo*.

Zaire headed into the prison kitchens, it was eerily silent and he had left Felicity and her friends alone with just one Guardian outside the cell. He hoped they tried nothing stupid, the Guardian he left with them wasn't part of his group, thcrcforc, he potentially backed Jaspar and would happily kill them on the spot.

He shuddered at the thought, in just two days, he had found a good friend in Felicity, it would pain him to see Jaspar kill her in all her innocence. She was only a year or so younger than him, yet he saw her as vulnerable and in need of his protection.

When he was younger, Zaire always knew he was different. He never believed they difference he attained to many of his family, friends and neighbours, could one day cause such an uprising across Pandoverse. Anthony always told him, growing up, that one day, the Quadrupedia: demi, fere and pure, would bring such a change to their worlds. He never would have thought it however, they were deemed dangerous, diseased, afflicted, jeopardous and formidable. There were times, in school, that the classes would take fieldtrips to Tampou, they would wander through the streets in groups, staring at the Quadrupedia like they were wild animals– with fear and intrusiveness. There were always one, at least, in his class who would then point at Zaire and laugh. *'You're just like them, you're cursed!'* … The worst part was, the teachers would not reprimand them, but laugh with them.

As he reached the archway, Jaspar rounded the corner, two Guardian's at his side, as usual. "Zaire Wentworth." His voice boomed through the corridors. "Why are you wandering away from your assigned duty?"

Zaire swallowed, looking up at the Elder with as much honest in his eyes as he could muster, "I was going to quickly get a drink, Elder Jaspar, I apologise." That wasn't true of course, he was sneaking food for the others.

Jaspar's blue eyes twinkled, "You're part Waterment, did you not think to get water yourself?"

"I didn't have a glass, sir, or I would have."

"Ah, that's understandable."

Jaspar gave a final nod, before pivoting to exit where he came from. Zaire released a breath he didn't realise he had been holding, before Jaspar stopped to face him once more. "I almost forgot what I came here for, I was looking for you." He smirked, "I have word that my son's little posse are in Pandoverse, preparing to fight us. So I have conjured up a little plan."

Zaire felt his entire body begin to quiver, trying to remain calm and not give anything away.

"I'm moving tomorrow's execution forward, to tomorrow morning. And as for you, young Wentworth, I am taking you for your procedure this afternoon rather than next week."

"Procedure?"

Jaspar cocked his head and shone an evil grin, "Why, my boy, the procedure to rid you of your Quadrupedia."

It took all of ten minutes for the group to realise Genesis had gone.

"She's gone to the Governing Parts; we can find her." Noah said, "I know she's there, she thinks that's were Theo and Amethyst are."

Xavier registered the expression that passed Elijah's face, before stepping forward with shame, "We can't go after her."

Elijah glared at him, "She's gone after Theo and Amethyst! We have to go after her! Any of them could get hurt, we need to protect them!"

"And get the rest of us killed in the process?" Xavier snapped, squaring up to Elijah with a set jaw, "I want to protect them all, just as much as you do, but if we go after them, all of us will alert Jaspar more than we probably already have. Genesis can handle herself, as can Theo and Amethyst. She has gone after them because she is worried, but I can assure you they know what they're doing, and when she finds them, she'll be safe too. We are *not* going after them."

Elijah turned away in a huff, before jumping back, pinning Xavier up by the throat against the nearest tree. "Do NOT tell me I don't need to protect my friends, *ever*." He growled, his admiral blue eyes burning with anger. "I lost Amethyst once, my God should I lose her again."

Xavier pushed Elijah back with a gust of air, "Don't fight me Kaimana, it won't be pretty."

Elijah went to lunge, but not before Eliza came between them both, her expression that of impatience.

"Enough!" She roared, pushing the boys apart from one another, "You have to stop! For the love of Zeus, we're about to fight in a war against an exceptionally large and dangerous army, why on Pandoverse do you think it's okay to fight amongst yourselves."

"Did you bypass everything he just said?" Said Elijah, sounding infuriated, "Don't you want to help them?"

"Think about it Eli, what would they tell us to do?" His sister said in a low yet patronising voice, "Would they ask you to go after them? Or would they tell you to continue with what we have set out to do? Don't you trust them?"

Elijah stayed silent, as did Xavier.

"Well? Don't you?"

Both boys nodded solemnly.

"Then let's get on with it, we have little time left and two more towns to visit, we need to do this fast."

Before anyone could counter her further, Jax came forward. "Fotia and Aeras are all that is left to visit." He scanned the remaining Artillery for a brief moment, Tiberius and Paisley had returned with the selected recruits from Nero, to join the others waiting in Tampou. "Half of us will go to each town. Icarus, Noah and Elijah, you will go to Fotia. Which leaves myself, Tom, Xavier and Eliza, to go to Aeras. Unless we want to walk straight past Jaspar in the Governing Parts, we will have to pass Fotia to get to Aeras, so Elijah and Xavier, try not to rip one another's heads off."

Eliza nodded, steering Xavier away from her brother and heading west, the outstanding Artillery following close behind.

It didn't take long for Elijah's half of the group to arrive in Fotia and the other half to continue toward the town of Air. He waited for everyone to gather together before turning to Noah for help.

He grew up in Fotia, he knew who to trust and who to steer clear of if they wanted their plain to work.

"Follow me." Noah instructed, heading toward his family's shop. The 'U' on the 'Duplex Trade' sign was missing, and he made a mental note to mention it to his mother when he got inside.

The door opened with its classic bell chime, alerting the workers of his arrival. It was growing late, so the store was practically empty aside from employees and one small family choosing their daughter's snake duplex.

"Noah?" A voice appeared from the back door, a middle-aged woman appearing from the darkness.

"Mother," Said Noah, stepping forward to hug her hello. "We need your help."

"Where's your sister?" Isabella, Noah's mother, asked in a panic.

"She's safe, in Tampou." He replied with a comforting smile, "Your friends, the one's whose son was Quadrupedia, where are they now?"

Isabella shook her head, "They were killed a few years ago in an Illecebra attack, did you not hear?"

Noah gave a stressful exhale, turning to his friends, "I thought they'd help and know who to trust."

"Noah." Isabella said quickly, causing him to turn to face her, "Their son is still alive. I can give you his address, he can help."

Noah grinned at his mother and pulled her into his embrace, "Thank you, we're very short on time."

She pulled back and headed to the counter to write down the address before giving it to her son and saying her goodbyes. "Just, be careful, won't you?"

Noah nodded.

"All of you."

"We'll be okay, I'll see you in a few days, when this is over." He went to turn away but stopped to briefly mention the broken sign.

She gave a low chuckle and one last hug before he headed outside with his friends and toward the address he had in his hand. He looked up at the ever-darkening sky and shuddered, at this point, they would need a miracle to get a whole army together in time. They would need a miracle to survive this entire war.

Zaire never returned.

Felicity paced by the cell door, growing more anxious by the minute. It had been an hour, and he hadn't come back. Where was he? Did Jaspar find out what he was planning? Did he get caught? Did he get reassigned? Perhaps he was just taking lunch break. The possibilities were endless and yet, Felicity felt an all too familiar pang of uneasiness in her stomach, telling her that she should worry. That Zaire was *not* okay.

She reached up to peer out of the window, the Guardian who was watching them, was staring down the hall, his expression blank, as usual. He must be on Jaspar's side, rather than theirs, or she was sure he would have said something to them by now.

"He'll come back, Felicity, don't worry." Adrianna soothed, stroking the young girl's hair.

"What if Jaspar has figured it out? What if one of Zaire's recruits are actually on Jaspar's side, and they've told him of our plans?" She replied, almost at a whisper, "Jaspar could have killed him."

Adrianna went to comfort her again but Felicity held up a hand, "Don't tell me it's going to be okay, it's not. I just know."

Adrianna bowed her head and turned back to the children, leaving Felicity to continue pacing until they had a visitor walk in.

Genesis.

Zaire sat in the large wooden chair, his hands, feet and neck shackled, making any attempted movements minimal. The room he was in was small and dingy. It smelt damp. The only thing he could see were Jaspar in deep conversation with the two Guardian's that brought him to the room. Within a few moments, Jaspar returned his attention to Zaire, with a grin that almost lit up the room. He was genuinely happy, he was going to cause him pain, and he was happy about it.

"Young Wentworth, thank you for cooperating with my men, it made this so much easier than I expected it to be." Jaspar complimented in a sing-song voice, rounding the chair and standing behind him.

Both Guardian's remained in the dim doorway, staring outward. One of them, Zaire recognised, was Tyson, a senior from Zaire's school. He knew that now he would be sixteen. Still a young age, just like himself.

Tyson occasionally looked over his shoulder at Zaire, he was unsteady when he had to bring Zaire to the room. He didn't want to be there; he didn't want to help Jaspar.

"What's with the restraints?" Zaire asked, tugged on the straps, "I willingly would have sat here."

"I don't doubt that," Jaspar replied bluntly, "But when the poison is injected, it may cause discomfort, I wouldn't want you to move too much."

Zaire swallowed his nerves, "Very well."

"We'll start with a small injection of less than a millilitre of poison, enough to extract some power, but not all, nor cause you any damage."

"Alright then." Zaire nodded, putting on a brave face. In his head, he kept telling himself it would be okay. The poison could kill him, but he was determined to survive. He would lose one of his abilities, but he would be okay.

Another Guardian appeared from the right, through a door Zaire had not previously noticed. In his hand, was a steel tray, syringes and needles laid across the metal surface.

"We will inject an antibiotic of sorts first, to lessen the inevitable pain, and make this a safer procedure." Jaspar explained as the medical Guardian began attaching a cannula into his arm. "Then we will up the amount of poison as of how you react."

Again, Zaire nodded.

Jaspar gave the medic the go ahead as the black liquid began pumping through the tubes and into Zaire's arm.

He muffled a scream as the poison began pulsing through his blood, making his veins feel like they were being cut open with a million white-hot scalpels. The pain was excruciating; unlike anything he had ever felt before. And it was in that moment, he knew he was going to die.

Nightfall.

The air had become cooler, less humid, and the town of Tampou had become inhabited by almost two hundred Elements.

Xavier stared out at the swarm of warriors, preparing themselves. He spotted his friends weaving in and out of the crowd, handing weapons to warriors who didn't have their own and explaining what was to happen over the next twelve hours.

Jax stood on the building opposite, his bicep-length dark brown hair fly behind him like a flag in the wind. He stared down at the Artillery, the same as Xavier. They were both on watch. There were enough Elements in the town centre at the present moment to make Jaspar aware of their plans. So many Elements, but not enough. Jaspar's army consisted of not short of a thousand soldiers. How many of them were actually against Jaspar and the Elders, they weren't sure, but it was still a huge risk. With their strongest warriors missing, they were all but facing peril. They just needed hope.

A whistle cut through the sounds of the crowds, catching Xavier's attention. It was Noah. Xavier was soon to begin descending the side of the building, jumping down the last few feet to reach the floor.

Before he could regain his posture, Noah was at his side, looking concerned. "We're out of weaponry."

"How many of us are without?"

Noah shook his head, "Too many. Over forty."

"Oh…" Xavier sighed, "Gather everyone according to their element. I need the Quadrupedia in one group, they're our strongest fighters, without weaponry, if there's enough; we will send them in empty handed."

Noah's eyes widened at his suggestion, "That's practically a death wish!"

"This whole thing is a death wish." Xavier huffed, "It's our only choice. We haven't got the time to find more weapons. There are none left back in Los Angeles either, so we can't send Tom back, this is the only answer."

"Theo and Genesis would know what to do, I can guarantee it." Noah admitted, "I wish they would come back."

Xavier's stomach churned, he was growing worried about them. Hoping Genesis had found Theo by now, that they were together and safe. "They'll return, Theo, Genesis and Amethyst. It'll be okay, they'll come back."

"Together?"

"I hope so."

"And what if Genesis hasn't found them yet?"

"We can just pray she has."

"Well," A voice interrupted their conversation, "she hasn't."

Xavier straightened up in panic, looking ahead of him.

"So," Said Theo, his tone bitter, "does anyone care to tell me where my wife is?"

Jax watched as Theo arrived, Amethyst walking strongly at his side. But no Genesis. He watched as a large crowd followed at the pair's heels, there were at least one hundred and fifty Elements, all walking proudly toward the army. It took a moment for him to work it out. Vampires and werewolves. The look of triumph on Amethyst's face told him that the mer-people were involved in some way too.

Theo's face contorted with rage as he approached Xavier and Noah, and within moments, he was shouting.

Jax didn't hesitate to jump down off the building's ledge, he wasn't high up– so the fall was short and the landing painless. He slipped through the crowds toward the commotion.

"You're supposed to be looking after her!" Theo screamed, Amethyst clawing at his upper arm and begging him to calm down. "She loves you, you are meant to protect her!"

Xavier's lip curled back in a snarl, "Excuse me? Coming from the doting husband who disappeared in the middle of the night with another girl and no answer to where he had gone?"

"Don't say it like I did something bad, Amethyst and I went to recruit some more Elements, the stronger kind. With people like you amongst us we're a sure fail!" Theo snapped.

"Theo, stop." Amethyst begged once more. She reached out for him but he pushed her away, stepping toward Xavier.

"You were meant to stop her doing anything stupid. That is your job, as her best friend!"

Xavier through his head back with laughter, "Is that my job now? Because if I did stop her every time she attempted something daft, she sure as *hell* wouldn't be married to you."

Jax wasn't quick enough, as Theo's fist collided with Xavier's jaw with an astounding thud.

Xavier smiled an unnerving smile, blood dripping from his mouth and nostrils, "Save your anger Theodore, save that for your father."

Another punch.

By this point, Xavier had passed caring, as he spat out insults and taunted Theo as much as he could, not caring about the consequences.

Theo stepped forward to swing at Xavier once more, this time, his fist colliding with Jax's hand. "That's enough." Jax growled.

Theo stepped back, glaring over the boys shoulder at a bloody faced Xavier. "He started it."

"Oh stop," Jax spat, "you sound like a four year old."

Theo shot him a look, before turning to walk away, soon stopped by Eliza. "Where are you going now?"

He shook his head, "I need to be alone, if you'll excuse me."

"No." She replied bluntly, "You will not be excused. What on Pandoverse, are you doing, Theo? Genesis went out to look for you and you're mad at Xavier for it? When have you been able to stop her from doing something she shouldn't? What makes you think he'd have the capability to stop her?"

Theo stayed quiet as Eliza continued to rant.

"She went after you because she loves you, be mad at her for loving too much. Be mad at yourself for given her a reason to run off like a lunatic. But don't be mad at one of your best friends for not stopping her when he didn't get a choice in the matter!"

"I have every right to be mad at him!" Theo snapped, brushing past the Waterment and stalking away.

"Why, what's he done?" Asked Eliza, growing impatient, "What's he done that's *so* bad?"

Theo stopped for a brief moment, looking over his shoulder, "I snuck onto the roof last night, I heard him. He was in love with my wife."

"The key word is *was*, Theo, why does it matter?"

"Because," He said, his voice etched with pain, "I heard it in her voice, and she was in love with him too." And with that, he wandered into the darkness, away from his friends, away from the Artillery, and away from all his troubles.

TWENTY EIGHT

MORNING CAME ALL TOO QUICKLY.

Zaire awoke in a small dark cell, his skin bloody and bruised. He panicked, clueless as to what had happened to him. His sculpes were fading, his chest hurt and he felt weak. His eyes scanned the room in a hurry, it was morning, therefore Felicity and her friends would soon be on their way to the execution. Theo and the Artillery still hadn't arrived, and he couldn't give his own army the go ahead on attacking Jaspar and his loyal minions. Everything that had been planned, was failing. He could almost taste the failure on his tongue, mixed with the metallic taste of blood: his lip was cut. Not just slightly, not just where you draw blood from chewing at the skin through nerves. It felt like his lip was hanging off, he touched a hand to check it was still intact. It was.

"You're still in one piece, don't worry." A familiar voice came from the shadows.

Tyson.

"What are you doing here?" Zaire stuttered, stepping back from the Guardian in fear.

"The same as you? Do you not remember?" Tyson replied, seemingly perplexed.

Zaire returned him the questioning look.

"After the procedure, you fought back, with all your strength. Jaspar ordered myself and the other Guardian to restrain you, but he asked the wrong people. We fought back too. Sadly, it didn't take long for a fresh batch of Guardian's to charge through the door and arrest us all. We're joining the others in the execution today."

"Who was the other guy? And where is he?"

Tyson shook his head wretchedly, "Jaspar killed him on the spot. He was the eldest, the, and I quote, 'most responsible, he should have known better'."

"Oh." Zaire squeaked, "We need to get to the others, they will help us."

"We're meant to be helping them, do you know how dangerous this all is? I doubt we'll make it out alive."

"What happened to me? With the Illecebra poison?"

"It worked, it removed your abilities."

Zaire shuddered, "Abilities?" He asked, emphasising the 's'.

Tyson nodded, "Zaire, I hate to break this to you, but you're mortal."

Theo had walked the perimeter of the Governing Parts, the smallest town in Pandoverse.

Pandoverse was mapped in an odd way. With the Governing parts in an almost perfect circle in the centre, and the other five towns around its perimeter. To walk around the outside of the Governing Parts took two hours exactly. Making the journey from town to town quick and relaxing. The deeper you travelled into the town, the further the journey to the next town across came, as the towns fanned out around the outside. He walked carelessly as he passed the entrance to Gi. In the next fifteen minutes he'd be back in Tampou, being bombarded with irrelevant questions and arguments. He couldn't deal with that. Genesis still hadn't returned, in the morning he had to kill his father– he wasn't ready.

He stared ahead in the darkness, shuffling his feet aimlessly across the pathway. He had a vision dome protecting him, making him invisible to all those around him. His second interaction with Genesis was when he first really began using vision domes. There were two types. One that protected you from everyone, and what that protected you simply of mortals. That was the type he had used that day, so only Genesis could see him. He never expected Margaret to be an Element, which through his plan entirely off track. Especially when it caused Genesis to run out on him.

Parked on the borders, the no-mans-land of Pandoverse, between Tampou and the Governing Parts, where the only cars in Pandoverse. They were Humvees. They had only a dozen, they stayed parked there most of the time, but each week, male final-year students at the school would be taught how to drive them. This was so they could drive on Earth.

Many Elements would be sent there during their lives, some to live permanently, as a job, some just for routine visits. Either way, it was an easier way of life, to drive on Earth. He made a quick mental note to suggest to Genesis that they allowed female Elements to learn also, when they won over the superiority of Pandoverse. Theo remembered when he learned to drive, it didn't take him long to pass his exams. He was a quick learner. It may be because he grew up in the Governing Parts, this gave him access to higher education, more intense physical training and many other perks.

The other thing this gave him, was the extra fun and games of having a murderous father. He thought about how much his life had changed in the past few years and laughed to himself. His chest stung at the thoughts of his mother and friends, but he found humour in how drastic everything had become. He was one of the most well-known Elements in all of Pandoverse. His father was head of the Governing table, he was strong, smart and the world was his oyster. Yet, here he was, walking discreetly through the towns, feeling sick at the thought of his wife's whereabouts and his friend's fates. And how did he go from being a local celebrity to one of the most wanted men on all of Pandoverse– most wanted, by his own *father*.

He gave a sigh as he reached Tampou, the new and improved Artillery were sat around small fires, all preparing for the following events. He removed the vision dome from around his body and proceeded to wade through the vast amount of Elements, Vampires and Werewolves, ignoring those who spoke his name or tapped his shoulder.

He didn't want to talk about what was to come. Nor did he want to engage in a conversation regarding his argument with Xavier just hours before. He wanted to sleep, then go out and find his wife before continuing to fight for the safety of Pandoverse. It seemed like something small, but somehow, it was a lot to ask.

Jaspar strode into the cell, facing Zaire and Tyson with an all too familiar look. "How are you both this morning?" He asked, strangely politely.

Zaire glared at him, "Mortal. But thanks for asking."

"I must apologise that it didn't go to plan, but at least you're not dead." He paused, looking at his watch for a moment, "Well, at least you're not dead for another two hours and forty-seven minutes, that is."

Tyson snarled, "Why are we in here?"

"Why do you think?" Jaspar gave a sarcastic chuckle, "You both, are traitors, I have no interested in keeping you at my side. You play with fire, you get burned."

"Damn straight." Zaire mumbled, a comment missed by Jaspar. "Will we be killed alongside the others?"

A gleam shimmered in Jaspar's eyes, "You want to die alongside that Felicity girl, do you?"

Zaire tensed, if Jaspar knew about Felicity, and the Artillery, their plans would be hindered. "I just want to know what is going to happen to us."

"Well that's the thing," Jaspar said with an unenthusiastic sigh, "I have different plans for you, Wentworth."

Both Tyson and Zaire looked up at the Elder in fear and curiosity.

"It's against the law to harm a mortal, not that it's ever stopped me, but still– I have decided to spare you."

A rush of relief washed over Zaire as he sagged his shoulders, releasing unabated tension.

"You won't be killed today Zaire Ra Wentworth," Jaspar continued, stepping aside to allow two Guardian's into the cell to collect the young boy. "You will instead be banished to Earth."

Claudia and Sophia sat in the dining room in silence. Today was the day the Artillery went to war. The day the children could be killed, or saved. The day that decided the future of Pandoverse. It was still early, there was still an entire day ahead of them, yet they already had begun to wait. For a contact, a sign, a flicker of hope. They prayed silently without making conversation. Claudia looked out of the window ahead of them.

It was winter, yet the air was humid and the sky was blue. Just like Pandoverse, Earth's weather worked in mysterious ways. Where the other side of the United States had blizzards across the city, California struggled daily through drought, the sun sucking up the life of everyone and everything in it. Aeras, was the town to get the bad weather. Despite neighbouring Fotia, the temperatures dropped below freezing throughout the winter months, whilst Fotia and Nero stayed sunny and warm all year round. The Governing Parts were slightly different, one day it would be sunny, the next– raining.

Gi, too, rained frequently, which was difficult for its citizens when most of their homes were built solely from nature, with mud and plants. Tampou didn't get much sun, rain nor snow. It was a very dry place to be. The skies would often be grey, yet the air warm, and the clouds so low that the fog enveloped the pathways. Pandoverse was different from Earth in many ways, mostly, it was home.

Claudia's thoughts were silenced when a sound attracted her attention. She and Sophia jumped up, running to the doorway, grabbing their weaponry off of the table as they passed. They prepared to assess where the sound had come from, and if necessary–fight.

They reached the back door, leading to the gardens and stared out. Hunched over one of the fallen's gravestones, was a young boy. A Guardian. He appeared to be sobbing, his shoulders moving rhythmically as he choked.

"Show yourself." Sophia ordered, holding a binarii over her shoulder, ready to pounce.

The boy turned to face them, and Claudia had to stifle a scream as she saw the figure stooped over the grave.

"*Anthony?*"

Theo watched with an ounce of excitement as Jax ordered the Artillery into lines: Airments, Earthments, Firements, Waterments, Demi-Quadrupedia, Fere-Quadrupedia and Pure-Quadrupedia. The latter consisted of only eleven Elements, unlike the rest of the groups which crowded through Tampou.

Theo didn't even realise that there were even Pure's left in Pandoverse. He had made the assumption his father killed almost all of them off. After the attack on Tampou and the constant urges to kill Genesis, it would only make sense if that was the reality. His stomach turned at the thought of Genesis being killed, it was his biggest fear, and with little knowledge of her whereabouts, his fear had escalated. His thoughts were soon abolished as Jax called for silence.

All the Artillery stood to attention, and Theo knew this was his cue to speak. He wandered forward, standing on the small box that Jax was once stood upon. He stepped up, his eyes scanning the tops of the heads in the crowd. He'd never seen so many Elements in one place.

It made him uneasy to know that his father had an army twice the size. He hoped that the vast majority of the Guardian's actually weren't on his side. That would make this war a lot easier than any of them had set out for it to be.

"Artillery." He said loudly, addressing the anticipating crowd, "I stand before you, as Genesis is not here. She would know what to say, what to do, and what to think, in a time like this. I do not, but I do know what to expect. We are going to go into a battlefield, but there are many things we should be ready for. We must save the children, we must protect them too." He paused, to assess those who stood before him.

"When we first reach the Governing Parts, it's down to the Outsiders to go in first." He nodded toward at the line of Vampires and Werewolves, they all looked excited, smug, even. "Once we reach the Hall, Earthments, you can go in first. You will try to corral them, so then when the Waterments come in second, they can help you in the first round of the attacks. Bearing in mind, this will be on Guardian's only, the Elders will stay away until they see fit. In their eyes, fighting last makes them stronger and us vulnerable. By this point, I hope to see at least one half of their Army down, so we can advance further into the Governing Parts and continue the battle. This is when the Firements come in. Again, another round of attacks. By the time that the Elders come out to fight, the Quadrupedia will come in. Round four of the attacks. Finally, with Genesis back at my side, the Airments will come in, then it will be down to the Quadrupedia to kill the Elders, after all, we're their biggest fear."

"Why are we going in last?" A voice came from the crowd, "We're the weakest Element."

Theo smiled at the Airment, "Trust me, you're all a lot stronger than you think."

Jaspar paced the length of the hall. Cliffio stood along one wall, waiting patiently for the Guardian's to return with the prisoners.

"We will win this." Jaspar said aloud, mostly to himself. "I won't allow my son and that girl of his to defeat us."

Cliffio stepped forward, "They have come further than any other chosen in history. I do believe we have a big fight on our hands."

"One which we will win." Jaspar countered, "I won't allow us to lose."

"Hades will go crazy if we lose."

"If we lose, we'll be dead, that will not matter, Cliffio."

Cliffio lowered his head, he felt guilty. He didn't want this war. He was in the same position as Jaspar. His Quadrupedia daughter was killed, and he wanted to avenge his death by settling the blame on every Quadrupedia's shoulders. He wanted revenge. But now, he was second guessing. He was putting himself in the same Army as those who killed his daughter. He was as bad as them. He thought he was doing the right thing, but as Jaspar ordered children to be sent to their executions, he realised, he was not.

He had to get out.

He was fortunate enough to be alive, after Gregor, Aeolos and Aegeus were killed before. He and Jaspar had a lucky escape. Next time, he worried, he would not be so lucky.

Cliffio stared up at the head Elder, his eyes pleading him to stop, but it was no use.

In the next few hours– they were going to die.

Theo stood at the borders of no-mans-land. The small piece of land between Tampou and the Governing Parts. Somewhere in the distant town was his father, and quite possible, his wife. He imagined the bridge into the Governing Parts that covered the lake, would be armed with Guardians. That would be their first obstacle. He set the plan out in steps in his mind.

Step one: *Werewolves*.

He turned to face the approaching Army, his chest puffed out and his head held high. "Artillery." He called, addressing the excited crowd, "Are you ready?"

They cheered in response.

"Today is the day, we fight and we avenge all those we have lost in the hands of these men." He growled, his chest aching at the thought of his mother. "We will fight for them, we will win for them."

Again, they cheered.

"Werewolves, get on the front line. Be ready."

A large group of Elements ran forward, shifting into large canines as they leapt ahead, lining up and facing the Governing Parts.

"Vampires, you will follow."

Another group, Calispar in the lead, wandered to stand behind the werewolves. Calispar grinned, his pearly white fangs glistening in the sunshine.

Theo wandered for a moment what made them stay so white, was it the blood? He shuddered, brushing the thought aside and turning back to the remaining Elements in their groups.

"Earthments next please."

Like the others, the group of Earthments filled the space behind. Theo didn't need to instruct any further as the others followed. Waterments, Firements, Quadrupedia and Airments. Theo stood at the front of the group once more, staring at them with a fire in his eyes. "Do not let the Illecebra fool you. Do not let the Elders manipulate you. Do not let the Guardian's make you feel guilty.

We are the champions. We are the Artillery, and *we are the future of Pandoverse."* He paused, as the army let out a chorus of whoops and cheers. "Artillery," He said one final time, turning to face the Governing Parts with his heart threatening to punch through his chest.

He gathered one final breath before shouting at the top of his lungs. "ATTACK!"

And with that, the Artillery charged through the grounds of no-mans-land and toward the bridge into the Governing Parts.

Zaire shivered as he limped through unfamiliar streets. Nothing was conversant. He was on Earth, that much he knew, but he had no idea where. Felicity had mentioned she stayed in California when she was on Earth, she said it was practically always sunny and warm. Wherever he was, it was freezing. He felt humiliated, walking the streets in his Guardian gear– which had now been ripped and shredded: people were staring.

He pulled himself into a nearby alley and tried to wave a vision dome over him, making him invisible to mortals. He understood Earth had a fair amount of Elements roaming it, but hopefully they would look at him with a less judgemental stare than the mortals did.

It didn't work, of course, he was mortal now. Zaire bit back tears and wandered back out onto the streets. He was scared. He was just a child, banished to another world and he was petrified.

As he walked some more, he noticed some strange landmarks. A tall clock, a large wheel, a river and more. He glanced at his surroundings, he recognised some of the buildings from pictures. In school, all Elements were taught about capital cities on Earth. Places they'd be likely to visit. He remembered many of them, Washington, Amsterdam, Bangkok, Canberra, Paris, Budapest, Beijing, Lisbon, Buenos Aires, Barcelona, Venice, Berlin, Washington D.C…

"London." He said aloud, realising suddenly where he was.

"That's right." A voice came from behind him.

He turned, facing a middle-aged man. He had blonde hair, with tints of grey and stubble. He was quite lean and tall, his eyes a fierce shade of Hazel.

"A foreigner, huh?" The man added, smirking.

"I– uh–"

"It's okay." He replied, pulling up his left sleeve, "I am too."

Zaire trailed his eyes to the man's forearm. Neatly marked on his skin was the sculpe for Fire. He looked back at the man, his face growing similar, "Why are you on Earth?"

"The same reason over half of the Earth's population are Elements, whether they know it or not." The man replied, tugging back down his sleeve. He paused for a moment, shrugging off his jacket and handing it to the young boy, "You need this more than me– I'm practically immune to London's weather."

Zaire looked at the sky. He couldn't locate the sun, perhaps London didn't really have one.

"I'm being sarcastic, kid. It's always bloody freezing, but I've gotten over it." He shrugged, "Anyhow, wanna tell me why you're here? And perhaps why you're a *kid* and a Guardian?"

Zaire reluctantly took his coat, pacing it over his shoulders. It was far too big for him, but the warmth was comforting. "I was banished."

"Oh, really?" The man asked, his lips quirked up at the sides, "What did you do wrong?"

"I fought back too soon."

The man's smile faded into a scowl, "Care to elaborate? I left Pandoverse because of that Government, for my niece's safety actually."

Zaire nodded, "I was taken from school to be a Guardian. Elder Jaspar said he would use the Illecebra treatment on me to rid me of my Quadrupedia. It didn't work, it rid me of my abilities completely. I am now mortal again. I had the plan to fight back, to protect my friends, but he banished me here instead." He noticed the man's face grimace at the mention of Jaspar's name. "You don't like Elder Jaspar?"

The man shook his head. "I know him all too well. He was a good friend, once. Now he is a monster, ever since his youngest son died. His eldest son, Theo, he hasn't sided with his father, has he?"

"His father is going to kill his wife's sister in the next few hours, and then go after his wife. I hardly doubt Theo would even consider it."

This time, the pain on the man's face was evident, "What about the sister?"

"Felicity Valencia." Said Zaire, he felt a twitch of pain at the mention of her name, she was due to be killed soon, and he couldn't protect her.

"When is her execution?"

"Noon, Pandoversian time."

"That's the same as GMT."

Zaire nodded. He didn't know if that was correct, but he presumed the man knew what he was talking about.

"In two and a half hours." He said, checking his watch.

Zaire nodded again.

"Alright, come back to mine with me, my wife and I will get you some nicer clothes."

The man was tense now, Zaire noticed, but he gave him a half smile and followed him anyway.

"What's your name by the way, kid?"

Zaire looked up at him with a raised eyebrow, "Zaire Ra Wentworth."

The man smiled, "Alright Zaire, we're going to get back to Pandoverse and help this war."

Zaire was shocked, but agreed nevertheless. "What is your name?"

This time, the man stopped walking to face him, a gleam in his eye. "My name, kid, is Richard Valencia, and I have to go save my nieces."

TWENTY NINE

A WOMAN WAS AT THE BRIDGE ENTRANCE.

She wore the Elder capes. Theo wasn't prepared for that. A female Elder, the first in Pandoversian history. He wasn't prepared to enter the Governing Parts easily, but neither was he prepared to deal with an Elder at the very first hurdle.

"Theodore Benedict." She smirked, "What a pleasant surprise."

He shook his head, "Who are you?"

"My name is Su, I am Elder Aegeus' replacement."

"You're a doorman?"

"Doorwoman. Although, I prefer the term *protector*."

"Right."

Su grinned, "I see you have brought your little army, how sweet. I can let you through, by the way. The trial starts in five minutes, I can guarantee you'd like to watch."

"We can get in whether you allow us to or not." Theo huffed, "You're vastly outnumbered."

Su sighed, "But, Theodore, you wouldn't hurt a woman, would you?"

Before Theo could respond, an arrow whizzed past his ear and embedded into Su's chest. The Elder slumped onto the floor, the life leaving her eyes instantly.

Theo turned to the Artillery, he noticed Eliza, perched on her brother's shoulders and holding an Arcus. She shrugged, "She was talking too much. I grew impatient."

Holding onto her calves, was Elijah, grinning at his twin behaviour and releasing her leg to reach up and give her a brief high-five.

Theo said nothing, he just smiled and turned back to the bridge. It was unnervingly empty, and he knew why. The trial was about to start.

The children were about to be murdered.

Jaspar stood outside the cell door, his prisoners inside, waiting to be executed. Beside him, stood Cliffio and the two new replacements, Adam and Caelestis. "Are you ready?"

The Elders nodded, even Cliffio, who had appeared distant for a while now. Jaspar grinned, reaching round to unlock the door when a Guardian rushed down the hall.

"Elder Jaspar!"

Jaspar snarled, "What is it, Irvin?"

"Elder Su is dead."

Jaspar stiffened, "How so?"

"Theo is in the Pandoverse, in the Governing Parts. And he's brought an army."

Jaspar roared, making the Guardian shrink back in fear. "Make him join me, or he'll die." He pulled open the cell door, revealing a small bloody and bruised figure in the corner of the room. Genesis. She squirmed in the chains and whined under the cloth that bound her mouth shut. "After he watches me torture the life out of his lovely wife."

Theo stopped as they reached the end of the bridge, turning to Jax. "I need to go alone."

Jax's eyes widened, "No chance. I won't allow it."

"If I go in alone, I can get to my father."

"Theo–"

"*Trust me.* Wait for fifteen minutes, then begin the attack. Send the OA undercover to the trial, they can stop it, I know they can." He replied, using Felicity's nickname for the *Original Artillery*.

Jax frowned, "I'm not sure this is a good idea."

Theo stared at him.

"But you're going to do it anyway, aren't you?"

Theo nodded. "I'll be back, be careful."

Jax patted the young boys shoulder, "And you my friend, see you on the other side."

Theo didn't respond, he flicked his eyes back to the Artillery before running off to find his father. He wanted to speak with him, he wanted to reason with him.

He didn't want him to die.

Adrianna looked around at the swarm of Elements crowded in the town square for the trial. She was tied to a post, beside her two boys. *They were just babies*, she thought, a lump rising in her throat. She could only pray someone would rescue them. She knew Theo, he would help them, surely? Beside the boys was Felicity, then Maggie, then Milo. Ahead of all six of them, was a lone post, ready for Genesis.

She felt the warm tears trickle down her cheeks as the twins screamed and cried. She failed as a mother. It was her fault they were here, and now they were going to die. She was going to die. They were all going to die.

The crowd began to cheer as Genesis arrived, being dragged by Guardian's. She was weak, Adrianna noticed, her skin was noticeably grey, her hair knotted, her clothes torn. Her skin was black and blue, stained with dry blood – and fresh blood too.

Adrianna watched as the young girl was hoisted up, and tied to the front post. Her hands above her head, as it rolled forward lifelessly. Her heart contracted vigorously at the sight of the poor, helpless girl. Genesis was a warrior, a hunter, a fighter, a survivor and a defender. She had to survive this. She was an oenomel. Something strong yet sweet. The epitome of power. But in that moment, she needed to be saved.

Come on Theo.

Jaspar appeared next, looking smug, as usual. The other Elders following behind. Adrianna noticed Cliffio looking solemn, he didn't agree to this, she thought, he didn't want this, he wanted out.

She watched him tentatively, as he approached her and stood to her left, between her and her sons. She stared at him still, watching his movements and body language. His eyes flickered at each prisoner, then back to the crowd. It was like they were small involuntary movements. His job was to look forward, but he seemed to look everywhere but. His jaw was tense, his lips pursed and his eyebrows somewhat furrowed. His fingers wiggled at his sides, shaking slightly as he danced lightly from foot to foot, his movements so miniscule, you could hardly notice them. But Adrianna noticed them. She knew what they meant too.

Cliffio was going to betray Jaspar.

Genesis forced herself to scan the crowd for familiar faces. Every time her eyes moved direction, a pain embedded itself into her skull, throbbing rhythmically with her unsteady heartbeat.

Her blonde hair appeared matted, falling at the sides of her face with streaks of dry blood. She could taste the metallic liquid on her lip, and feel the stiffness of her skin, from the wounds, beneath her clothing. She imagined herself. Her petite yet muscular frame, grazed and battle-worn. Would Theo love her now?

Her thoughts became averted when she spotted an acquainted face in the audience. Rushing through the back of the crowds, headed toward Jaspar.

Theo.

She wanted to scream for him. She tried. Her throat was too dry to conjure up any sounds or words, and she couldn't even find the strength to move her lips to form them.

She followed the dark haired boy as he waded through the crowed, strangely unnoticed. His eyes locked with hers for a moment, and she felt a twinge of hope, before he glared, and looked away. All the pain in her body faded and appeared in her chest all at once. Like a blow to the heart, a newly healed wound, ripped open at the stitches. He looked at her like he hated her. Did he? Was it because of how bad she looked? Because she ran away to look for him? Because she wanted to kill his father? There were endlessly possibilities. But as he approached Jaspar with a smile, she knew there was just one answer.

Theo was on his side.

Jax watched from the side-lines as the werewolves began their ascent into the Governing Parts. He prayed silently that they'd make it in time.

As he stood, staring, his long dark hair billowing in the wind, he realised it was now or never. If the wolves didn't reach the square in time, Adrianna, the children, they'd all be dead. He trembled at the thought. His sons. His wife. He had to help them.

He peered over his shoulder at the remaining Artillery, they all stood anxiously, staring at him, waiting for the go ahead. They wanted in. They wanted to attack. But Theo had a plan, and it didn't involve sending the entire army into the deep end straight away. However, as Jax stared at their anticipation, and listened to his conscience as it spoke in his mind, he knew he had to do something.

He turned to the Artillery with a smirk, "Artillery," he said softly, before preparing to shout. "Attack!"

Adrianna watched in horror at the scene ahead of her. Theo approaching Jaspar. Jaspar embracing Theo in a hug. Cliffio stepping forward to untie Genesis from the post. Genesis gathering all the strength she could muster. Genesis running at Theo. Genesis' fist colliding with Theo's jaw. Adam wrapping vines around her body as she thrashed and fell to the floor. Jaspar pulling a gladio from its scabbard. Jaspar killing Cliffio.

She screamed as Genesis fell to the floor. The twins were sobbing, Felicity was shouting. Even young Maggie was yelling minor profanities at the Elders. Genesis head bounced as it hit the concrete, knocking the very last, yet small amount of consciousness from her body.

Adrianna stared at Theo, half expecting him to rush to his wife's aid. Yet he didn't. He stood beside Jaspar, his expression blank as he stared at the young girl writhing on the floor.

Adrianna felt a low growl leave her throat as she bellowed. "You bastard! That is your wife!"

Theo glanced her way without showing any remorse.

Adrianna felt outraged. Theo was her cousin, she loved him with all her heart. But in that moment, she wanted him just as dead as she planned to have his father.

"Theodore, assist Caelestis and Adam as they tie up Genesis once again, won't you?" Jaspar asked in a sweet, sickening tone. "Shame our dear Cliffio had to betray us like that. What a waste."

Theo nodded and abided, following the Elder's as they carried Genesis' almost lifeless body to the post, tying her up once more as Theo held her up.

It was in that moment that Adrianna felt hope, the flicker of affection mixed with pain, that passed Theo's eyes as he held onto his wife's torso. The moment soon passed, as his expression returned to that of his fathers. Evil, twisted and somewhat unprepared.

Trevor led the pack of wolves as the vampires caught up.

Calispar arrived swiftly at the front of the two clans, his footwork identical to Trevor's as they marched forward.

"Are you prepared, wolf boy?" Calispar grinned.

Trevor shot him a look. The vampires and werewolves had never quite seen eye to eye. They weren't like the stories, rivals, nemesis', enemies. They just weren't quite best friends. They could live amongst one another but they wouldn't socialise if it could be helped. "The question is, are you ready?" Trevor snickered. He wanted to respond with more wit, or sarcasm. Perhaps with an amusing nick name for the vampire clan. But his mind was solely focused on the battle ahead, not on pet names and humorous come-backs.

"When this is over, and we've won, I hope that Genesis and Theo will allow me back into the main towns of Pandoverse. Living amongst caves and psychotic born-vampires is quite exhausting."

Trevor laughed at this, his chuckles creating a low howl. "I'm sure if we win, you'll have earned the right to ask. Your little posse, however, I'm not sure it's safe for them to be here."

Calispar stared at the group of born vampires. They were different from the others. More dead, less lively. Paler skin, darker hair. Their eyes, unlike turned-vampires, were more of a dull, mustard yellow. They were the half of the clan that weren't enclosed in an air dome, keep them protected from the Pandoversian sun. Born-vampires could survive in the natural sunlight. It was the turned-vampires that could not.

Aeris arrived at Calispar's side in a haste, his canary-yellow eyes gleaming with sheer panic. "Can you hear it?"

Calispar stared at the vampire in confusion, "Hear what?"

He turned to Trevor, who had stopped in his tracks, his head held high and alert. Whatever Aeris heard, he heard too.

"What is it?" Calispar asked, trying hard to listen. It took a moment but he soon heard the commotion in the town square.

He spun to look back at the Elements following the clan, all prepped and readied with their weapons. Ready to fight.

He looked back at Aeris, "Genesis is in danger."

Aeris nodded, "And I think Theo put her there."

Genesis regained consciousness quickly. Looking over her shoulder at her sister as they exchanged comforting nods. It didn't take long for Jaspar to realise she had awoken, and he was by her side with the same twisted smile he wore always.

"Miss Valencia, how kind of you to join us once again." He grinned, "Bit of a mess before, don't you agree? Now is much better. No more traitorous Elders to help you against me, huh?"

Genesis went to correct him. She was a Benedict now, just like he was. But as she stared over at his son, his *ally*– she chose against it. "What do you want, Jaspar? You have me, don't you? Isn't that what you've wanted all this time? Me? Well here I am. Let the children go."

Jaspar stared at her with a bemused expression, "Very well." He said, all too quickly. "I will spare the children's lives." He waved a hand and two Guardian's appeared in an instant. "Move the children to the cells again, and bring young Adrianna up front, beside Genesis.

If we're going to make a spectacle of this, at least allow them to both share the centre stage."

The Guardian's nodded, scurrying off to abide by his rules.

Felicity screamed as the Guardian grabbed her, kicking her legs out and twisting her body in almost impossible ways, in attempts to get free.

"Felicity, trust me." Genesis cried, as her younger sister began to be dragged away, "It'll be okay, I promise."

Her cheeks were now hot with tears. The pain growing unbearable. All the open wounds, fractures and bruises, felt like nothing compared to the emotional pain she felt in her heart. Theo had betrayed her, and now he had come to watch her die.

"Is there anything you'd like to do or say, in your final moment, Miss Valencia?"

Genesis shot a sideways glance to Theo, before nodding. "I want to speak with my husband: privately."

Jaspar's face contorted with displeasure, before he gritted his teeth and gave a nod. "I guess it would only be fair, if that is your final wish."

"It is."

"Alright then." He responded, turning to his son. "Theodore, come."

Theo took long strides onto the execution area, arriving at his father's side.

"Genesis' final wish is to exchange private words with you. You have three minutes."

Theo nodded as his father stepped down and away, leaving them alone.

Before he could say anything, Genesis spat at him. "Gen–"

"What on Pandoverse is wrong with you?" She said through gritted teeth. All the pain replaced with fury. "You betrayed me. You betrayed *us*. For *him*?!"

"He is my father, Genesis."

"And I am your *wife*." She replied, the words tasting bitter on her tongue, "And he is going to kill me in cold blood."

"I'm sorry it has to be this way."

Genesis shook her head in disbelief. She thought he would hold her in this moment. Tell her it was all an act. He wasn't on his father's side, he was on her side. Instead, he stared emotionlessly into her colourful eyes, his expression unreadable. "In two minutes, my final wish will be over and I will be dead. Is there anything you need to say to me?"

Theo pulled his hand out of his pocket, revealing a long pointed pink stone. Which she had made into a pendant. *Athena's stone*. Genesis didn't recall losing it, but she didn't remember much anyhow. She looked down at his palm in confusion. Was this how he said goodbye? Returning her own necklace, her wedding gift. Her family heirloom?

She half-anticipated him to place the shard pendant around her neck, allowing her to feel the coolness of the rock as it fell down upon her breast. She waited to feel his hands touch her skin one final time as he closed the clasp of the pendant and let it hang. She stared, wordlessly, as he held the stone in front of her eyes, the point, glistening in the sunlight.

And then she felt the pain as he thrust the sharp end into her chest, as he whispered the words, '*I'm sorry*', and the world went dark.

Felicity heard the screams. Adrianna's screams. She knew, instantly, it was Genesis. She pulled back, the Guardian's holding her in place.

"Let me go, something has happened to my sister!"

The Guardian on her left glanced at her, then back at his acquaintance, before tugging her arm toward him and away from the elder man. "Run." He said quickly, pushing her away and preparing to fight to loyal Guardian.

Felicity stared for a moment in shock, trying to process what to do. She could go after the other children, or Genesis. She knew, being in the cells, the children would be safer. She had to get onto the battlefield. She stifled a scream as the Guardian that helped her get away fell to the floor, a lamina protruding from his chest.

Now she had no choice but to run, before the other Guardian killed her too. Without thinking, she pivoted, sprinting down the hall, the Firement at her heels. The hall was open planned. One side was a wall, the other, concrete columns. She could run through the gaps and out into the courtyard, but she had a goal. Ahead of her, in the arch way, hung a labrys. She flicked her sight sideways, catching a glance of the gaining Guardian. The archway was twenty metres away.

Her chest began to burn as her legs insisted they continued to sprint. Her heart was beating faster than she thought possible, seemingly threatening to push through her ribcage.

Fifteen metres.

The Guardian was closer now than ever. She could almost feel his breath on her neck. If she faltered in the slightest, he would have her. If he stopped, he could use his abilities against her. But he was too hot on her tail, too indulged in the chase.

Five metres.

It was almost accessible. She had just one issue. The archway stood at twelve feet tall. Felicity was just short of five foot four. Even if she jumped, she would only reach ten foot with her arms extended. She had to think, and fast.

One metre.

Felicity side stepped toward the column, kicking up her legs and running almost vertically along the concrete. With a quick mid-air twist, she grabbed the labrys and swung around at the Guardian, beheading him before she even hit the floor.

She landed at a crouch, holding the labrys in one hand, using the other to steady herself. Ahead of her approached three more Guardian's. They soon stopped as they acknowledged the dead Elder at the young girl's feet.

"Take one more step, and you're next." Felicity growled, sending a glare their way. The trio scurried away, and she made a silent prayer that the children were safe. Zaire created an army inside the Governing Parts, she could only hope some of the soldiers were going to keep the kids safe.

Without hesitation, she ran out onto the courtyard and began to climb the trellis to gain roof access. It was the safest way to cross into the town square unnoticed. And the only way she was going to have even a slither of chance at saving Pandoverse.

THIRTY

BLOOD. LOTS AND LOTS OF BLOOD.

That's all Adrianna could see. The Artillery entered as Genesis fell to the floor. Jaspar dragged Theo away by the wrist as the war unfolded. Sapiens began pecking at the rope around Adrianna's wrist. She didn't know where the owl came from, with Genesis unconscious on the floor, she couldn't have sent for her. Within moments, she was free. It took her all of ten seconds to register where the Artillery were, before she ran to Genesis side, feeling her neck for a pulse.

She was alive.

Adrianna conjured up all her strength and lifted Genesis so she sat upright against the wooden post. She couldn't lift her out of the square. It would be too obvious, too dangerous. Although it didn't seem as though anywhere was safe. She scanned the crowd for Alexandrus, before giving him a thumbs up, allowing him to know his daughter was safe.

She began to panic now, with no weapon other than her abilities, she was bare. She skimmed the battle, looking for any fallen weapons. Her choice weapon was always a Hastam, but she would use whatever she could find. The thought of leaving Genesis, vulnerable, alone, petrified her. But she had no choice. If she wanted to fight people off with more than just the power of the Earth, she would need a weapon.

She watched as an Artillery member killed a Guardian, his weapon clattering onto the pavement and glistening in the light. An Acutam. The worst of the weapons. It's short, sickle blade meant that to kill a man with it, would mean to be so close to him that he could easily kill you first.

She stepped up to run for the weapon. She had a plan. Dart through the crowd carefully, retrieve the weapon, return to Genesis' side and guard her all whilst keeping her alive. It sounded a lot simpler than it actually was. But there was no plan B. It was all or nothing. She brushed loose hair from Genesis face, she was entirely unconscious, but she was alive. "I'll be right back and I'll keep you safe. I'm sorry my cousin did this to you." She whispered, before turning and sprinting into the battlefield.

Jaspar watched as two Guardian's stood against the doorway. Besides them, just he and Theo were in the room.

"Father, why are we hiding out here? Shouldn't we go and fight?" Asked Theo, pacing to cancel his anxiety.

"Theodore. Sit down for Hade's sake. Let them battle it out, eliminate that little army you brought in."

"I had to make them think I was on their side, don't you understand?"

Jaspar smirked, "You did well, my son. I'm sorry you had to harm Genesis, I prayed I would have to do that, and not you."

Theo glanced over at him, "You would have tortured her first, I wanted to make her death sweet."

"I always knew you'd choose me over her."

"How so?"

"She was new to this world, a weakness. A flaw. You're a strong boy. You have goals and aspirations.

You didn't arrive in Pandoverse and set out to destroy authority. You were born and raised here, you were going to grow up and work for the Government, in the army. She would have taken that dream from you. Despite your infatuation with the girl, it's clear, ridding Pandoverse of her is the best thing you could have done. I'm proud of you, son."

Theo's heart swelled for a moment. For years he had prayed to hear his father say he was proud of him. When he excelled in school, he fished for compliments. When he killed his first Illecebra, he waited for a 'well done', but it never came. "Thank you, Dad."

"Now, when we get the go ahead about the battle beginning to settle, we will go out there and finish it off. Our biggest threat was eliminated, thanks to you. Therefore it should be pretty simple."

Theo nodded. "Let's wait it out."

Jax grabbed Adrianna's wrist and hoisted her up from the floor where she crouched. "Ade."

She looked up, her eyes staring into his. Her throat burned at the sight of him. The man she loved, the man she married, the man who fathered her children, the man she betrayed, the man who probably hated her more than anything on Pandoverse.

They stared, wordlessly, for a moment. Before he pulled her close and pressed his lips to hers.

For a moment, just a moment, everything around them had faded. The battle, the dead bodies, the cries and screams. All faded. The only thing noticeable was the sparks that flew and the desire that melted them into one another.

Jax withdrew, breathing hard. "I still love you."

Adrianna allowed a small smile to play onto her lips as he spoke, "I'm sorry. You know, I always knew you were Quadrupedia."

"You didn't hate me?"

"I couldn't hate you. The Quadrupedia are the future of Pandoverse."

Jax gave a low chuckle, "What changed your mind?"

"When I realised, all along, I was the weak one in our family."

"You're much stronger than you think."

"Strong enough to protect Genesis?" She glanced at the still unconscious girl, "She's still alive."

"Theo stabbed her." Jax mumbled, his tone indicating his shock.

"She's okay, she'll be okay."

"In the heart."

"We can't let her die."

Jax planted a chaste kiss on Adrianna's forehead, "We won't."

Before she could respond, he disappeared into the battle to fight. Adrianna stared for a moment, before turning on her heels and wading through the fighting Elements and toward Genesis. Slashing the Acutam at whoever stood in her way.

She would not let her die.

Athena rounded the corner in her battle gear. He arms swinging with every beat of her marching feet. Behind her, Hecate, Ares, Poseidon, Peitho, Eros, Dionysus, Asclepius, Apollo, Artemis, Eirene, Hermes, Hephaestus, Persephone and Aphrodite.

"Brother, fetch Theodore and his father, bring them out. Cowards." She snapped, sending Ares on his way.

"Are you going to start bossing us around like usual?" Said Hecate, rolling her eyes.

"Dad left me in charge, so yes, yes I will."

Hecate sighed, very well, what can I do?"

"Currently, just wait. Apollo, find Felicity. Hephaestus, Persephone and Aphrodite, find the rest of the children, keep them safe."

The Gods abided, scurrying away to follow out their instruction.

"Hecate, we need to find Genesis."

"You saw Theo stab her, right? What if she's dead?" The Goddess of Witchcraft replied, her tone laced with worry.

"She's not dead." Athena replied simply, as she marched ahead, the other Gods at her heels.

"How can you be so sure? She might be okay now, but–"

"Hecate." Athena said sharply, stopping to face her friend, "Genesis isn't dead, *yet*. But she's going to be okay, I know."

"That makes literally no sense!" Hecate cried as they resumed their march toward the town square.

Athena didn't reply, she just pulled down the front of her armoury, to mask her face, and headed into battle.

After ten minutes of emotional reunions. Zaire and Anthony were ready to fight. Richard Valencia, Jemima Valencia, Claudia Benedict and Sophia Pelagius all stood at the edge of the Governing Parts.

They came through the Atrium at the same time. All for the same purpose.

To save Pandoverse.

Richard led the group to the town square. He hadn't been in Pandoverse since before his niece was born. Not a lot had changed over the past two decades, but he noticed the little differences.

"How are you alive?" Zaire asked his cousin as they walked, "Felicity said you were dead."

"Seth Valencia." Anthony replied, raising his eyebrows at the young boy, "Hades punished him, I'm sure. But he sent me back to rescue his sister."

"After she killed him?"

"After she killed him." Anthony repeated.

"Is that allowed?" Zaire asked, seemingly perplexed.

"No, it's not." Anthony explained, "But Seth sent Charon for me, he used his loyalty to Hades to do that. Charon brought me back to Earth, then I found my way to the farmhouse to find Claudia and Sophia, we came here and that's when I found you."

Zaire stared for a moment, bewildered. "You were reincarnated?"

"Basically."

"It doesn't matter right now," Richard replied, holding a hand out to stop the group in their tracks. "Genesis is on the floor."

Jemima let out a strangled cry, "Is she…?"

"I'm not sure." Richard replied, his tone harsh but the pain evident in his eyes. "Are you all ready?"

They nodded.

"Let's fight."

Katherine stood there, beside Seth. Beside Margaret, Sally, Sabrina, Harry, Konner, Jessabelle, Crystal, Yale, Paignton, Fabia, Lael and May.

Genesis shook her head. Seth looked different from what she remembered, he looked kinder. His expression was soft, he was beside their mother. He was smiling. "What's going on?" She asked, stepping toward the group.

"Genesis," Katherine came forward, taking her daughter's hand, "You're not going to die, you must know that."

Genesis' eyes scanned the line of Elements, all dead, because of her. "Theo betrayed me. He stabbed me, he wanted to kill me."

"He stabbed you with Athena's stone." Seth explained.

Genesis glared at him,

"Gen, you can trust him. He's just like us." Margaret added.

"Marge." Genny sniffled, wrapping her arms around her old friend. It had been so long, she had forgotten how it felt to hear her voice.

"Genesis, please listen to your brother." Katherine demanded.

She pulled back from the elder woman and turned to Seth, "Go ahead."

"Theo stabbed you with Athena's stone. I'm not sure if you noticed, but it shattered, after he stabbed you. Its power has embedded in you. In a moment, you will wake, stronger than ever, your wound will have healed, you mustn't hesitate.

Ares is bringing Theo and Jaspar to the square as we speak. Amethyst has placed a Lamina beside you. As soon as you wake, do not vacillate to take the weapon and fight. You must fight."

"What about Theo? Is he really on Jaspar's side?"

Seth shook his head in dismay, "I'm not sure, Gen, I really don't know."

"Will I have to kill him?" She squeaked.

Katherine placed a reassuring hand on Genesis' shoulder, "You'll know what is right or not. I know you will."

Next to speak, was May. Genesis rarely conversed with her prior to her death, but she knew that Adorjan cared deeply for her, she was like a sister to him. "He loves you." May said honestly, "I don't know if this betrayal is an act or real, but no matter what is happening, he does truly love you. He told me once, he told me a lot."

Genesis didn't know if this made her feel better or worse. Knowing he truly loved her, that perhaps he wasn't truly betraying her, made the thought of killing him, harder. "What did he say?"

May smiled, "It was over the summer, he was sat outside and I brought him some lemonade, I sat with him, asking how he was and all the usual small talk. He was telling me how he was going to ask you to marry him again – properly, when this was all over. He said the wedding you were having was far less than you deserved. He said how he wanted to spend his life with you. Going by Theo's track record, you can imagine why this came as such a shock, not just to me, but to everyone who ever knew him. I told him to do it, that you'd appreciate it.

I could see how much you loved one another, love that strong is rare." She looked over at Yale with a smile, "When you return to Pandoverse, please say hello to Adorjan for us, won't you?"

Genesis sniffed and nodded. "Thank you for telling me that. I'm sorry, for everything."

"Hey, it's okay." Yale grinned. He was a handsome boy, with deep auburn hair, so dark it was almost brown, and a perfect pearly white teeth. "It's not actually too bad up here."

The group laughed, and Genesis felt a pang of hurt and guilt. When she woke up, she would not see them ever again. This was it. "Where's Anthony and Liz?" She asked, realisation dawning on her. Her hands began to fade in colour, turning transparent.

"Anthony is alive, on Pandoverse. In fact, he's leaning over you right now." Seth smiled, "He's also the reason Hades hates me. But I'm okay, as long as you're okay."

Her arms faded too, as did her feet, ankles and calves.

"Liz isn't here. I haven't yet seen her." He continued, "I'm sure she's somewhere and that she's okay."

Now her abdomen.

"Genesis, wake up. Gen, wake up!" A voice called in her ear.

Her chest.

"Genesis." Seth said one final time, "Remember what I told you. The Lamina. Be ready."

Her neck and shoulders.

"Don't let your emotions get in the way, you're Pandoverse's last hope." Margaret added, "You're the prophecy, Genesis. Not the Artillery. It's you. You are the future of Pandoverse."

Genesis' eyes snapped open and her chest heaved with pain. She scanned the area. Beside her lay a Lamina, ahead of her was Anthony.

Don't hesitate. Her brother's voice echoed in her mind.

She flung her arms around the young boy's neck, "You're okay." She whispered, before pulling back, "You're actually alive again?"

"A story for another time." Anthony replied, passing her the Lamina and helping her up, "You ready to win this thing?"

Genesis smirked as she locked eyes with her Uncle. He gave her a mock salute, before setting alight the cloak of a nearby Guardian.

"I'm ready." She replied, watching as the God of War marched Theo and Jaspar out into the square, their hands were tied, their faces set with an angry expression. "Let's save Pandoverse."

Nothing had ever hurt more than seeing Theo stab Genesis. Nothing hurt more than seeing her pain, written all over Genesis' face as she realised Theo's betrayal. And nothing angered Xavier more, than knowing there was nothing he could do in that moment, to protect his best friend.

Genesis woke up after a while of being unconscious. Anthony was there to greet her, as she came back into the world. Her stab wound had not only faded, but disappeared completely. No blood stain, nor scar in its place. She should have died, but there she sat, in typical Genesis fashion, without even a hair out of place.

Xavier snapped out of his daze when the commotion begun. The current ratio was at least three to one for the Artillery versus the Government. So when Ares marched Jaspar and Theo out into the square, their hands tied, their abilities guarded. There was a lot of noise from the now-paused battle. A mixture of boos and cheers filled the crowd as the God of War led the pair up onto the trial area, where Genesis and Adrianna were previously tied. He placed them both up against the post, tying their hands above their heads before stepping back to admire his handy work.

"You're my mentor, why are you doing this?" Theo spat.

Ares smirked, "You chose the wrong side, buddy."

Theo shot the God a glare as he walked off.

Xavier went to advance toward Theo and the Elder, his anger clouding his judgment, but an arm pulled him back suddenly.

"Don't do it." Said Genesis, almost at a whisper. "Don't hurt him."

"Gen, he stabbed you." Xavier snarled, "You could've died."

"But I didn't."

"That's just pure luck!"

"No, it's because he knows what he's doing. Athena's stone. Athena told me it was the key to winning this war. He stabbed me with it and I didn't die but I returned to consciousness with more strength than ever. It's going to help us, he knew that."

Xavier shook his head, "How do you know this? How do you know this is an act, if that is what you're implying?"

Genesis looked over at her husband with a sigh, "I don't I just hope I'm right." She turned back to her friend, "But just, please, trust me?"

With a groan, he nodded. "Alright, what's next?"

Ares arrived at their side with a solemn expression.

"What's wrong?" Gen asked, noticing something wasn't right.

The God's face didn't change as he looked at her, he still seem worried. "Athena has spoken with Zeus. We can't kill Jaspar this way." He said, gesturing at the Elder tied to the post. "It has to be a fair fight, that's what the prophecy says." He shook his head and stared at the floor, "We have to clear the square, you and Jaspar need to fight to the death. *Alone*."

"No." Said Xavier, before Genesis could respond. "It's too dangerous, she almost just died!"

"I understand that but–"

"No!"

"I'll do it." Genesis spoke quietly, staring blankly toward Theo and Jaspar, "I'll fight him."

"Genesis." Xavier said with a low growl, "I don't want you to do this."

She shot him a soft glare, "You don't get a say. I'll fight Jaspar. This is my war."

"You're wrong!" He cried, throwing his hands up in surrender, "This is our war! The Artillery's war!"

Genesis gave a half-hearted laugh. "No, *you* are wrong. This is *my* war." She thought back to Seth's words, staring proud, majestically and blood-thirsty at Jaspar. "And *I* am the future of Pandoverse."

Everyone arranged themselves at the perimeter of the town square. Genesis stood at one end, Jaspar at the other. Xavier took place beside Genesis, Theo beside his father.

"I mean it, Gen, you don't have to do this." Xavier said into her ear, holding tightly onto her forearm, as though it would keep her away from trouble.

"I do, he is the last Elder – he is the key to winning this war. And I need to be the one to kill him."

Xavier shook his head, "Theo was so scared you'd kill his father, I think that's why he took his side, to protect him. I think he wanted you to just lock him in a cell and leave it at that."

"I would if I could." Genesis admitted, "For Theo's sake. But I cannot. He is the reason my mother, my brother, Elizabeth and many more friends of ours are dead. He tried to kill me. I need to avenge their deaths, defend myself and protect Pandoverse, just like the prophecy said."

Xavier stared deep into her eyes. She was right. And she was stubborn. He couldn't stop her, no matter how hard he tried. "Alright." He said softly, "Be careful."

Genesis smiled, "I'm always careful, am I not?"

"Never." He chuckled, kissing her on the forehead, for everyone to see.

Genesis didn't care how Theo would feel when another man planted a kiss upon his wife. If she died in this war, she would never hold her best friend again. Without a second thought, she wrapped her arms tightly around his torso, burying her face into his chest, "If I do die, look after Felicity and my father, won't you?"

She looked up as a lone tear fell across Xavier's cheek, "You'll survive, Gen you always do. You were made for this. You're a *warrior.*"

Genesis pulled back, "Wish me luck," She grinned, turning her attention to the Elder ahead of her, "Although I believe it's he who will need it."

Jaspar got the first punch, theoretically.

He caught Genesis off guard, sending a whirlpool of ice cold water around her, making her cold, tense, weak and dizzy. When the water drained, she fell to her knees.

Another blast of icy water.

This knocked her backward, crashing into the crowd with a groan. Anthony pulled her back onto her feet and eyed her from head to toe, "Go. Win."

She nodded, brushing herself off and returning to face the Elder with an angry glare. "It's game time." She mumbled, pulling all her energy into her palms and thrusting them forward. A surge of air knocked the Elder into the far wall, making the concrete crack and crumble before he fell to the floor. "That's for being an Elder, the creatures who killed my friend Margaret."

Jaspar scrambled up, shooting icy and boiling blasts of water toward Genesis. Each one missing her by centimetres as she ducked and dived.

Before he could attack again, two vines appeared, wrapping around his ankles and knocking him to the floor with a thud. "And that," She stated, "Is for ruining the wedding dress I wanted."

Jaspar had started to panic now, his expression fearful and anxious, "Genesis, I am your father in law, you do not have to do this."

Another shot of air. "That's for being the reason Seth killed my mother."

An icy blast of water. "And that I had to kill Seth."

"Genesis, I promise you, we can work this out. As Theo's wife, I will hand over my power to you both, you can rule Pandoverse together, I'll let you and all your friends live."

Genesis looked at Theo, whose expression was hopeful. She shook her head, flicking her wrist and setting alight Jaspar's cloak. "That's for Liz."

Jaspar extinguished the fire quickly, looking at her with wide eyes. "Elizabeth? Don't make me fight back, Genesis."

"You've had no problem before." She spat, circling him with anger and revenge, clear in her eyes. "So why change your attitude now? Worried I might actually win?"

"You can't win. Not against me."

Genesis smirked, "Is that what you think?"

Jaspar threw up his hands, a wave coming toward Genesis at a hurtling speed. Without a second of hesitation, she mimicked his actions, a blast of air holding back the water before it washed her into the ground.

Air.

She shot out another hand, before drawing it close to her chest and pushing her palm toward the Elder.

Fire.

A flaming wall appeared up against the wave, pushing it closer to Jaspar without fail.

She reached another hand out, drawing it back and toward him once more.

Water.

A wave appeared alongside the fire, colliding into one without extinguishing the flames. Jaspar's wave dowsed, the three of her own Elements creating a hurricane of colours, heat and power in the centre of the square.

"You know what's left?" She asked, grinning wickedly, "Earth. The name of the world I was born and raised in. The place I was happy in. The place I would still be, with my entire family, happy, if you and your little Governing friends didn't pose such an uncertain threat to Pandoverse. I can use air, fire, water and Earth. Because I'm Pure Quadrupedia." She seethed, drawing her hand back as cracks formed in the pavement.

Theo jumped forward, "Genesis, don't do this."

Her usually coloured irises, turned an unusual shade of pale pink, pupils and whites included, as she stared his way, "Don't try and stop me Theodore, it won't be pretty."

"Gen, please. Lock him up and throw away the key, I do not care. Just don't kill him, he's my father."

"He killed your mother!"

"He didn't! He never killed her! I don't know where she is but she's not dead!"

Genesis let out a growl, "Don't defend him!"

"Genny," Theo pleaded, his eyes searching hers for a miracle, "Please. I'm your husband, your best friend. If you loved me, you'd grant me this one wish. *Please*."

Genesis tilted her head, "You're right." She said honestly, causing Theo's shoulders to sag in relief.

"But *I don't love you.*"

And with that, she blasted the hurricane toward Jaspar, watching him with pure pleasure as he screamed and writhed beneath the Elements. The ground soon opened slowly around him, the screeches of Hades burning souls echoing in the courtyard. It was terrifying, to say the least, but Genesis had no chance to falter. This was the moment she had waited for. The moment she was born for. This was the beginning of the end. This was love, pain, fear, revenger and anger, all tired together. This was triumph. Within moments, Jaspar disappeared into the underworld, as scorched souls clawed at every piece of him, dragging him down until he was out of Pandoverse *forever*.

EPILOGUE

A<small>THENA EMBRACED</small> G<small>ENESIS IN A WARM HUG</small>, "You've made me so proud." She said fondly, "All of us, so proud."

Genesis smiled, "It's all thanks to you. I didn't know I had the ability to conjure up all four Elements at once."

Hecate grinned childishly, "You don't. Well, at least you didn't. You have Athena's stone to thank for that."

Genesis looked at the Goddesses' with wide eyes, "You mean–? That's what you meant, when you said it would help us triumph."

"That's exactly what I meant." Athena smiled.

"Genesis!" A voice cried.

Noah.

He ran to her side, pulling her close to congratulate her on her success. "You were awesome out there, you know that, right?"

Genesis grinned and nodded, "I know."

"So modest." He teased.

"How's Theo?"

Noah's smiled dropped, "Ares has him tied up once again."

"It's down to you what happens to him." Said Athena.

Genesis stared at them before heading toward the boy, the others following close behind. "Why is it down to me?"

Hecate clapped, "Can I announce it, please?"

Athena nodded, placing to fingers in her mouth and whistling a deafening sound. "Listen up!"

Hecate stood on some rubble, capturing everyone's attention. Including Theo's. "People of Pandoverse, with orders from Zeus himself, we are here to make an announcement. Following Genesis' success, we are pleased to tell you that Zeus has decided that forthwith, Genesis will be your successor, your leader, your Elder, your Queen. You will obey and abide, worship and cherish, love and follow your new monarch with full loyalty. She is not like the Elders. Things are going to change massively. So I want three big cheers for Lady…" She glanced at Genesis with a questioning look.

Gen stared at Theo for a moment, before looking back to the Goddess. With a lump in her throat and a pain in her chest, she pushed through a smile, "Lady Valencia." She announced.

Theo's expression was that of pain, but in that moment, she did not care.

"Lady Valencia!" Hecate cheered, the civilians of Pandoverse echoing her chants.

Genesis smirked and walked over to Ares and Theo. "May I speak with him? In private."

Ares nodded, "Of course my lady." He gave her a brief wink, before turning to his friends and leaving the pair alone and ordering the Artillery to fetch the last of Jaspar's loyal guardians.

"Genesis." Theo said dryly, "You killed my father."

"He killed my friends, my mother, my brother, your mother too."

"He didn't kill your mother, Seth did that. And you killed Seth. He also didn't kill my mother."

Genesis laughed and shook her head, "Seth did what he did because of Jaspar! And if he didn't kill Liz, who did?"

Theo stared up at her with wide eyes. For the first time, she noticed how dishevelled he looked. His face was taught, dark circles surrounding his eyes and the sparkle she knew and loved, was now gone. "My mother isn't dead. I'm not sure where she is, but she isn't dead."

"I saw it, Theo!"

"She isn't, please trust me!"

"How can I trust you when you sided with him, over me?"

"He was my father!"

"And I was your wife!"

Theo flinched at her tone, "*Was*?"

"I want an annulment." She said gravely, not sympathising as Theo's lip trembled and his eyes began to water. "I don't want to be married to a traitor."

"I didn't betray you, Genesis, I was always on your side."

"You have an extremely humorous way of showing it!" She chuckled sarcastically, "Siding with your demonic father and allowing him to try and kill me! Or perhaps the part where you stabbed me, made me feel betrayed…"

"Genesis, I did that because I knew the story behind Athena's stone, she told me, the other night when you were at the beach!"

"How did you know for certain it would work?"

"I didn't–"

"So you *could* have killed me. I mean, not for certain. But potentially. Fifty-fifty. The odds were pretty poor but you took the risk anyway." She spat back sarcastically.

Theo sighed, "Gen, listen to me. I had to make my father believe I was on his side, so I could trick him."

"Then why did you try to stop me killing him?"

"I wanted him to live, no matter what, he is still my father. Wouldn't you have spared Seth, given the chance?"

Genesis snarled, "I killed Seth for a reason. As I did your father, and many others. I have blood on my hands that will never leave. I will live the rest of my life remembering those I murdered, killed, destroyed. But I tell you something, I don't regret any second of it. Perhaps being in charge isn't the greatest thing. Perhaps I too, am too twisted and evil for my own good. But we will see, right? Pandoverse survived this long with evil leaders, what's another fifty or so years?"

Theo stared wordlessly at her, unsure on what turned her into the person she had become.

"I have been given the choice to kill you or spare you, and right now, I'm not too sure." She spat, turning on her heels and marching away in anger.

Ares stood atop the rubble that Hecate had previously been on, staring out at the gathering crowds in the town square.

Genesis turned her attention to him, but was soon disrupted by Felicity and Apollo.

"Lady Valencia." Apollo greeted, bowing his head politely.

"Please, spare me the niceties, I'm just Gen! You're the God here." Genesis replied honestly, "Is everything okay?"

Felicity smiled, "Look what we found."

The young girl held out her hand, a sapphire stone in her palm. Genesis took it, holding it in front of her eye-line. "What is this? It's beautiful."

"It's an Elemental stone." Apollo explained, "For Water."

"As in, one of the Elements of Pandoverse?"

The God nodded. "One of four. It was left in Jaspar's place."

Genesis raised her eyebrows, "I killed Jaspar and gained a gem."

"It's as though Hade's planted the stones amongst people."

"And every time I, or someone, kills one of those specific people, the stone is left in their place."

"Death is the key to the stones."

Genesis furrowed her eyebrows in confusion, "What does it mean, though? To have all four stones?"

"To have all four stones makes us Gods, and all in Pandoverse, a lot stronger than you could imagine."

"So there's three more?"

Felicity stepped forward, placing a hand on Genesis' necklace, "Its opal."

"Like the Elemental stone of Air." Apollo noticed.

The young girl smiled up at her mentor, "Could it be? Or is it too small?"

Genesis glanced at the pair of them in bewilderment. "What?"

"Can I?" Felicity asked, gesturing to the small pendant.

Gen smirked, "Theo bought me it, so by all means." She undone the clasp, handing the piece of jewellery to her younger sister.

For a brief moment, both Felicity and Apollo stared at the pendant, before Felicity handed it to the God and he enveloped it in his palm.

Seconds later, a small light appeared through his fingers and he pulled them open. Revealing what once was Genesis' small pill-shaped Opal pendant, "What happened?" She asked.

Apollo grinned, "Genesis, this whole time you wore another Elemental stone on you. The Elemental stone of Air, you have two of the stones."

"Now I just need two more."

Apollo nodded, "And I am sure you will find it."

Ares addressed the crowd in a loud tone, catching everyone's attention immediately. "Hecate will open an Atrium to my right, and the following must enter." He said with a blunt tone, his eyes scanned the crowd. "Genesis, Felicity, Theo, Eliza, Elijah, Tom, Xavier, Zaire, Anthony, Adrianna, Noah and Paisley." Adrianna looked at Jax in confusion, before the God continued, "Please head through the Atrium in the next three minutes."

Genesis looked around at her friends, "What's going on?"

"Zeus' orders." Areas announced, before standing down and wandering to Hecate's side.

"I guess we should go." Genesis said to Xavier with a shrug, "Go where? I do not know, but... Zeus' orders."

Xavier nodded, "With Theo?"

Genny glared over at the boy, he heart aching and her mind abundant with anger. "Keep him tied, Noah and Anthony can keep hold of him."

"I'll let them know." Felicity added from beside her sister, before tottering off to inform their friends about their instructions.

Genesis headed over to the Atrium, Xavier in pursuit. "Where are we going?" She asked Athena, who stood beside the black hole. "And why is only a few of us going?"

Athena pulled Genesis into an embrace, "I'm sorry. Be careful, you're an amazing warrior, I'm so proud of you."

Genesis pulled back, looking at the Goddess, "But–"

"It's time to go." Xavier said from behind her, pulling her wrist toward the Atrium. One by one, their friends entered the darkness.

"Good luck." Athena said solemnly, as Genesis wandered beside Xavier and followed the group into the unknown.

Genesis didn't know what to expect when she arrived on the other side of the Atrium. She didn't know what would greet her, or whom.

But it wasn't this.

Darkness, was the first adjective to come to mind.

Desert surrounding them.

Death was the stench that besieged their nostrils.

Genesis grasped onto Xavier's bicep, ignoring the stares from Theo and walked forward, taking in their surroundings, trying to figure out where they had ended up. It wasn't Pandoverse, or even Earth, for that matter. "Toto, I've a feeling we're not in Kansas anymore." She said in a soft American accent.

Xavier grinned in recognition of her quote, whereas others cast her a befuddled look. "I honestly have not the slightest idea of where we are." He admitted.

Genesis sighed, "Neither do I."

She stared around her. To her left was extensive desert. The sand was a deep shade of rust, similar to that of the sky. To her right, mountains, volcanoes and endless caves.

And it was from one of the caves three figures emerged from the shadows.

"Someone else is here." Genesis whispered, standing her ground with her hand rested on the hilt of her Lamina.

Xavier loaded his Arcus and pointed it toward the strangers.

"Stand down." A voice boomed.

Genesis stared at each of her friends with wide eyes. Unsure of whether or not to follow. She raised her hand, ordering her friends to halt.

"I said," The voice continued, "Stand down. We will not harm you, unless you intend to harm us."

Genny gestured the group to do as they were instructed.

Immediately, they all lowered their weapons, urging the strangers to come closer and into the very minimal light of the desert moon.

"Who are you?" Asked Xavier loudly, "Show yourselves."

A girl, around Genesis' age, stepped forward. She had deep olive skin and long, thick dark hair. On either side of her, two more youngsters. One boy with even darker skin, and on the other side, a fair haired, blue-eyed boy. They both stood close to the girl, in attempts to protect her and intimidate the others.

"Where are we? Why were we sent here?" Genesis added, demanding answers. She stepped forward, both Xavier and Tom at her sides.

The blonde haired boy spoke first. "My name is Blake, and you're on the outskirts of the Underworld."

The other boy gave a wicked grin at the group's confusion.

"We defeated the Elder's, we saved Pandoverse, yet we're here?" Gen questioned, seemingly perplexed, "I don't see why?"

"It's not as bad as it sounds." Blake explained, "Through those caves is our home, and it's nothing like you'd imagine. It's also far from Hades, I promise."

"But why were we sent here?" Xavier questioned, "We should be allowed home, surely?"

"This place is a labyrinth, the only way out is to get through." The other boy explained, "My names Sheldon, by the way."

Genesis nodded, "My name is Genesis Valencia." The trio from the caves stared at her with shocked expressions, but said nothing. "Well, may we enter your home, if we are to get out?"

Sheldon nodded, leading them toward the small cave, which soon opened up into a lighter world, one just like Pandoverse.

Xavier stared, "It looks like–"

"Home." Genesis finished, with slight amusement.

The girl, whom had yet to speak, smirked at Genesis, as she stood in front of the group at the entrance to the new world. "Lady Valencia," She said with a wicked grin, "We've been expecting you."

Genesis raised an eye brow in confusion, "But, I don't know you?"

The young girl shook her head, turning half way to face the world. "My name, is Nadia." She explained, gesturing out an extended hand,

"And welcome, to *Guardlaterra*."

ACKNOWLEDGEMENTS:

There are no specific people I can really thank,
because I am grateful to everyone.
Every reader.
Every friend.
Every relative.
My partner.
My pets.
And every one who has supported me throughout
writing and publishing this novel.

You are all warriors.

I hope you enjoyed book two and are ready for
book three.

Thank you, for returning
To
PANDOVERSE

In loving memory of:

Roh,

My beloved hedgehog.
1st October 2011 – 7th July 2017
Who sat upon my shoulder many a
time as I wrote.

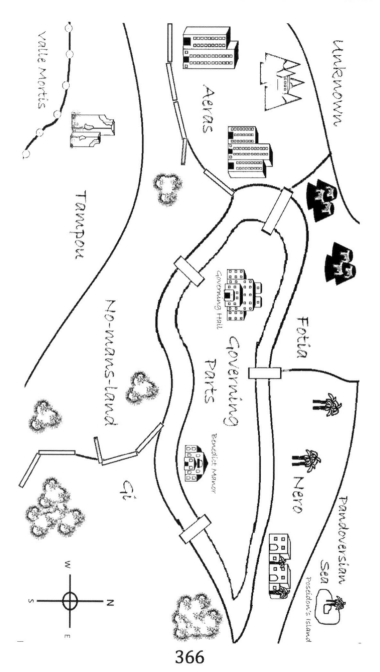

Printed in Great Britain
by Amazon